Born in Paris in 1947, Christian Jacq first visited Egypt when he was seventeen, went on to study Egyptology and archaeology at the Sorbonne, and is now one of the world's leading Egyptologists. He is the author of the internationally bestselling RAMSES and THE MYSTERIES OF OSIRIS series, and several other novels on Ancient Egypt. Christian Jacq lives in Switzerland.

Also by Christian Jacq

The Ramses Series
Volume 1: The Son of the Light
Volume 2: The Temple of a Million Years
Volume 3: The Battle of Kadesh
Volume 4: The Lady of Abu Simbel
Volume 5: Under the Western Acacia

The Stone of Light Series
Volume 1: Nefer the Silent
Volume 2: The Wise Woman
Volume 3: Paneb the Ardent
Volume 4: The Place of Truth

The Queen of Freedom Trilogy
Volume 1: The Empire of Darkness
Volume 2: The War of the Crowns
Volume 3: The Flaming Sword

The Judge of Egypt Trilogy
Volume 1: Beneath the Pyramid
Volume 2: Secrets of the Desert
Volume 3: Shadow of the Sphinx

The Mysteries of Osiris Series
Volume 1: The Tree of Life
Volume 2: The Conspiracy of Evil
Volume 3: The Way of Fire
Volume 4: The Great Secret

The Vengeance of the Gods Series
Volume 1: Manhunt
Volume 2: The Divine Worshipper

The Black Pharaoh
The Tutankhamun Affair
For the Love of Philae
Champollion the Egyptian
Master Hiram & King Solomon
The Living Wisdom of Ancient Egypt

About the Translator

Sue Dyson is a prolific author of both fiction and non-fiction,
including over thirty novels both contemporary and historical.
She has also translated a wide variety of French fiction.

The Vengeance of the Gods

The Divine Worshipper

Christian Jacq

Translated by Sue Dyson

SIMON & SCHUSTER

LONDON · NEW YORK · TORONTO · SYDNEY

First published in France by XO Editions under the title
La Divine Adoratrice, 2007
First published in Great Britain by Simon & Schuster UK Ltd, 2008
A CBS COMPANY

1 3 5 7 9 10 8 6 4 2

Simon & Schuster UK Ltd
Africa House
64–78 Kingsway
London WC2B 6AH

www.simonsays.co.uk

Simon & Schuster Australia
Sydney

A CIP catalogue record for this book is
available from the British Library

HB ISBN: 978-1-84737-058-7
TPB ISBN: 978-1-84737-059-4

Typeset by Rowland Phototypesetting Ltd, Bury St Edmunds, Suffolk
Printed and bound in Great Britain by CPI Mackays, Chatham

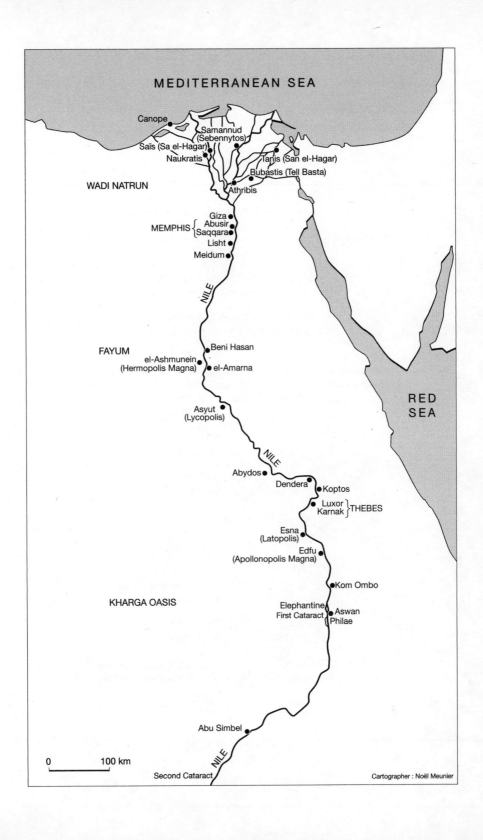

MEDITERRANEAN SEA

Canope

Samannud
(Sebennytos)

Saïs (Sa el-Hagar)

Naukratis

Tanis (San el-Hagar)

Bubastis (Tell Basta)

WADI NATRUN

Athribis

Giza

Abusir

MEMPHIS {
Saqqara

Lisht

Meidum

NILE

FAYUM

Beni Hasan

el-Ashmunein
(Hermopolis Magna)

el-Amarna

Asyut
(Lycopolis)

NILE

Abydos

Dendera

Koptos

Luxor
Karnak } THEBES

Esna
(Latopolis)

Edfu
(Apollonopolis Magna)

Kom Ombo

KHARGA OASIS

Elephantine

First Cataract

Aswan

Philae

RED
SEA

Abu Simbel

0   100 km

NILE

Second Cataract

Cartographer : Noël Meunier

1

On the orders of Judge Gem, head of Egypt's whole judicial system, guards and archers moved silently into position around the abandoned brick-works. Armed with clubs and short swords, the guards were preparing to arrest a criminal who had been on the run for several weeks: a monster who was accused of having murdered all his colleagues at the interpreters' office, wiped out his accomplices and organized a conspiracy against Pharaoh Ahmose.*

The elusive murderer was a young scribe named Kel, a gifted young fellow who had apparently been destined for a brilliant career but who had turned into a cunning, merciless and ferocious creature. He had succeeded in slipping through the net put in place by the forces of order. In the whole of Gem's long career – and he was now an elderly man, though still tireless and rigorous – he had never come across a killer like this one.

The archers had been ordered to kill Kel on sight if he threatened the lives of the men trying to catch him. The judge hoped to be able to interrogate him and find out the motives for his actions. But would Kel talk? And if he did would he tell the truth? When a man sank to this level of barbarism, he was clearly no longer in full possession of his reason.

* Ahmose II ascended the throne in 570 BC.

It was just before dawn.

The land surrounding the brick-works was overgrown with weeds, some with sharp-bladed leaves, and it presented numerous pitfalls: shattered brick-moulds, broken shards, scorpions ... The guards must advance slowly, careful not to wake their sleeping quarry.

The judge turned back to his informant, a storekeeper at the Temple of Ptah. 'Are you sure he's hiding here?'

'Absolutely sure. I recognized him as soon as I saw him near the temple, thanks to the portrait of him that has been circulated everywhere, and I followed him here.'

'Did he see you?'

'Fortunately for me, no. As soon as he entered this old brick-works, I made myself scarce and ran to the city. I thought I was going to be chased and killed at any moment. When I reached the main barracks it took me a long time to get my breath back, and I was so frightened that my explanation was rather confused. When do I get my reward?'

'As soon as he is arrested,' promised the judge. 'Did you spot any accomplices?'

'All I saw was the killer,' replied the informant, 'but I didn't dare get any closer. If there'd been a lookout, I wouldn't be standing here now. Don't all the risks I took deserve an extra reward?'

'We shall see. Now, stand well back and do not interfere in any way.'

'No sooner said than done!'

The informant hid behind a clump of thorn bushes. His mouth was watering at the prospect of seeing this monstrous criminal executed.

The judge, though, was worried that one or more members of the network headed by Kel might be in the vicinity. Destroying the interpreters' service, which was vital for Egyptian diplomacy; stealing Ahmose's legendary helmet, which his soldiers had used as a crown when they proclaimed him pharaoh; and playing games with his pursuers ... these achievements implied the existence of a group of determined, battle-hardened criminals.

Henat, head of the pharaoh's spy service, a shadowy individual whose methods were somewhat dubious, disagreed. He thought a man on his own would be able to evade even the best-organized search for a long time. Nevertheless, fugitives always made a fatal mistake in the end. Kel's had been to prowl the area near the Temple of Ptah.

Was he trying to meet new allies? Had he been establishing contact with someone offering him refuge? Or had he simply been searching for food? Many aspects of this alarming affair remained unexplained.

Although he was on the point of arresting Kel at last, Judge Gem had not forgotten the trail of disasters and failures of the past few weeks. He had felt obliged to offer the king his resignation, but Ahmose had continued to trust him. A faithful servant of the state, who set great store by justice, Gem was also a tireless investigator. Never would he let go of his prey.

'My men are in place,' the commander of the archers informed him. 'The criminal cannot escape.'

'If he tries to run away, aim at his legs.'

'And if he attacks us?'

'Kill him.'

Those were the king's orders. There had already been too many dead bodies, and no more men must fall victim to this uncontrollable wild beast.

Gem had once met the wild beast, outside the framework of official legal procedure. Of course, the scribe had claimed complete and utter innocence, despite all the evidence that had piled up against him. How could anyone believe such a fable? Kel had proved intelligent, and a good speaker with a lively mind. He had been almost convincing, but the judge had sufficient experience not to fall into that trap.

There was not a breath of wind, and not a hint of birdsong. Their nerves tensed almost to breaking point, the raiding-party waited for the command to attack.

'Now,' ordered the judge.

The attack was perfectly coordinated. Two men entered the brick-works, followed immediately by five others, who spread out inside the building.

'Over there!' shouted one of them.

Spotting the figure of a man armed with a spear, an archer fired. Despite the darkness he did not miss his target, striking him full in the heart.

There was no reaction from any accomplice of Kel's. He must have been alone. The guards halted. They had not expected to succeed so quickly and easily.

It was the judge's turn to enter. He alone could formally identify the murderous scribe and put an end to the investigation.

'He threatened us,' explained the commander of the raiding-party.

Preceded by two archers, Judge Gem approached the corpse, which lay stretched out across a heap of broken bricks. Despite the half-light, there was not the slightest doubt: it was a dummy, a kind of scarecrow made of rags and straw, holding a pointed stick.

'So now,' fumed Gem, 'that damned scribe is poking fun at us!'

As he emerged from the brick-works, the informant hurried over.

'Well, did you kill him? Can I have my reward now?'

'Guards, arrest this man,' ordered the judge. 'I must interrogate him and satisfy myself that he is not one of the assassin's accomplices.'

2

Sweet-Lips was both buxom and commanding. In the full bloom of her thirties, she ran one of the largest bakeries and breweries in Memphis, Egypt's economic capital. Rising before dawn, she summoned all her workers together and gave them precise instructions. One mistake led to a reprimand, two to a reduction in wages, and a third meant dismissal. Nobody protested, for Sweet-Lips behaved fairly and paid well.

She never failed to meet the daily delivery of grain and to check both its quality and quantity. If a supplier tried to deceive her, she flew into such a rage that he never did so again.

Once checked, the grain was crushed, pounded, kneaded and sifted. Experienced specialists took care of these stages in the making of loaves of varying shapes and sizes. Sweet-Lips herself carried out the delicate operation of adding the yeast; then she oversaw the baking process, using the city's finest ovens.

Seeing the hot, crusty loaves emerge filled Sweet-Lips with justifiable pride. Customers were queuing up to buy, her business was flourishing, and she had acquired a luxurious house near the centre of the great city, where Egyptians, Greeks, Syrians, Libyans, Nubians and other races lived side by side.

While the deliverymen hurried away with the loaves, their

employer moved on to her brewery, which produced delicious, sweet* beer at an unbeatable price. The keys to success were hard work and constant vigilance. Sturdy fellows kneaded the paste for a long time by trampling it with their feet, then experienced women workers filtered and sieved it. The fermentation vats had just been improved, and Sweet-Lips had bought many jars with pointed bases, lined with carefully beaten clay in order to purify and clarify the beer.

Since orders were pouring in, she was forever enlarging her trading-office and counting-house. She regarded with suspicion the scribes who manned them, and liked to employ young ones, whom she could train in her own way, to meet her demands.

At the end of an exhausting morning, she returned home for the midday meal. And there, for the last few days, an appetizing sweetmeat had awaited her: her new lover, an infinitely resourceful actor.

Sweet-Lips had separated from her husband, a puny fellow who whined all the time, and had decided to enjoy the fruits of her labours on her own. Although she had no desire for children, she was a passionate lover, who delighted in men without becoming too attached to them. And this one was positively succulent.

'My darling!' Bebon exclaimed, greeting his mistress with an affectionate embrace. 'Did you have a good morning?'

Sweet-Lips certainly deserved her name. The kiss was endless and delicious.

'I was so busy that I didn't notice the time passing. What about you, my treasure?'

'As you wanted, I took care of all your domestic chores. A good, thorough clean, fumigation, perfumes, scented flowers, then I bought meat and fish, fetched the laundry from the washer-man and prepared the lunch. Are you pleased?'

* Or 'mild' – translator's note.

'You are a perfect housekeeper.'

Neither of them was under any illusions: their dalliance would not last long. They would enjoy as much pleasure as possible until Sweet-Lips grew bored. In the meantime, the actor must make himself useful.

If Bebon was happy to undertake these domestic tasks, it was in order to thank the gods for providing him with unhoped-for lodgings, which also benefited his friend Kel – who was playing the part of his servant – and their donkey, North Wind.

Heeding his instincts, Bebon had sensed that their previous refuge, the former brick-works, was no longer altogether safe. A curious passer-by might mention their presence to the authorities, who would be sure to take action. It was better to come back to Memphis and lose themselves in the general population.

As he was buying bread, the actor's eyes had met those of Sweet-Lips, and a sensual spark had passed between the generously endowed baker and the seducer with the charming smile. First they had talked of this and that, then they had met privately and enjoyed the joyful, inventive games of pleasure.

Invited to stay at his new mistress's home, Bebon had at first been hesitant. But persuasive caresses had overcome his reticence, and he had described his forthcoming tour during which, wearing the masks of the gods Horus, Set, Anubis or Thoth, he would act out the public sections of the Mysteries on temple forecourts.

Reduced to the status of a plaything by the voracious Sweet-Lips, Bebon was enjoying the benefits of a comfortable house: a large entrance hall, reception chamber, four bedchambers, two washrooms, a kitchen, cellar and terrace, all put together with good taste. She insisted that he keep himself impeccably clean – after all, cleanliness was the secret of good health, and she was counting on that health.

When she undressed her lover, he did not resist her.

'Today,' she confessed, 'I'm too hungry to wait for the sweetmeats.'

Once her appetite had been temporarily sated, she asked Bebon to pour two cups of white wine from the Delta.

'Let us drink to our pleasure, my darling.'

The actor did not need to be asked twice. But his expression remained grave.

'You look troubled,' she observed.

'Memphis is becoming a dangerous city.'

'What has happened to you?'

'To me, nothing. But your cook told me that a young woman has been kidnapped.'

'Where from?'

'The port.'

'That's unbelievable!'

'Ask her. People everywhere are talking about this horrible affair, and the authorities don't seem to be interested. It's worrying, isn't it? Myself, I like peaceful places.'

'My house is peaceful,' whispered Sweet-Lips.

'Yes, it is, but I used to like walking along the quays and visiting the little markets that are held at the bottom of each gangplank.'

Fearing that her lover might leave suddenly, the baker felt obliged to do something.

'Memphis is my city,' she declared, 'and nothing goes on here that I don't know about. I'll soon find out the truth and you'll be reassured. Rumours are often nonsense. In the meantime, let's have our meal.'

3

Kel was staying in the stables along with North Wind, a robust and cunning donkey. His fellow donkeys respected him, and allowed him to occupy the best stall.

Since the disappearance of the priestess Nitis, the woman with whom he had just been united for all eternity, the young scribe could no longer sleep. Who had kidnapped her? Was she still alive? Nothing now remained of the brilliant scribe destined for high office: just an unshaven boy, grown prematurely old.

Mad with worry, Kel forgot all about his own situation. Not only had he been accused of murdering his colleagues at the interpreters' office, and his apparent accomplice, a Greek scribe named Demos, but he was suspected of fomenting a conspiracy against King Ahmose. He ought to have gone immediately to Thebes to beg for help from the Divine Worshipper, the only person who – if she believed him – was capable of taking up his defence. But he would never abandon Nitis. It was here, in Memphis, that he would pick up her trail, and nobody would prevent him from freeing her.

North Wind licked Kel's cheek gently. The attention comforted him. He thought of the coded papyrus that was at the origin of all his misfortunes; the second part of it remained indecipherable. According to a voice from the world beyond, only the ancestors possessed the key. But where were they?

Perhaps the Divine Worshipper knew the answer to the question . . .? According to the text, which Kel had discovered in a shrine dating from the time of the pyramids, conspirators were rejecting Egypt's traditional values, wanted to alter the exercise of power and encourage 'modern' progress. There was one last obstacle in their path: that same Divine Worshipper, the high priestess who ruled Thebes and preserved the ancient rites.

Alas, it had proved impossible to dicover the conspirators' names and find out their precise plans. Only one thing was certain: in order to mask their abominable crimes, the murderous band had chosen the ideal culprit in the form of a young scribe only recently recruited to the prestigious Interpreters' Secretariat. But they had not foreseen his ability to resist adversity or his determination to re-establish the truth.

Nitis's love had given Kel greater strength, and Bebon's staunch friendship had enabled him to escape from his pursuers. Injustice, corruption, a criminal conspiracy: could Nitis, Bebon and Kel really overcome these horrors without help? In any case, the disappearance of the young priestess had reduced their fragile hopes to nothing.

North Wind's ears pricked up, but he did not bray. The new arrival was no threat to them.

'Dinner,' announced Bebon.

'I'm not hungry.'

'It's lentil soup, and a paste of onions and leeks with garlic, dill and coriander: take just one mouthful, and your appetite will come back.'

For his part, the donkey was more than willing to munch his fresh lucerne.

'You'd better do likewise,' advised Bebon. 'If we're to win our battle, you need to build up your strength.'

'Nitis didn't go to the Temple of Ptah,' mourned Kel. 'The captain of the *Ibis* lied, and then ran away. He was in league with the conspirators, and we fell into their trap.'

'It's pointless to keep going over the past. The important thing is to find the clue that will lead us to Nitis's prison.'

'What if they've killed her?'

Bebon seized his friend by the shoulders. 'Do you love her?'

'How can you doubt it?'

'Then you must feel her presence. If she were dead, you'd know it.'

Kel closed his eyes for a few moments. 'No, she isn't. She's alive.'

'You're certain?'

'Absolutely certain.'

'So stop lamenting your fate, and let's get on with our investigation. First of all, eat. Our protector's cook is excellent, so take advantage of her skills before we set out on the road again. Tomorrow we'll probably have to be content with a flat-cake and an onion.'

'I must go back to the port and question all the captains. One of them must know the captain of the *Ibis* and be able to tell us his destination.'

'There'd be no better way to get yourself arrested! Thanks to Sweet-Lips' unwitting help, the guards have lost our trail. They think we're trying to reach Thebes and must be searching every boat.'

'But can't you imagine Nitis's distress?'

'Her soul is stronger than yours and mine put together. She'll never lose her trust in you. And I'm going to acquire some interesting information.'

A glimmer of interest awoke in Kel's eyes. 'What are you going to do?'

'Sweet-Lips knows Memphis very well – not a single significant event escapes her attention. Now, she hasn't heard anything about a kidnapping, which is an exceedingly rare crime. In other words, the authorities are trying to lay a cloak of silence over a highly embarrassing affair.'

11

'Has she got friends in the city guards?'

'She has friends everywhere, and especially among the ordinary folk. However, somebody must surely have seen something – even in the middle of the night the quays aren't deserted. I pretended to be alarmed at this lack of security, and said I'd be leaving soon. As Sweet-Lips still appreciates my charm, she'll try to find out the truth to stop me leaving.'

'She won't succeed!'

'Success is unlikely, I agree, but she'll find me the name of a witness and then we'll follow the lead to its source.'

North Wind signalled his approval with a trusting look.

Bebon's persuasive abilities were so great that Kel wanted to believe this improbable plan might work.

'There aren't too many curious folk around you, are there?' asked Bebon worriedly.

'The other donkey-drivers regard me as your servant. North Wind and I run errands according to your instructions and spend the rest of the time sleeping. Given my current appearance, nobody would ever imagine that I'm a scribe.'

'So much the better. I'm sorry, but Sweet-Lips is waiting for me.'

Seated with his eyes half-closed, Kel thought back to the happy time when he had looked forward to a fine career as an interpreter-scribe in the service of the pharaoh. Life had promised to be peaceful, pleasant and exciting. And then the anger of the gods had been unleashed upon him, shattering his future and plunging him into the middle of an affair of state.

The anger of the gods ... And yet they were protecting him. First, they had enabled him to escape his pursuers, who were now determined to kill him since Judge Gem himself did not believe in his innocence; then they had made him meet Nitis. Was it not a priceless gift to experience such great love? Even in the depths of misfortune, that love could not be swept away. And that tiny glimmer of light would continue to guide him.

4

The presence of the king's court in Memphis did not hinder the conspirators; on the contrary. By deciding to stay in the great city, which was known as 'the Scales of the Two Lands' because it was the balancing-point between North and South, Ahmose was making their task easier.

When their leader called them to a meeting, well away from prying eyes and ears, they were clear in their minds about what lay ahead. All of them envisaged a long, delicate process before they could succeed, and regretted the deplorable error that had obliged them to kill the entire staff of the Interpreters' Secretariat. The coded papyrus ought never to have reached those remarkable scholars, who would have been able to decode it and thus discover both the names of the conspirators and their plan. By ensuring that the young scribe Kel was accused of the murder, the traitors had provided the authorities with an ideal culprit and should have put an end to the incident.

Unfortunately, Kel had proved much more resourceful than they had expected. Despite an overwhelming security presence he was still at liberty, and he had even dared to proclaim his innocence, although he had not convinced anyone. The evidence and charges accumulated against him left no room for doubt. Sooner or later Kel would be arrested, tried and sentenced to death.

Nevertheless, the leader sensed a certain fear in the other conspirators. In order to escape from the forces of order in this way, the young man must surely have the benefit of the gods' protection. If that were so, they murmured, would he not survive all the attacks upon him and eventually gain the upper hand?

'We must not be slaves to old superstitions,' their leader warned them. 'Kel has been extremely lucky, but he is merely a doomed human being, hunted and perpetually on the alert.'

'I believe it's vital that he's eliminated,' ventured one anxious conspirator. 'He's trying to follow the trail back to us in order to prove his innocence, and he has nothing left to lose.'

'What's more, he clearly has help from friends or allies,' added his neighbour. 'Without it, he couldn't possibly keep evading us.'

'Yes, and for that reason I have taken a radical decision,' said the leader.

The conspirators hung on every word.

'Evidently, Kel found support at the Temple of Neith in Sais, initially from High Priest Wahibra, who fortunately has since died. The successor chosen by that honest old man was his pupil Nitis, Superior of the chantresses and weavers, an intelligent, honest and determined woman. In my opinion, she agreed with the High Priest and believed in Kel's innocence, so she became his principal supporter. We therefore contrived to block her appointment to the post of High Priestess, and instead installed as High Priest a man of straw who won't hinder us. But that did not seem adequate, so I decided to have her kidnapped, entrusting the task to one of you.'

'Mission accomplished,' declared the man responsible. 'The operation went marvellously well.'

'Any witnesses?'

'Apparently not. And if anyone did see something, they'll keep quiet and the guards' investigations will lead nowhere.

Moreover, Nitis is in a place where nobody will ever look for her.'

'But won't that damned scribe try to free her?' asked the anxious conspirator.

The kidnapper laughed. 'He'd have to be madly in love and completely insane. Anyway, even if he did try, Nitis is far beyond his reach.'

'Has her interrogation begun?' asked the leader.

'The priestess has character. She hasn't yet given the names of her accomplices or revealed the location of Kel's lair. But the experts will be able to make her talk.'

'If necessary, torture her.'

One of the conspirators was appalled by this. 'But she's a priestess of Neith! Surely you aren't planning to—'

'Don't be a fool!' snapped the leader. 'The woman is going to disappear without trace, once we've verified the information she gives us. That way, we'll eliminate Kel's last sources of support, and as a man on his own he will make easy prey.'

This ferocity chilled the conspirators' blood. All of them realized that it was no longer possible to leave the conspiracy and that they must pursue it to the very end.

'Kel will try to reach Thebes and win over the Divine Worshipper – our worst enemy – to his cause,' said the anxious man. 'In my view, he's probably left Memphis.'

'If so, there's nothing to worry about,' replied the leader. 'All the river and land routes are closely watched, and we have set the necessary traps.'

'He's already shown he can avoid our traps.'

'He'll never reach Thebes. And if by some miracle he does, he won't meet the Divine Worshipper. I have taken suitable precautions.'

For once, a conspirator rebelled. 'We have already spoken of a horrible plan concerning the queen of Thebes, and I am formally opposed to it.'

The leader smiled. 'Do you think she'll live for all eternity?

But don't worry. We probably won't have to kill her because Kel won't have an opportunity to try and convince her. But, whatever happens, nobody will prevent us from succeeding. I say again: nobody.'

A long silence was followed by a final question.

'King Ahmose's helmet still hasn't been found. Is Kel keeping it, in the hope of wearing it and proclaiming himself pharaoh at the head of his faction?'

'A ridiculous idea!' declared the leader. 'Now, don't worry about that detail. We control the situation, which will keep developing in our favour for as long as we continue our efforts and maintain absolute secrecy.'

5

Menk was deeply worried. The organizer of festivals in Sais, the dynasty's capital, was usually charming and affable, but now he wore a sad expression. And yet he was succeeding in the mission entrusted to him by the king: to work with the priests of Ptah and Hathor to ensure that the great rituals in Memphis were perfect. Menk had managed to avoid coming into conflict with the priests, always speaking tactfully to them, and they had come to like him. Together, they were working to satisfy the gods and the king. Some predicted that he would soon be promoted.

Normally, Menk would have revelled in his professional success, but his pleasure had been spoilt by the disappearance of the beautiful priestess Nitis, whom he loved and intended to marry. True, she had not yet given her consent, but that was merely a question of time, for she quite understood that one did not turn down a husband like Menk. Sometimes, the independence and freedom of choice enjoyed by Egyptian women posed serious problems. The Greeks, by contrast, knew how to enforce the decisions made by their men.

Nitis did not have an easy personality. Intelligent and cultivated, she ought to have become High Priestess of the Temple of Neith following the death of her mentor, High Priest Wahibra. But in her place the king had chosen an obscure courtier, probably because of the priestess's unwise actions. She was suspected of believing that the scribe Kel was innocent, even though he was clearly guilty of all those monstrous crimes.

At her request, Menk had ventured to speak to the king about an imaginary traffic in weapons, a fable designed to prove the killer innocent. It could have ruined Menk's career, but he felt no resentment towards the too-credulous Nitis. Now disabused of her illusions, she would never again see that fearsome murderer and would no longer defend him.

Unfortunately, her regrettable mistake had brought the young woman temporary disgrace. By marrying Menk, she would recover her honourable status and once again lay claim to high office.

But first he must find her. Where could she be hiding?

Menk went to the Temple of Ptah and questioned several ritual priests. Nobody had seen Nitis for several days. He was asked to check the quality of the incense that had recently been delivered, and the quantities of sacred oils, and did so – but his mind was elsewhere.

'A message for you from Sais,' announced the temple messenger, handing it to him.

Nervously, Menk broke the seal on the small papyrus. Its contents filled him with consternation. According to the High Priest, Nitis had not returned to the temple in Sais, and there was no trace of her in the capital.

Alarmed, Menk excused himself by pretending to be over-tired, abandoned his checks and rushed to the head steward's office. Judge Gem was still in charge of arresting Kel the scribe and conducting an in-depth investigation, and had set up his own office there temporarily.

He did not keep Menk waiting long.

'You seem shaken,' said the judge when his visitor was shown in.

'Nitis has disappeared!'

'That's putting it rather strongly.'

'She isn't in Memphis or in Sais, and nobody has seen her for a long time.'

Gem grunted. 'That is strange, I grant you. Could she have left on a journey?'

'Nitis has specific duties to carry out,' Menk reminded him. 'She is to help me prepare for the forthcoming festivals of Ptah and Hathor. Her knowledge of the ancient rituals will be invaluable. She has no reason to absent herself, especially if she wants to regain the king's trust.'

'Do you think she has run away?'

'Run away? Certainly not. I fear she has been kidnapped.'

The judge looked astonished. 'Who would do such a thing?'

'I don't know. I fear . . .'

'Do you suspect someone?'

'Perhaps it's Kel the scribe. Perhaps he wanted to get revenge on Nitis.'

'Why?'

'For not helping him.'

'Interesting . . . Are there any definite clues?'

'No, only suppositions, but I think the situation is very serious.'

'We must not be over-dramatic, Menk. Imagination often plays bad tricks on us.'

'Nitis has well and truly vanished! Don't ignore the facts, I beg of you.'

'That is not my custom.'

'What do you intend to do?'

'I shall appoint investigators to question temple employees, riverboat captains and overseers of the roads.'

'That will take ages!'

'I shall promise a substantial reward to anyone who gives me information about Nitis, and I will send out official messages alerting my colleagues in every province. After that is done, we must simply wait and hope.'

'Hope, yes, but wait?'

'Given the exceptional nature of the kidnapping, I shall use all the means at my disposal.'

'Thank you, Judge.'

'Do not do anything foolish, Menk. If Nitis really has been abducted, and if the man responsible is Kel, we are on dangerous ground. Leave this to the professionals.'

'I promise you I will.'

Shoulders slumped, Menk left the judge's office.

Gem was perplexed. First there was the Kel affair, which he had not managed to resolve, and now the disappearance of a priestess of Neith, an incredible event liable to unleash the anger of the gods. Up to now, despite the difficulties of handing down equitable justice, his career had proceeded peaceably and he was within sight of old age and well-deserved retirement. But now a vicious killer, allied with a seditious figure determined to overthrow Ahmose's throne, was defying the state and the law. And it was up to Judge Gem to destroy him.

In view of the new circumstances, he must question one of the kingdom's principal dignitaries, who might know a considerable amount about all of this.

6

It was years since Udja, first minister of Egypt, had entertained any thoughts of rest. In addition to being head doctor at the prestigious Sais school and personal physician to Pharaoh Ahmose, he was also governor of the capital, inspector of the court scribes, head of the prison administration and responsible for developing the war-fleet, a formidable deterrent weapon by which the king set great store.

With his broad shoulders, energetic manner and innate authority, Udja imposed his natural power on others and handled his responsibilities without a word of complaint. He exhausted his colleagues with his iron constitution and ability to get by with little sleep, and he would not tolerate either laziness or incompetence.

Moving the royal court to Memphis had brought with it a deluge of work, for Udja wanted to check everything and ensure that certain sleepy officials were put back to work. At any moment, the king must be able to move into any one of his palaces, which must be perfectly run.

Despite the development of Sais, the dynastic capital, the ancient city of Memphis, founded by Pharaoh Djoser, remained the key to the economic prosperity of the Two Lands. So, like the finance minister, Pefy, Udja was delighted by this royal sojourn, which would enable him to re-energize the various public services and favour trade, crafts and agriculture.

Concerned about the king's personal safety, Udja had issued strict instructions: all visitors were to be searched on entry to the palace, guards were to be hand-picked and relieved every three hours, the validity of all requests for audiences must be checked, the names of all visitors were to be written in an official register, and everyone must have a final meeting with one of Ahmose's secretaries before gaining access to the pharaoh's office. As long as Kel was at liberty, the most stringent precautions must be taken.

'Judge Gem wishes to speak with you, my lord,' an officer informed him.

'Send him in.'

Udja got up to greet the judge. 'Good news, I hope?'

'I am sorry to disappoint you.'

'Has Kel committed another crime?'

'I cannot say for certain, but he may be responsible for the abduction of the priestess Nitis.'

'The pupil of High Priest Wahibra at the Temple of Sais?'

'The same.'

'That's annoying.'

'So you didn't know about the incident?'

'Not until you told me. In Egypt, people are not abducted, especially not priests and priestesses. Is this crime an established fact?'

'Merely a probability, First Minister. The investigation has only just begun.'

'Ah. So there is still room for doubt.'

'I was hoping you might be able to enlighten me.'

Udja stiffened. 'I do not understand.'

'The king wanted perfect cooperation between Henat, head of the spy network, and the judiciary. At my age, I no longer believe pious promises. Henat will never pass on to me all the information he has, and on reflection I would not criticize him for that. He deals with state security, I with the strict observance of the law. In the Kel affair, our spheres of operation come into conflict. If this insane scribe has indeed abducted Nitis, I must add that crime to his file and, above all, find her. Might the head of the king's spies not have information vital to that success?'

'I don't know.'

'Question him, I beg you.'

'Why not do so yourself?'

'Because he won't tell me the truth.'

'Judge Gem, think what you are saying!'

'I am doing so, my lord. If we had cooperated, Kel would be in prison.'

'Are you accusing Henat of hindering your investigation?'

'Certainly not. He and I are both in the service of the state, of order and of justice, but our methods differ and the lack of unity leads to ineffectiveness. The worst killer in the land is still at large, and I fear he may commit other crimes. So your intervention seems vital to me.'

'What good would it do?'

'It might persuade Henat to provide me with information he is reluctant to give to a judge. I am prepared to overlook the sources of his information, although doing so conflicts with my conscience and my integrity as a judge. Kel is a dangerous murderer, very dangerous. We still do not know the names of his possible henchmen or his true goal. If he is merely an enraged madman, the throne is not at risk. On the other hand, if this scribe commands a group of rebels, our king will be their target. And I cannot believe that Henat knows nothing at all.'

'You are making serious accusations, Judge.'

'Not at all. I am simply concerned about the kingdom's security and I beg you to help me to preserve it.'

The solemnity of this declaration impressed Udja. 'In accordance with His Majesty's demands,' he assured Gem, 'I shall ask Henat for his full and entire cooperation.'

'I am afraid,' whispered the old judge. 'Abducting a

priestess ... Never before has such a crime been committed. The gods will not forgive us.'

'Do not be so pessimistic, and do not endow this killer with too many powers.'

'He has amply demonstrated his capacity for doing harm.'

Udja let out a long breath. 'I am not ignoring that. But our institutions stand firm and have resisted much more violent attacks. We shall not lower our guard, and we shall put an end to his crimes.'

'The gods are listening to you, First Minister.'

7

In his capacities as head of the king's spy network, palace director and priest of Thoth, who was the patron of scribes and scholars, Henat was privy to all the king's secrets. With his penetrating gaze, he had a gift for making people uneasy: in his presence, they immediately felt that they were suspects.

The enforced stay in Memphis had enabled him to recruit two new interpreters who spoke five languages fluently, including Greek and Persian. Recreating the department destroyed by Kel required time and caution, so Henat took no decisions without King Ahmose's explicit agreement. Little by little, the mainspring of Egyptian diplomacy was regaining its strength and vigour. The interpreters translated messages from foreign lands and wrote letters addressed to the king's allies in their own languages, for hieroglyphs – the embodiment of divine speech – could not be exported.

The Interpreters' Secretariat was not yet operating at full strength, but its activities were expanding from day to day, and Egypt was no longer deaf and dumb. Kel's attempt to reduce the country to silence and isolation had failed.

A meticulous and well-organized man, Henat did not allow dossiers to pile up. Only one document at a time lay on his work-table, where it was studied in depth and memorized in its entirety. The smallest detail might be important, and the service of the state demanded absolute thoroughness.

On his way to a working lunch hosted by Udja, Henat met Menk, who looked worried. Henat commented on the fact, and Menk said, 'Haven't you heard about the new drama? The priestess Nitis has disappeared.'

'Disappeared? Isn't that word a little excessive?'

'I think it may even be an abduction.'

'Is there any proof?'

'No, I just have a feeling of foreboding.'

'That is a little insubstantial, my dear Menk.'

'I have confided my fears to Judge Gem.'

'An excellent idea. He is just the man to deal with the matter.'

'And so are you, Henat.'

'This kind of problem is not really within my domain.'

'But you know about everything!'

'Let's not exaggerate.'

'You entrusted me with the task of spying on the senior priests at the Temple of Neith in Sais, especially Wahibra and Nitis. Wahibra is dead, and now Nitis has been abducted. She must be found.'

'Your reports do not contain any charges against them, and they have not attacked the security of the state in any way. So allow Judge Gem to act; he has excellent investigators at his disposal.'

Leaving the downcast Menk, Henat headed for the reception hall, where Udja was awaiting him along with a few royal scribes and Judge Gem.

A frugal meal was served. Henat drank only one cup of light beer and ate little. The talk was of different matters requiring the attention of Udja and Henat; then the scribes withdrew.

'We almost caught Kel,' said the judge.

'I doubt it,' objected Henat.

'What do you mean?' asked Gem.

'Someone was hiding in the abandoned brick-works, I agree, but was it really the killer?'

'Only he could sneer at the forces of order by leaving a decoy in his place,' declared the judge.

'In that case, he must have been warned that we were coming.'

A heavy silence followed this declaration.

'We must not veil our faces,' urged Udja. 'If Henat is right, Kel has allies and informants right at the heart of the forces of order, and that is why he continues to evade us.'

'In which case we are facing a true conspiracy with hitherto unsuspected ramifications,' said the judge. 'Kel is aiming to destroy the state and overthrow the king. It falls to the palace director to ensure the absolute loyalty of each of the guards charged with the king's safety.'

A half-smile appeared on Henat's face. 'I did not wait for your injunction, Judge Gem, and I have gone through every dossier with a fine-tooth comb. Two suspect soldiers have already been rejected. You may be certain that I shall not take any risks. I consider myself personally responsible for safeguarding the king in all circumstances, and I shall surround him with men who are perfectly sound, ready to give their lives to defend him.'

The judge's expression was grim as he finished his cup of red oasis wine.

'Henat, have you heard about the disappearance of the priestess Nitis?' asked Udja.

'One of my informants has just told me about it.'

'Menk, I assume?' Gem ventured.

'Permit me to maintain the secrecy of my sources.'

'The king has ordered your entire and perfect cooperation.'

'I obey his orders.'

'Then what do you know about this new tragedy?'

'Absolutely nothing.'

'That's impossible!'

'I am not omniscient, Judge. If there really was an abduction, it was carefully prepared, and my men had no warning of it. Of course, I shall initiate an investigation and keep you informed of the results. On the other hand ...' Henat hesitated.

'Please continue,' said Udja.

'We should not exclude the possibility that it's a case of one of Kel's accomplices fleeing. Nitis did speak in favour of his innocence. Perhaps she belongs to his network.'

'Is this suggestion based upon any evidence or clues?' asked Gem.

'It is merely a possibility,' admitted Henat.

'We are dealing with an affair which is far more serious than we imagined,' went on Udja. 'An enemy is threatening the integrity of the kingdom from within, and we must fight him to the very last of our strength. We must put aside personal differences and petty rivalries between state secretariats. Our foremost priority remains to eliminate Kel and his supporters.'

Udja's speech was interrupted by the sudden arrival of Queen Tanith, who looked terribly shaken.

'I need your help immediately,' she said.

'What has happened, Majesty?'

'The king has disappeared.'

8

Bebon's presence delighted Sweet-Lips. Always attentive, never bad-tempered, always ready to make love to her and satisfy her every desire, he was almost too perfect. There was, of course, no question of marriage, but the parting of their ways would be painful. Still, she would have wonderful memories of a devoted and attentive lover. While she awaited that unpleasant moment, she was taking full advantage of this fine male.

As they lounged together, naked, on a pile of cushions, Bebon looked worried.

'I hardly dare walk through Memphis any more,' he said. 'That story about the abduction is very frightening. Did you manage to learn anything about it?'

'Nothing pleasant,' she admitted.

'So it really did happen, then?'

'There are persistent rumours that it did.'

'Are the authorities investigating?'

'Apparently not. They even refused to take witness statements, on the pretext that they were not serious. Officially, there has been no disappearance.'

'But there has – you know there has.'

'What's the point of bothering with these horrors? From now on everyone will hold their tongue, and eventually the incident will be forgotten.'

'Not by me! The killer could strike again at any time, and you or I might be his next victim.'

Sweet-Lips was troubled.

'I have a friend in the guards,' said Bebon. 'If I speak to him he'll listen, but I must give him some concrete information. Is there anyone who'd be willing to testify?'

'A woman trader who has a shop on the quays would probably speak to you. But if you fail, don't persist.'

'I promise,' said the actor, putting his arms round her.

Bebon felt a bit ashamed of living in such comfort while his friend had to make do with a stable. But at least Kel was safe, thanks to North Wind's vigilance.

'I have a lead!' announced Bebon. 'We must go to the port.'

Sweet-Lips' words left no room for ambiguity: the city guards were obeying orders from above. No abduction, so no investigation. The conspirators' power was taking on enormous dimensions. How could two lone men possibly fight against it? Preferring not to think about it, Bebon followed Kel and the donkey, his nerves on edge.

'We'll pretend to be itinerant traders,' he said. 'Stay behind me and keep calm.'

'Did Sweet-Lips describe the trader to you?' asked Kel.

'She's a small redhead with a generous bosom.'

'What does she sell?'

'Lettuce from Memphis, onions and pots of fat.'

On the quayside, the market was in full swing. There were shops and temporary stalls, which sellers were allowed to erect when the boats arrived and unloaded their cargoes of fresh produce.

North Wind suddenly stopped dead. Two guards were cutting a swathe through the crowd. One of them had a baboon on a leash; its duty was to spot thieves and apprehend them by biting them on the leg. The trio changed direction.

'The baboon might think we look suspicious,' whispered Bebon. 'We'd better start trading right away.'

An old lady was shouting at an engraver. As she walked angrily away, Bebon asked, 'Can I help you?'

'I want an inscription on this alabaster bowl, in memory of my husband. That ruffian is demanding an exorbitant price!'

'My colleague can write in black ink,' said the actor. 'You can fix his fee yourself.'

'Two pairs of good sandals: will that be enough?'

'Perfect.'

Kel took his writing-materials out of one of the leather satchels carried by the donkey, and drew beautiful hieroglyphs as the widow dictated.

'That's splendid!' exclaimed the old lady in delight.

'The baboon's gone,' Bebon whispered in Kel's ear, 'but we'd better not stay here because he'll be back.'

The cheerful atmosphere of an Egyptian market dispelled all forms of sadness. People chatted, haggled for pleasure, told each other family stories, complained about the abuses of officials, and sought out good bargains. Seated on three-legged stools, many women ran shops, sheltered by a roof whose beams were adorned with pieces of fabric, belts, tunics and kilts. At the end of a successful purchase, people rushed off to the beer stall, where charming girls in short skirts served cool beer.

The redhead with the generous bosom was seated opposite the *Ibis*'s berth, although a different boat was now moored there.

'It's wonderful. My lettuce from Memphis is wonderful,' she called out to attract the attention of passers-by who would enjoy its delicate flavour.

'Your lettuce looks good,' purred Bebon, 'and you are positively delicious.'

The compliment took the trader by surprise. 'Are you ... buying?'

'Of course. Here are two pairs of brand-new sandals. In exchange, give me as much as you think fit.'

Still rather puzzled, the redhead selected several fine lettuces.

'I'm a close friend of the baker Sweet-Lips,' said Bebon. 'Would you be willing to help me?'

'How?'

'Something very serious has happened. A member of my family, a beautiful young girl, has vanished. Rumour has it that she's been kidnapped.'

The lettuce-seller looked down. 'I don't know anything.'

'I believe you, but please understand why I'm so upset. The guards refuse to investigate, and I'm dying of worry. The missing girl is my sister. We had a wonderful childhood together and were hardly ever apart. Because my mother was ill and hadn't long to live, my sister came to Memphis to find help. And then suddenly she disappears. Life can be cruel, can't it?'

The redhead wiped away a tear. 'Somebody did see something,' she confessed.

'Someone close to you?'

'No, the man who supplies me with pots of fat.'

'Did he really, or is he just boasting?'

'He drinks a lot, and at night he wanders the quayside with a bellyful of beer. But even when he's drunk he's clear-headed, and what he told me was appalling. Frankly, I'd rather forget it.'

'But I must find my poor sister. Where can I meet the trader?'

'Late in the evening, he gets drunk at the Good Luck inn. But it's no use: he won't talk.'

'What's he afraid of?'

'The guards delivered a message: absolute silence. Anyone with a loose tongue will be in serious trouble.'

Bebon kissed the redhead tenderly. 'Thank you for your help.'

9

Despite his abrupt and even brutal personality, General Phanes of Halikarnassos was popular with senior officers and men alike. He spent much of his time travelling from one garrison to the next, checking the Greek mercenaries' well-being – their pay had just been increased – their ability to fight and the quality of their equipment.

His tours of inspection were not merely a humdrum administrative routine. Following large-scale manoeuvres in which a number of incompetent soldiers were sometimes killed, he took on the best footsoldiers in single combat, and always emerged victorious from these duels. Despite his general staff's urging to exercise caution, Phanes was eager to spend time on the ground. Under his command, there was no question of shirking or forgetting one's military duties. In addition to the footsoldiers and cavalry, there was now an impressive war-fleet, thanks to constant hard work by Udja.

The general recognized the deterrent power of these forces, but thought they should be improved and, above all, kept on a war footing. The first moment of relaxation could prove fatal. The destruction of the Interpreters' Secretariat and the escape of the murderer and conspirator Kel represented very real threats. And then there was the vexing disappearance of Ahmose's helmet, the symbol of his accession to power. Phanes was sure none of his officers had either the intention or the opportunity to overthrow the throne and unleash a civil war. Nevertheless, he remained vigilant, ready to slit the throat of any man who rebelled.

The sojourn in Memphis enabled Phanes to study in detail the enormous barracks there and to rectify shortcomings in discipline. He was also working on developing the city's defence plan, in collaboration with the admirals.

As he was observing archers in training, a scribe asked him to go immediately to the palace. When he arrived he was greeted by a grim-faced Udja, who told him, 'The king has disappeared. Place our troops on a state of highest alert.'

'Disappeared? When and how?'

'He seems to have left his bedchamber during the night. The queen did not find him there this morning.'

'And what about the guards?'

'None of them saw him.'

'That's impossible. Let me question them.'

'You have my authorization to do so, General.'

'My best soldiers will search Memphis from top to bottom. There's not a moment to lose.'

Udja rejoined Queen Tanith, who was utterly distraught. She asked, 'Have you learnt anything?'

'Not yet, Majesty. The guards and the army are out in force, searching the city.'

'Have you searched the palace?'

'We are checking every nook and cranny.'

Henat interrupted them. 'At last, we have a credible witness report. A gardener saw the king setting off, alone, along the tamarisk walk towards the canal.'

Udja, Henat, the queen and a large number of armed men set off in the same direction.

The man in charge of the landing stage was dozing.

Udja roughly shook him awake. 'Did His Majesty come this way?'

'I don't know. You'll have to ask my superior.'

The superior was cleaning one of the court's pleasure-boats, designed for pleasant trips on the river.

'The king? Yes, he took a boat early this morning.'

'How many men forced him to do it?'

'There weren't any men, only some young girls – a bit saucy they were, too. And I had to fetch ten jars of rough wine for His Majesty. Look, there's the boat now.'

The female crew steered the boat skilfully to its moorings.

Udja dashed up the gangplank. 'Is the king on board?'

'In his cabin,' replied a pretty brunette.

Udja forced open the door.

'You, already!' Ahmose exclaimed.

'Majesty, we were very worried.'

'Do I not have the right to enjoy myself? Oh, this is awful!' The king held his head in his hands. 'I've got a terrible headache. I've drunk too much, and it was the hard stuff. But at least the girls were happy, and they didn't bore me too much with their chatter.'

Udja had to support the king, who could barely stand upright. 'Do you wish to return to the palace, Majesty?'

'No doubt you have arranged a council of ministers?'

'General Phanes awaits your agreement regarding the new defence plan for Memphis.'

Ahmose straightened up. 'The security of the state must not be neglected. We shall go.'

At the foot of the gangplank, the queen greeted her husband affectionately, then told him, 'I was frantic with worry.'

'It was only a short boat trip. A king who never enjoys himself becomes grim and loses touch with reality.'

'How do you feel?'

'Apart from the headache, very well. I needed to escape from the stifling atmosphere in the royal apartments.'

'Do you wish to return to Sais?'

'Not yet, sweet Tanith. I want to visit the main barracks, meet my Greek mercenaries, listen to their grievances and give them satisfaction. Arrange several banquets so that I can forget about council meetings and my never-ending administrative tasks. And tell my cupbearer to select only the finest wines!'

10

The man who roasted the meat at the Good Luck inn was not short of work. Untroubled by sensitivity, he wrung the necks of ducks and fat geese, plucked them and put them on a spit above a brazier, which was fanned by his assistant. Then he salted the poultry and added fine herbs.

The quality of the food attracted many customers, who also enjoyed delicious chunks of beef boiled in an enormous cauldron. As the prices were reasonable, everyone was eager to secure a chair at one of the low tables.

The fat-seller was a regular customer, who never tired of the good food but always enjoyed every mouthful. For him the noon meal was the best time of the whole day. He forgot all his troubles, his wife's bad mood and the whims of his children.

When Bebon and Kel found him, the chairs opposite him were empty.

'May we sit here?' asked Bebon.

'The seats are free.'

'All the food smells good,' said Bebon. 'What do you recommend, goose, duck or beef?'

'The roast goose couldn't be better. The next time you come, try the duck. And the beef is well worth a third visit.'

'I wouldn't say no.'

'What do you two do for a living?'

'We're travelling traders. We sell fabrics, sandals and mats.'
'That's hard work.'
'We don't complain, as long as we enjoy our trips.'
'Me, I sell pots of bull's, goat's and goose fat, and two sorts of butter: one for eating straight away, and one for keeping. My pots are numbered and dated, and the wealthy customers fight over them. I supply the best inns in Memphis, too.'
'You're quite a success,' said Bebon admiringly. 'You must work very long hours.'
'One can't skimp on quality.'
'You sound like Sweet-Lips the baker. Once you've tasted her bread, everyone else's tastes second-rate. It's lucky life has those kinds of pleasures to offer us, isn't it? Mind you, because of the increasing insecurity, we're sometimes afraid to travel the roads – or even to walk along the quays in Memphis.'
The fat-seller stopped chewing. 'Have you had problems?'
'Not personally, but my little sister recently disappeared.'
Kel was silently watching the fat-seller, and saw the affable expression vanish from his coarse face.
'The guards will find her.'
'They're refusing to investigate. Strange, don't you think?'
'Everyone has his own trade and his own problems.'
'You like walking on the quayside in the evenings, don't you?' ventured Kel.
'That's my concern.'
'You saw some men abduct a young woman, didn't you?'
'You're talking nonsense.'
'Judging by your reaction, I'm certain you saw it all.'
'Don't talk rubbish!'
'We know you did,' Bebon claimed. 'I want to find my little sister, and you're going to help us.
The fat-seller looked cautiously around. 'Come outside. There are too many curious ears in here.' He led them over to a cauldron where bacon was cooking, in the shelter of a straw roof. 'You're city guards, aren't you?'

'No, we aren't. Don't worry,' Kel reassured him.

'I know your game. If I don't keep my mouth shut, you'll send me to prison.'

'No, we won't. We don't belong to the forces of order and all we want is to find someone very dear to us.'

'Liar!' Seizing the cauldron, the man threw its contents at Kel.

In the nick of time Bebon pushed his friend out of the way, and the boiling water narrowly missed them both.

The fat-seller took to his heels, but just when he thought he was out of reach North Wind charged at him and knocked him over. By the time he had regained his wits and stood up, Bebon and Kel had come racing up, and they were determined not to let him get away again.

'You're part of the kidnap gang, aren't you?' demanded Bebon furiously.

'You're mad!'

'And you wanted to boil us alive!'

'I'm afraid of prison!'

'How many times do we have to tell you? We aren't guards. You saw everything, didn't you? So tell us.'

'What if I refuse?'

'I'll smash your head in with a stone and we'll find another witness. But if you talk we'll let you go.'

The fat-seller swallowed hard. Dry-mouthed and trembling with fear, he gave in. 'I was a bit drunk and I'm not sure I—'

'Hurry up, friend! Our patience has run out.'

'It happened beside the *Ibis*, a trading-boat. A young woman was stepping on to the gangplank when four burly fellows grabbed her. The poor girl had no chance of escape.'

'These men, did you recognize them?'

The fat-seller hesitated. Kel, sensing that the man had vital information, picked up a rock.

'No, no, wait! I know one of them.'

'What's his name?'

'Palios.'

'A Greek?'

'Yes, a . . . a . . .'

'A soldier?'

The fat-seller nodded.

'The four men were Greek mercenaries,' suggested Kel. 'Is that it?'

Another nod.

'Where do we find this Palios?' demanded Bebon menacingly.

'He lives in the main Memphis barracks, but when he isn't on duty he often goes to the alehouse near the potters' district.'

'Does he see a girl there?'

'Yes, Guiga, a nice little thing.'

'Do you go there, too?'

'Oh no, hardly ever! I'm married and—'

'Nobody will say anything to your wife. Now, my friend, forget all about us. If you make the unwise move of warning Palios or alerting the authorities, you won't live long.'

11

Pharaoh Ahmose could not stop thinking about the decisive moment when, as a mere general, he had allowed himself to be crowned with the helmet which, by the grace of the Egyptian army, had been transformed into a royal crown.

Despite having no desire to reign – he had wanted only to win a quick victory in the civil war against the hated and discredited Pharaoh Apries – he had accepted his destiny and taken in hand the fate of the Two Lands, with one fixed idea: not to suffer the same fate as his predecessor. So he had surrounded himself with reliable men, faithful servants of the state, and rewarded them according to their efforts. Nevertheless he was still wary: he constantly observed them and weighed up their actions. Up to now, they had applied his directives to the letter.

What had become of his helmet? A would-be usurper would surely have already tried to take power by force? Unless, as the investigation led him to believe, the thief was also the murderous scribe Kel, who had been weakened too much to succeed.

The pharaoh enjoyed living in Memphis. Even though he preferred his capital, Sais, he liked the cosmopolitan nature of the great city, which was always able to transform itself in accordance with events.

Understanding developments and adapting to them: that seemed to be Ahmose's genius. And the key to the future was

Greece. Old Egypt lacked a spirit of innovation and was bogged down in its respect for the ancestors. By entrusting the security of the country to an army of well-trained and well-paid Greek mercenaries, the king deterred any would-be predators from attacking the Two Lands, whose wealth made many people envious. And he had been able to undertake important legal reforms, not forgetting the imposition of a tax on personal income, which no Egyptian could escape. The upkeep of his armed forces cost a great deal, and it would have been a grave mistake to reduce it.

Ahmose continued to be suspicious of Nitetis, daughter of the late Pharaoh Apries. Her husband was the wealthy Kroisos, head of the Persian diplomatic secretariat. A friend to Egypt, Kroisos advocated peace, but his wife might well harbour a lasting hatred of Ahmose, whom she accused of having assassinated her father. At their latest official meeting in Sais, Nitetis had promised to forget the past. But was that promise sincere or merely a tactful lie?

Towards mid-morning, Henat brought the king a pile of files to read.

'Anything important?' asked Ahmose.

'Only a letter from Kroisos.'

'Good news?'

'He suggests lowering certain customs duties in order to facilitate the development of trading exchanges between Asia and Egypt. It is an interesting idea, Majesty, worth examining closely. We must not strip ourselves of our prerogatives or destroy our system of protection. If you are in agreement, we could grant him a few crumbs, examine the results and then have further discussions.'

'Very well,' replied the king, scanning the various reports.

Capable of brief but intense concentration, Ahmose wanted to be informed about everything, notably the smallest initiative by his ministers. Accustomed to reading quickly and extracting what was important, the king only appeared to delegate, even if he sometimes neglected certain details.

'Has there been any progress in reorganizing the Interpreters' Secretariat?'

'I have two new candidates for you, Majesty. They both speak several Asian languages and have spent time in our protectorates. I examined their files closely and found nothing that would cause concern.'

'Have you interviewed them?'

'At length.'

'Bring them to me tomorrow, and I will give you my decision. Now, is there any news from our agents in Persia?'

'Coded messages, following the usual procedure.'

'And is the information reassuring?'

'They corroborate what our friend Kroisos says. Emperor Cambyses has apparently have given up all desire for war and territorial conquests, in order to devote himself to the economy and to trade.'

'You sound sceptical.'

'That is the basis of my profession, Majesty.'

'What makes you doubt the emperor's sincerity?'

'To be honest, there's nothing specific, but I'm still cautious. The volume of our trade with Persia has indeed increased, and our diplomatic exchanges have grown in strength.'

'I hope that that is merely a beginning.'

Commander Phanes requested an audience; he was accompanied by Greek envoys laden with gifts.

The king received them in the great pillared hall of the Memphis palace, and greeted them warmly, one by one.

Never had relations between Egypt and her Greek allies been better. The queen held a sumptuous banquet for the envoys, and far into the night there was talk of poetry and music as cultural traditions were compared. The Greeks had been drunk for a long time when Ahmose called for a jar dating from Year One of his reign.

'Permit me to be the first to taste this wine,' suggested Phanes in a low voice.

The sovereign was surprised. 'What do you fear?'

'The banquet is a success, the atmosphere is relaxed, and friendship reigns. A warrior must be wary of such moments.'

'Do you think . . .?'

'I would prefer to check.'

'Not you.' Ahmose turned towards the oldest Greek envoy and asked, 'Will you do me the pleasure of judging the quality of this exceptional vintage?'

'It is a great honour, Majesty.' When he tasted it, the envoy went into raptures. 'I know my wines, Majesty, and this one is wholly exceptional – absolute nectar.'

The other guests also extolled the wine, which the pharaoh was last to enjoy.

At the end of the enjoyable and successful evening, Ahmose made three announcements: first, he was creating hundreds of posts for mercenaries in the garrisons of the Delta and Memphis; second, the elite Greek troops would be exempted from taxes; lastly, their pay was once again to be increased.

All these decisions were greeted with great enthusiasm.

The king had another jar of Year One wine opened, in order to celebrate the strengthened links between Egypt and her allies. The military power thus created would discourage any would-be aggressors, starting with the Persians.

12

Walking along beside North Wind, who was laden with vegetables purchased at a market in the old town, Kel spotted the alehouse frequented by Palios. It was bustling. Many customers, mostly Greeks, thronged the place. There they could drink strong beer, laugh and joke at their leisure, and above all take advantage of the charms of Libyan, Syrian and Nubian girls who openly adorned themselves with tattoos, a characteristic of women of ill repute.

In only a short time, Kel saw two guards patrols pass by. At the slightest sign of trouble, they would take action and apprehend the brawlers.

As he was moving away, about twenty guards armed with clubs and accompanied by a detachment of archers invaded the district.

Frightened, the housewives who were chatting in the middle of the narrow streets scooped up their children, ran indoors and closed their doors and shutters. Any itinerant traders and passers-by in the streets were caught in the net, along with the customers of the inns, taverns and houses of pleasure. Not a single district of Memphis would escape the meticulous sweep ordered by Judge Gem.

Sensing that the archers were ready to fire, Kel made no attempt to run and escape. North Wind stood stock still, urging him not to move a muscle, even though his nerves were at breaking-point. A short time from now, Kel knew, he would be in the hands of his accusers and would lose his freedom for ever. Nitis had been kidnapped, and he would soon be sentenced to death . . . Their happiness had been nothing but a fleeting dream.

An officer came up to Kel and looked him over suspicuously. 'Name?'

'Bak.'

'Who do you work for?'

'Sweet-Lips, the baker. I fetch food for her household and deliver it to her cook.'

'I buy bread from Sweet-Lips, and I haven't seen you in her shop.'

'You wouldn't. I only deliver to her house.'

'Where is it?'

Kel gave the address.

'Have you been to the market?' asked the officer, still suspicious.

'Yes.'

'So your donkey's carrying food.'

'That's right.'

'Open the panniers.'

Kel did so.

At the sight of the vegetables, the officer seemed disappointed. 'One of my men will accompany you to the baker's house and check what you've said.'

This was a disaster. Kel was Bebon's servant, not Sweet-Lips'. She would deny knowing him, talk about her lover, and the guards would arrest the two friends.

'Come along,' said the sturdy fellow ordered to escort him.

Kel wasn't strong enough to get deal with the guard, who was armed with a heavy staff and a short sword and would make short work of him. Besides, the trio kept meeting more and more soldiers and guards, who had been deployed all over the city in order to question as many suspects as possible.

Aware of the seriousness of the situation, North Wind dragged his feet. Kel wondered if the donkey would take the wrong direction, trying to mislead the guard. But he'd be sure to realize and take brutal action.

As Kel was desperately searching for a solution, a commotion broke out. Two soldiers shouted to the guard, 'A fugitive! Come with us – we must catch him!'

'I've got my orders, I—'

'They're being changed. This is an emergency!'

The guard obeyed, and ran to join them.

Suddenly free, Kel and North Wind hurried off towards Sweet-Lips' house. They must warn Bebon at once and then leave their refuge, which was now a trap.

Judge Gem had struck hard. Unable to bear the sight of justice being taunted by an escaped murderer, he had put all his efforts into organizing a vast search operation, hoping for impressive results. If Kel and his accomplices were hiding in Memphis, they would be caught up in the sweep or else be denounced by someone who was frightened by the deployment of so much force. Eventually tongues would wag and nobody would dare shelter a wanted criminal with such determination.

At the end of the hectic day, the men responsible for the operation appeared before Judge Gem. Their spokesmen was general of footsoldiers.

'Positive results, Judge,' he said. 'The operation went perfectly, and we made many arrests: around twenty thieves, five of them repeat offenders, foreigners with illegal status, anti-social people trying to evade their compulsory work obligations, unworthy fathers refusing to pay a food pension, and itinerant sellers who have been avoiding taxes. A few offenders attempted to escape, but we caught them all.'

'Excellent,' said the judge morosely. 'Did you arrest the scribe Kel?'

'Unfortunately, no.'

'Did you get any information about him?'

'Not a word.'

'And the missing priestess, Nitis?'

'Nothing, I'm afraid. But your plan has succeeded brilliantly, Judge. Not a single criminal in Memphis feels safe any longer, and they all know we may act at any moment. Thanks to you, their morale is at its lowest point and that of the forces of order is at its height.'

'Congratulate your soldiers and guards, General.'

The officers withdrew.

Alone, Gem wondered how he was going to present this crushing failure to Udja. There was only one solution: the truth, combined with his resignation. After such a blunder, the old judge could no longer remain in his post. So many cases solved, so many court cases brought to a just conclusion, so many guilty parties put under lock and key ... And now this murderous scribe was sneering at him, putting a shameful end to his career ...

No, Gem would not give in like this. Instead of humiliating himself, he would emphasize the positive aspect of this vast operation and draw conclusions from it: either Kel had left Memphis or else he had an enormous network of accomplices capable of endangering the state.

The coded papyrus discovered in Khufu's chapel had still not been deciphered. And there was no trace of Ahmose's helmet. The existence of this text seemed to speak in the scribe's favour ... But no, it must be a decoy.

Strengthened by his experience and perseverance, the old judge would see this battle through to the end. It would probably be his last, but he would bring down the monster threatening Egypt.

13

By a stroke of good fortune, Bebon was at Sweet-Lips' house. Still drowsy after waking from a long midday nap, he had no idea of the gigantic operation that had been mounted to capture his friend.

When Kel delivered the vegetables to the cook, he said, 'I have a message for the baker's guest.'

'I'll go and tell him.'

Bebon soon arrived, and Kel explained the situation to him.

'Did you find the alehouse?' asked the actor.

'Yes, but we can't get anywhere near it.'

'Don't panic. The guards and soldiers will soon go back to their barracks. We'll make our attempt in the middle of the night.

'I can't stay here.'

'Yes, you can – nobody will look for you in the stables. I'll wait for Sweet-Lips to come home, then we'll have dinner and I'll do my duty as a lover. After that I'll go to my own room, escape via the roof and come and fetch you.'

'What if the city's still being patrolled?'

'We shall check.'

As North Wind showed no signs of anxiety, Kel lay down on the straw and waited. At the least sign of danger, the donkey would warn him.

Nitis was still alive; he was certain of it. He could feel

her anguish and hear her call – and time was against them.

At last Bebon appeared. 'Let's go. Sweet-Lips thinks I'm asleep, and the district seems calm. If there are still too many guards around, we'll beat a retreat.'

'And go where?'

'We'll see. But our first priority is to free Nitis, isn't it?'

Cut to the quick, Kel dashed out of the stable.

'Take care!' Bebon urged him.

North Wind had already set off towards the alehouse, choosing the shortest route. To judge from his brisk pace, there was no danger.

The guards and soldiers had indeed withdrawn, restoring the city's tranquil yet happy atmosphere. The relieved inhabitants were emerging from their homes and discussing the strange events of the day. They all expressed their own opinions, and vehement criticisms were voiced.

As the trio neared the alehouse, the donkey slowed down. All their senses on the alert, Kel and Bebon scrutinized their surroundings. There were no guards lying in wait.

'Wait at the corner of the street,' said Bebon. 'I'm going to see what I can find out.'

He knocked at the door of the alehouse. It opened slowly, and a Nubian stuck his head out. 'What do you want?'

'A drink and a bit of fun.'

'Are you alone?'

'Too alone.'

'Can you pay?'

'I know the prices.'

The Nubian looked up and down the narrow street. 'Come in.'

The large room was filled with revellers, most of them drunk.

'Is Guiga free?' Bebon asked the Nubian.

'Not a chance! That little one's in good hands.'

'Those of my friend Palios, I'll wager.'

'Ah, so you know him?'

'What a man he is, that Greek! Give me a drink, and I'll wait for him. And he's paying.'

'No girl for the time being?'

'We'll see afterwards.'

Bebon settled himself comfortably and sipped his beer.

Half an hour later a couple appeared: a pretty brown-haired girl and a heavily built man with the look of a soldier. He kissed the girl, drank down a cup of date wine and headed for the door.

Bebon slipped over to him and jabbed the point of his knife into the man's side. 'We're leaving together, Palios. If you resist, I'll kill you.'

Tired and drunk, the Greek obeyed.

When they got outside, North Wind crushed him against the wall of the alehouse and Kel seized him by the throat and demanded, 'Talk, you piece of filth! Where did you take Nitis the priestess?'

'We'd better move further away,' advised Bebon.

They dragged their prisoner into a darkened alleyway.

'You've got the wrong man,' Palios protested feebly.

'You're a mercenary, aren't you?'

'Yes, but—'

'And you and some others like you abducted a woman, didn't you?'

'No, I didn't!' Palios tried to run away but, charging at him, North Wind butted him hard in the lower back and he fell face down on the ground.

Bebon immobilized him and ran his blade across the back of his neck. 'If you lie, I'm going to cut you into pieces! And I'm in a hurry, a very great hurry.'

'It was an order. They made me do it.'

'Who gave the order?'

'I don't know. All I did was obey the commander of the group.'

'What's his name?'

'I don't know that, either.'

'Don't joke with me, Palios!'

'I'm not, I swear! I'd never seen any of those men before in my life.'

'What did you do?' Kel demanded.

'We intercepted the girl at the bottom of the *Ibis*'s gang-plank.'

'Nitis is not a girl,' raged Kel. 'She is the Superior of the chantresses and weavers of Neith!'

'All right, all right! I didn't know anything about that. When you're a soldier you carry out your orders without questioning them.'

'Where did you take her?'

'To a big house south of the city.'

'Right, you're taking us there now,' Bebon ordered.

'I can't. I have to go back to the barracks.'

The point of Bebon's knife sank into the Greek's neck.

'I said: you are taking us there. Now.'

14

The moon was full, so the quartet were able to move fast. Suddenly, though, North Wind stopped dead.

Kel immediately realized why. 'You're trying to mislead us, Palios. One more trick like that, and you won't see dawn break again.'

'You'd better understand something,' added Bebon. 'To us, one death more or less doesn't matter. But if you take us to the right house, you have a chance of survival.'

Defeated, head bent, the Greek set off in the right direction. There were no guards or soldiers in sight.

Shortly before sunrise they came to a narrow, slumbering street, at the far end of which stood a sumptuous two-storey house protected by high walls. Hundred-year-old palm trees provided shade for the house, and it stood in the middle of a huge garden.

North Wind halted, his ears pricked up.

'Who lives here?' Kel asked.

'I don't know,' said Palios. 'There were other soldiers waiting for us at the entrance. We handed over the girl – I mean, the priestess – to them, and then dispersed.'

'As you don't know anything,' observed Bebon, 'you're pretty worthless.'

'You promised . . .'

Reaching into one of the donkey's panniers, the actor took

out a rag, which he stuffed into the mercenary's mouth, then a length of ship's rope, with which he bound him securely. Kel and Bebon left him at the back of a storehouse where jars were kept.

'Someone will find you eventually,' the actor told him. 'Take care to hold your tongue. If you don't, our people will execute you. Understood?'

The Greek blinked and nodded.

'Now,' said Kel, 'let's get in there.'

'I wouldn't advise it,' said his friend. 'In my opinion, it's probably a trap. We must examine the place carefully, then we can work out a plan of action.'

Although boiling over with impatience, Kel had to listen to reason. He did not want to spoil any chance, however small, of freeing Nitis.

Bebon had been sure the house would be heavily guarded, but he eventually had to acknowledge that he was wrong. There were no soldiers or police officers nearby, only a door-keeper sitting in a wooden kiosk covered with coarse cloth, which during the day would protect him from the sun's fierce rays.

'It's too good to be true,' Bebon said. 'Let's go round and check again.'

The place was particularly quiet, because it was at some distance from the busy streets and districts.

'A perfect prison,' observed Kel.

'If so, the soldiers will be inside. How many of them do you think there are?'

'Let's get rid of the door-keeper and go in.'

'That fellow's bait. At the first sign of trouble, a horde of Greeks will descend on us.'

'Then let's climb over the wall.'

'Same result. There must be patrols and lookouts. And we don't know where to go. We need accurate information.'

'We'll get it from the door-keeper.'

'No, we won't!'

'Nitis has already waited so long . . .'

'If we get ourselves killed, she'll have no hope left.'

Once again, Kel fought back his longing to rush into the damned house. Could Nitis sense his presence? Did she still believe he would free her?

'Even Greek mercenaries have to eat and drink,' said Bebon, 'and that means deliverymen are going to come to the house. They may know something useful.'

'But what if they don't?'

'Look on the bright side. The sun's nearly up, so we shouldn't have to wait long.'

Kel's patience was sorely tried by the waiting, but at last a water-carrier appeared. He exchanged a few words with the door-keeper, who allowed him to enter the grounds, from which he re-emerged almost immediately.

Kel and Bebon intercepted him in a nearby alleyway while North Wind stood guard.

'We're thirsty,' said the actor.

'Sorry, but I've sold all my water.'

'To the people in the big house?'

'That's right.'

'They're Greeks, aren't they?'

'I don't know. I'm standing in for my employer, who's ill, and I don't know this area very well.'

Kel and Bebon returned to their observation post.

The next to arrive was a man delivering hot flat-cakes stuffed with chickpeas. He, too, was given permission to cross the threshold.

When he left, Kel approached him as soon as he was out of sight of the door-keeper. Bebon remained some way back, checking that nobody was following them.

'I'd like a flat-cake,' said Kel.

'I haven't got any left. But you'll find several sellers not far from here.'

'Those Greeks have all the luck!'

The cake-seller looked surprised. 'What do you mean?'

'You've sold them all your famous flat-cakes! And they must be very rich to live in such a fine house.'

The seller relaxed. 'Oh, you're quite wrong. The owner of that house isn't Greek.'

'Do you know who he is?'

'The finance minister, Pefy. His staff pay me well. Judging from the number of flat-cakes they buy, there must be at least ten servants in there. But I must get on. Good day to you.'

15

Queen Tanith looked both beautiful and elegant, her face exquisitely painted, her only jewellery a lapis-lazuli necklace and bracelets of gold. Although the court had reached Sais only that morning, she had arranged for a banquet to be held in the evening, to mark the pharaoh's return to the city. Ahmose greatly appreciated these moments of relaxation, which enabled him to forget the burden of his duties for a while. Admittedly he drank too much and sometimes indulged in regrettable whims; but he always steered the ship of state with a firm hand and to pursue his goals of economic prosperity, alliances with the Greek kingdoms and principalities, and the growth of Egyptian military power.

After complimenting the queen on her appearance, Ahmose grumbled, 'I am suffering from another terrible headache.'

'Did you forget to take the remedies Udja prescribed?'

'It's possible. I do prefer a nice light, fruity white wine, which has the power to dispel all ills.'

'The court is delighted that we are back. Memphis is a beautiful city, but our capital has especial charm, hasn't it?'

'And it has not stopped growing, I assure you. From now on, this is where the fate of the world will be played out. Memphis will continue to be a trading centre, and Thebes a repository of outdated traditions.'

'Isn't the Divine Worshipper still extremely popular?'

'Our people appreciate the glorious past of the city of the god Amun, and remember the golden era of the Tuthmosids, the Amenhoteps and the Ramses. But the future lies elsewhere, Tanith. We must turn towards the Mediterranean and towards Greece. Thanks to intellectuals like Pythagoras, we are strengthening Greece's links with Egypt, which will never be distanced from progress.'

'Tonight, several Greek envoys have been invited to your table.'

'Excellent! See that our head cook shows he is equal to the occasion.'

'You can count on my vigilance.'

Although everyone at court admired the queen, they also knew that she was very strict. She was unforgiving of professional errors and set great store by a rigorous respect for protocol: Egypt's reputation depended on it. Ahmose congratulated himself daily on having her at his side. She had even succeeded in calming Nitetis, wife of Kroisos and, more importantly, daughter of his erstwhile rival Apries. By soothing that lioness's resentment, Tanith had shown herself to be a perfect negotiator.

'Before the banquet,' grumbled the king, 'I have many boring duties to perform.'

Tanith smiled. 'The prosperity of the Two Lands depends upon it.'

The couple parted and Ahmose went to his office, where he received Judge Gem.

'Despite its encouraging results,' said the judge, 'the operation in Memphis did not enable me to arrest Kel. However, security has been improved by it and criminal activity will be considerably reduced. Some dangerous individuals are now in custody and I have established one certainty: Kel has left the city and is trying to reach the South. If he succeeds in crossing the border at Elephantine, he will take refuge in Nubia and attempt to stir up the tribes against you.'

'Have you taken the necessary steps?'

'I have asked Phanes and Henat to place their men on a permanent state of alert. For my part, I have ordered all the guards forces in the kingdom to exercise even greater vigilance. Land and river routes have never before been so closely monitored, Majesty. I cannot see how an insurrection could take shape.'

'And yet that accursed scribe has slipped through our fingers again, and my helmet has still not been found.'

'Since you have placed your trust in me, I shall prove equal to my task, and I will bring that murderer back to you, dead or alive. His cunning will not defeat my patience.'

'The new High Priest of Neith is much less stubborn than his predecessor, so the Temple of Neith is now completely open to us,' said Ahmose, 'and it will no longer serve as a refuge for those who oppose the authorities. Make another detailed search, Judge. Perhaps we shall be pleasantly surprised.'

'A really detailed search?'

'No building is to be spared.'

'Not even the shrines of the royal tombs?'

'I have already told you: none.'

The judge seemed embarrassed. 'Nitis, the favourite pupil of the former High Priest, Wahibra, has vanished, Majesty. There are no clues, and no witnesses.'

'Vanished? Or run away?'

'Nitis may be a remarkable young woman and destined for a brilliant career, but, despite the absence of concrete evidence, I have always been suspicious of her. If Wahibra did protect Kel in some way, she would have obeyed him unquestioningly.'

'If she is in league with the murderer, has she gone to join him?'

'I believe so, Majesty.'

'A strange thing for her to do. Was she not Superior of the chantresses and weavers of Neith?'

'Indeed, but the appointment of a new High Priest convinced her that she would soon be dismissed from her offices
and returned to a lowly rank. In my opinion, there is a
convincing explanation for this curious disappearance.'

'What explanation, Judge Gem?'

'A simple case of love, Majesty.'

'Nitis has fallen in love with Kel?'

'And he with her, unless he is using her as an ally in order to
move about and hide. We are looking for a man on his own,
not a couple.'

'A convincing explanation,' said the king. 'Issue new
instructions.'

'I have already done so, Majesty. Kel's skill rests not on
chance but on effective and discreet help. And this is doubtless
one of its aspects. If others exist, I shall discover them.'

'My trust in you is renewed.'

The old judge felt rejuvenated. Once again he had become a
merciless hunter, patient and clear-sighted, from whom not
even the most cunning of criminals could escape. Forgetting
the honours, titles and comfort of a comfortable life, he had
rediscovered the energy and ferocity of the young investigator
who had wanted to see justice done and fight evil. Pleasantly
surprised, Ahmose knew that the fugitive couple's days were
numbered.

16

Kel and Bebon were thunderstruck by what the cake-seller had told them. The conspirators' leader, the man who had given the order to destroy the Interpreters' Secretariat and who would not hesitate to kill again in order to satisfy his ambitions, was Pefy, the finance minister! They couldn't believe it. As director of the Double House of gold and silver, director of fields and overseer of the floodlands, Pefy managed the Egyptian economy and had always given complete satisfaction to King Ahmose.

'Pefy served Ahmose's predecessor, Apries,' Bebon recalled. 'Perhaps he's still loyal to Apries and wants to avenge his death by seizing power himself. Age and wealth don't necessarily snuff out ambition.'

'Nitis told me that Pefy knew her parents well,' said Kel. 'He smoothed the way for her to enter the Temple of Neith. She regarded him as a protector, so she wouldn't have been suspicious of him. And it was Pefy who invited me to the banquet during which – on his instructions – I was drugged so that I would oversleep, arrive late at the Interpreters' Secretariat and thus become a killer in the eyes of the law.'

'There's something else,' said Bebon. 'He often goes to Abydos, where a garrison of Greek mercenaries is stationed. He probably recruited the kidnappers there.'

Kel seethed with anger and impatience. 'That monster made

a fatal mistake when he attacked Nitis,' he said. 'Now I know how to free her.'

Bebon bit his lip, fearing the worst.

'First,' Kel went on, 'we must find Pefy, assuming he hasn't left Memphis. We'll kidnap him and then simply exchange him for Nitis. After that, we'll take stock of how things stand.'

'With respect, I think your plan is insane and impracticable.'

Kel ignored him. 'We must go to the palace at once.'

North Wind chose the shortest route, as always, and – in view of the urgency of the situation – set a fast pace.

Kel approached the first guard-post. 'I have come from Abydos,' he said, so calmly that he surprised himself, 'and I must deliver a message into the hands of Minister Pefy himself.'

Impressed by the scribe's bearing and serious demeanour, the sentry did not dismiss him out of hand.

Anxiety gnawed at Bebon, who was watching nearby. This course of action was suicidal. If a soldier recognized Kel, there would be a stampede! However, North Wind was munching some of his fodder, looking quite serene.

An officer arrived, obviously a man of some importance. He and Kel had a long discussion, without any apparent animosity. Then the scribe walked calmly back to Bebon. Nobody stopped him.

'We're going to the port,' said Kel. 'Pefy's boat is preparing to leave Memphis. We still have a chance of intercepting him.'

'That's impossible. He'll be protected by hordes of guards!'

'We'll see.'

North Wind consented to interrupt his meal, and chose a clear, open route to the port.

When they got there, Bebon turned out to be right. It was impossible to gain access to the official landing-stage. Only authorized persons could pass through the military checkpoints.

A magnificent vessel was preparing to cast off. In the centre of the desk stood a large cabin, charmingly decorated with flowers and a chequerboard pattern.

'That's Pefy's boat,' said Bebon. 'Unfortunately we'll never get near it.'

'Give me the Greek knife.'

'What idea have you got into your head now?'

'There are too many soldiers on the quayside, I agree. But there's still the river – and I'm an excellent swimmer.'

'Either you'll drown, or the archers will kill you when they see you climbing aboard.'

'Nobody is watching the other side of the cabin. Give me the knife.'

'Don't do this, Kel. It's madness!'

The look in the scribe's eyes was so commanding that Bebon was obliged to hand over the knife.

'Don't move from here. We'll take Pefy to the house and free Nitis.'

Speechlessly, Bebon watched Kel move away, thinking that this was the last time he'd see him alive. Swimming underwater for a long time would not be easy; reaching the boat without being spotted would be quite an achievement; and climbing aboard would be close to a miracle. As for the eventual outcome, that was an utter impossibility. Pefy would never agree to go with Kel. He'd alert the soldiers, and the scribe – who was incapable of cutting a man's throat – would be killed.

North Wind and Bebon both kept their eyes fixed on the boat. The sails were being hoisted, beer and food were being taken aboard, and the captain was addressing the oarsmen.

Bebon bitterly regretted not having stopped his friend. But how could he have reasoned with him? Kel's overwhelming love for Nitis had blotted out all sense of danger, and he'd rather die trying to free her than accept reality. They couldn't possibly fight Greek soldiers or a powerful minister of the state.

For a moment, Bebon thought of causing confusion by

shouting incomprehensibly. He would attract the attention of some of the guards, then he'd be arrested and Kel could continue his mad attempt. He really was an odd fellow! To all appearances he was controlled, level-headed, cut out for high government office, yet he was capable of this immense love which had transformed him into an adventurer.

Suddenly, he saw him. With startling athleticism, Kel scaled the veritable wall of the vessel's hull and, with the aid of some rigging, managed to reach the deck. There was no reaction, either on board or on the quayside. Nobody had noticed the intruder.

Crouching down, Kel seemed to hesitate for a moment. He would now have to cross the open deck and rush towards the door of the cabin, in the hope that it was not bolted on the inside.

'Don't do it!' whispered Bebon. 'Give up and come back.'

Kel darted forward. The surprise was complete. The crew and soldiers saw a kind of wild animal, swifter than a jackal, rush into the minister's cabin. Before they could react, the door had closed again.

Pefy, who was sitting reading a papyrus concerning state accounts, looked up in astonishment. 'Who . . . who are you?'

Kel brandished his knife. 'My name cannot be unknown to you: I am Kel, officially accused of having killed the interpreters.'

Someone hammered hard on the cabin door.

'Tell them to stay back, or I'll cut your throat.'

'Keep calm,' Pefy ordered in a loud voice. 'There's nothing wrong.'

'Are you sure?' called the captain anxiously.

'Obey me and await my instructions.'

The din ceased.

'What do you want?' Pefy asked, his gaze not faltering for a second.

'Can't you guess?'

'What on earth do you mean?'
'I know exactly what you're going to do. You're going to help me free Nitis. If you don't, I'll kill you.'

17

Imperturbably, Pefy looked his attacker in the eyes. 'So you really are the murderer.'

'I haven't committed any crimes yet. You, on the other hand, are responsible for an appalling one.'

'What are you talking about?'

'The kidnapping and imprisonment of the priestess Nitis.'

'The Superior of the chantresses and weavers of Neith?'

'Yes.'

'You're talking nonsense, my boy.'

'Don't try to deny it,' snapped Kel. 'I picked up the trail of the Greek mercenaries who abducted her, and I know she's being held in your house in Memphis.'

The minister looked very worried. 'That's ridiculous. I hold her in the highest esteem, and I'm proud of having helped her to follow her vocation. Wahibra hoped she would succeed him, but the king decided otherwise. That was a regrettable error, in my opinion; but sooner or later it will be rectified.'

'That's enough talk! Your sole ambition is to depose Ahmose and take his place, so you devised a diabolical plan, choosing me as the ideal culprit. I should have been arrested, tried quickly and sentenced to death. But here I am, free, standing in front of you. Your attack on Nitis was stupid: it turned me into a merciless predator.'

'Do you mean ... Are you in love with her?'

'We are married.'

'Nitis cannot possibly be the wife of a murderer! Unless ... unless you are innocent and she's trying to prove it.'

'Don't try to play clever games. We're going to your house together, and you are going to order the Greeks to free her. Otherwise, I tell you again, I shall kill you.'

'You're wrong, Kel. I've neither plotted against the pharaoh nor organized Nitis's abduction.'

'I was expecting that lie. Don't take me for a fool, Pefy. You thought that, by inviting a young and inexperienced scribe like me to your banquet and having a doctor drug me, you could attain your goal. You never imagined that I'd escape from Judge Gem, your accomplice, did you?'

'You're utterly wrong about Gem! He has devoted his whole life to the search for truth and to punishing the guilty. Nobody – not even the king himself – could corrupt him.'

'You're still taking me for a fool.'

'No, I'm not. Actually, I'm beginning to wonder. Could you possibly be the victim of some terrible plot?'

'Very clever, Minister Pefy! Your doubts and your sympathy overwhelm me.'

'Think, Kel. I am old, wealthy and respected, and I have served the pharaoh loyally for many long years. Soon he will replace me, but before he does my main concern is to restore the temple at Abydos and celebrate the cult of Osiris. Don't you believe that the house of death, the house of eternity, belong to life? I disagree with Ahmose's policies, which I think are too favourable to the Greeks, and I make no secret of my opinion. Power and politics no longer interest me. Egypt is taking the wrong path, and I am unable to stop it. All I can do is use my position and my wealth to encourage the craftsmen who take their inspiration from the golden age of the pyramids and keep those traditions alive. If the king does not demand my resignation, I shall give it to him and retire to

Abydos, to be with Osiris. That is what my sole ambition really is.'

Disorientated, Kel gripped his knife tightly. 'You're trying to put me under a spell, like a magician. Abydos houses a barracks of Greek soldiers and you hired some of them to kidnap Nitis.'

'Ahmose has ordered them to be stationed in as many places as possible, large or small. According to him, that is the price of the Two Lands' security.'

'Do you doubt it?'

'I am concerned with Egypt's finances and agriculture, not its defences.' Pefy stood up. 'To prove my innocence, we shall go to my house together.'

'At last we'll be getting to the truth. But one false move, one call for help, and I'll stab you.'

'I shall give you a scribe's palette, and you are to walk two paces behind me. In the name of Pharaoh, I swear a solemn oath that I will not hand you over to the guards.'

The oath shook the young man. Pefy knew the consequences of violating his word once it was given: his soul would be torn to pieces by demons and condemned to nothingness. Was he really so cynical and perverse as not to care?

Pefy held out a palette. Kel took it.

'During the government's stay in Memphis,' explained Pefy, 'I didn't use my house. Instead, I lived in one of the official apartments at the palace. If something untoward has happened in my home, we shall find out together.'

He seemed sincere, thought Kel, but was this yet another cunning trick?

'Time to go,' said Kel.

Pefy opened the cabin door. The captain, crew and soldiers were standing in front of him. One word, one sign, from the minister and Kel was dead.

'All is well,' said Pefy calmly.

'Who is this man, my lord, and why did he charge into your cabin?' asked the captain.

'He is an emissary from Abydos who is under serious threat from a band of evil-doers. He wanted to inform me personally and feared he would be intercepted. I am taking him to my house in order to consult some documents, so our sailing will be delayed.'

'When do you intend to return?'

'As soon as possible.'

'Do you require an escort?'

'That will not be necessary.'

Flabbergasted, Bebon saw Pefy walk slowly down the gangplank, followed by a scribe carrying a palette. Kel seemed to be at liberty.

'Incredible,' murmured the actor. 'He isn't even threatening his hostage. Whatever did he tell him?'

Bebon fully expected the soldiers to take action, but Pefy and Kel passed by a few paces from Bebon and North Wind, who gave a perfect impression of indifference. No one was following them.

The actor and the donkey tailed the duo, keeping well back but ready to intervene if guards tried to arrest Kel. But nothing happened, and Pefy, closely accompanied by Kel, reached his fine house, where Nitis was being kept prisoner.

18

Pefy gripped the door-keeper's shoulder firmly and shook him awake.

'My lord, it's you! I thought you'd left.'

'And you took advantage of that fact to laze around and not bother watching over my house any longer.'

'Don't think that! It was just a moment of tiredness.'

'Have you anything to report?'

'No, absolutely nothing.'

'A young woman was brought here,' cut in Kel impatiently, 'and Greek mercenaries are holding her prisoner.'

The door-keeper's eyes opened wide in incredulity. 'What are you talking about?'

'Don't lie. I know all about it.'

The man gazed at his master. 'My lord, this man is out of his mind.'

'Are saying that nobody has entered my house in my absence?'

'Nobody, my lord, except the cleaners who work each morning, according to your instructions, and your steward, who has to check that everything is in good order.'

'We shall go in,' said Pefy, 'and question him.'

The steward, a skinny fellow with dark eyes, came to meet the new arrivals and bowed before his master. Fearing an ambush, Kel kept a constant watch on his surroundings.

'I am happy to have you back, my lord,' said the steward. 'Will you be dining alone or will you have guests?'

'We shall see later. Have a young woman and a number of Greek soldiers been staying here?'

The steward's jaw dropped. 'I don't understand . . .'

'If you have been threatened, say so.'

'Threatened, my lord? No, indeed not. I have done my work, as usual, not forgetting to oversee the gardeners and order jars of beer.'

'And there have been no unusual visitors?'

'None, my lord.'

Sensing Kel's frustration and scepticism, Pefy invited him to inspect the whole house, from the cellars to the roof terrace. The scribe even examined the bedchambers and the washrooms. There was no trace of Nitis.

'You have been deceived, Kel,' said Pefy.

'That's impossible. The soldier was too afraid to have made it up.'

'Look at the evidence: he was trying to throw you off the scent by telling you a pack of lies.'

'No, I still believe him. Your servants are accomplices, and you're the one who is lying.' He brandished his knife again. 'My patience has run out. Where are you hiding Nitis?'

'Nowhere – I did not abduct her.'

His nerves at breaking-point, Kel became menacing, but the sound of a donkey braying rooted him to the spot. 'So this was an ambush.'

'I did not inform the authorities,' Pefy assured him.

Kel cast a glance at the garden through the window. North Wind was walking in front of Bebon, who was gripping the shocked door-keeper and the steward by the collars of their tunics.

'They were trying to run away,' explained Bebon. 'We had to stop them.'

Astonished, Pefy went outside, accompanied by Kel.

The door-keeper had a large lump on his forehead, and the steward was bleeding from the nose and mouth.

'Two good kicks by North Wind,' said Bebon. 'These servants don't seem to have clear consciences.'

Kel put his knife to the door-keeper's throat. 'Talk, you scoundrel! A young woman was brought here, wasn't she?'

'Yes, she was. But I'm not guilty! I just obeyed the steward's orders.'

His gaze unfocused, the steward seemed only semi-conscious.

Bebon slapped him and pulled his hair. 'Wake up, my lad, and answer the questions or my donkey will give you a new face.'

The steward retched. 'Some Greek soldiers threatened me,' he confessed, 'and you don't refuse those people anything.'

'Threatened you – and paid you?'

'A little.'

'Did your employer know about this?' Kel demanded, looking hard at Pefy.

'No. They took advantage of his absence to bring a prisoner here and question her for a whole night.'

'Did they treat her roughly?'

'I don't know.'

'How could you betray my trust in this way?' Pefy cut in, his eyes filled with cold anger.

'My lord, the Greeks gave me no choice.'

'What are their names?'

'I don't know.'

'Where did they take their prisoner?'

'I don't know that, either.'

'You really are ill-informed. Perhaps the donkey's hooves will refresh your memory.'

The steward dropped to his knees. 'I'm telling the truth, my lord.'

'When they brought the woman,' yelped the door-keeper,

'one of them said something about their camp at Saqqara.'

'What else?' said Pefy icily.

The door-keeper knelt down, too. 'I've told you everything I know, my lord.'

'You and your accomplice, be off with you.'

'You mean . . . we can go?'

'Get out!'

The steward and the door-keeper scuttled away.

'Shouldn't you have handed them over to the guards?' said Kel.

'They will hold their tongues. And I do not want to be mixed up in the abduction of a priestess. Well, you have the information you were seeking, so act on it.'

'If we leave you free,' said Bebon, 'you'll have us arrested. You know too much now.'

'That is why I, too, shall say nothing and do nothing. I very much doubt that Kel is guilty, but I have no intention of conducting my own investigation or interfering in an affair of state which is too big for me. It is up to Judge Gem to establish the truth. I must return to Sais and my duties. Our meeting never took place.'

Kel and Bebon exchanged looks.

'Very well,' said the scribe.

Pefy walked unhurriedly away.

'You've made a fatal mistake,' said Bebon. 'Whether or not he was the leader of the conspirators, you should have killed him.'

19

The new High Priest of the Temple of Neith opened wide the temple doors to Judge Gem and his team of investigators. The judge undertook a detailed search of all the buildings making up the vast temple, the sacred heart of the rapidly expanding city of Sais.

This time, he easily gained access to the restricted places, such as the underground chambers of the House of Life, and was confirmed in his suspicions: the late High Priest Wahibra and his pupil Nitis had helped Kel to hide. So there really was a conspiracy, in which a priest of the highest rank had been involved. Was Wahibra the mastermind? Did he have accomplices at the palace? Had Kel succeeded him? These and many other questions remained unanswered.

One thing was certain, though: the temple no longer housed a nest of conspirators, and the priests were confining themselves to their ritual tasks.

Gem inspected the 'House of Morning', the place of purifications, the flint chamber where the cult objects were kept, the 'Castle of Linen Fabrics', the temples of Neith, Ra and Atum, and the shrine of the Bee. Here, the Mysteries of the resurrection of Osiris were celebrated. At the centre of the innermost shrine lay the mysterious chest containing the divine mummy.

'Open it,' Gem ordered the High Priest.

Despite his docile nature, the priest protested, 'You must wait for the next celebration, as—'

'I have full powers.'

His hands trembling, the High Priest did as he was bidden and stood aside. Violating the secrecy of the great Mysteries in this way would provoke the gods' anger, and their vengeance would be terrifying.

Gem saw what he ought not to have seen: a gold sarcophagus, one cubit long, containing Osiris's body of light, wrapped in a fabric created by Isis and Nephthys. But he found no documents or other things relating to the investigation.

Shaken, the High Priest asked permission to withdraw, and Gem, himself uneasy, continued his search. Upon it rested the security and future of the kingdom.

The last stage involved the tombs of the pharaohs who had made Sais their capital. Resting inside Neith's enclosure, they benefited from the goddess's protection. Their houses of eternity were very grand, each having a portico, palm-shaped pillars, a vast chamber leading to a shrine and a vaulted burial chamber. Ahmose's had recently been finished, and was magnificent. Judge Gem entered it slowly, crossed the courtyard and walked to the prayer-chamber.

Endowed with intense life, the statue of the king's *ka* gazed at him.

Taking his inspiration from the works of the Old Kingdom, the sculptor had succeeded in capturing the power and stern demeanour of the rulers of the golden age.

The judge approached.

On Ahmose's death, this shrine would be filled with offerings, and every day a *ka* priest would celebrate the deceased's memory. Embodied in this statue, his soul would take flight in order to regenerate, and then return to inhabit his never-changing body of stone.

The judge went round behind the statue to read the texts

inscribed on the pillar at its back. As he leant closer to them he stopped dead. Carefully rolled and placed behind the statue was a papyrus.

Intrigued, Gem seized it. There was no seal, just a string, which he quickly untied. He found himself looking at a completely incomprehensible text. It was made up of hieroglyphs, which were certainly drawn by a skilled hand but which as a whole conveyed no meaning at all.

The judge thought of the last words written by the head of the Interpreters' Secretariat in his death throes: 'Decipher the coded papyrus.' Was that what he had found, and was it the cause of the murders? He must face facts: this text was identical to the one already in his possession, the one belonging to Kel. Who had hidden the original here? It must have been either Wahibra or Nitis. They would have been sure nobody would ever dare to search here, and he now had proof of their guilt and their complicity.

The conspirators must have further use for the papyrus, perhaps at the moment when they took power. But what did it contain that was so important?

'Have you found something, Judge?' enquired an ice-cold voice.

Gem jumped and turned round.

'I was unaware of the presence of that papyrus,' said Henat. 'You must make sure that it isn't an offering.'

'What are you doing here?'

'I am overseeing the completion of the pharaoh's house of eternity. He is not happy with certain details, and we must make sure everything is perfect.'

'His Majesty ordered me to search every part of this temple in the hope of uncovering a clue,' explained the judge.

'And you have succeeded,' acknowledged Henat.

'Yes and no. The text is incomprehensible.'

'Will you permit me to try and decipher it?'

The judge hesitated.

'My dear Gem, the king has ordered us to cooperate. In exchange for your goodwill, I shall pass on some interesting information to you.'

The judge handed him the papyrus.

After examining it at length, Henat conceded defeat. 'It is indeed incomprehensible at first sight. It's clearly in code, and so should be entrusted to the specialists at the Interpreters' Secretariat, if you agree.'

'After showing it to the king, I shall give it to them myself.'

'I understand that you have questioned Minister Pefy, and have doubts about his integrity. Remarkable intuition, Judge Gem. He is an excellent manager but he criticizes the king's policy as being too favourable to the Greeks and to innovation and progress. So I have ordered my men to watch him discreetly.'

Gem frowned. 'You should have spoken to me about it.'

'It is a slightly illegal course of action, I admit, but we are searching for a criminal in the service of dangerous conspirators.'

'I do not approve of your methods, Henat. Violating procedure can lead to serious abuses.'

'You know that I am moderate, prudent and loyal to the state. In my view, in a serious crisis only the result matters. Now, Pefy was a friend of Wahibra, who was probably in league with the killer, Kel. And that is sufficient reason to suspect him of being the mastermind behind the conspirators.'

'Have you any proof of that?'

Henat hesitated. 'That is putting it a little too strongly. Nevertheless, Minister Pefy's behaviour continues to interest me. Just before returning to Sais, he delayed the departure of his boat and went to his house, accompanied by an emissary from Abydos. After their visit, the house was locked up.'

'Pefy carries out his duties scrupulously, it seems to me.'

'I agree, but is he trying to deceive us? While working as a

model official and conscientious minister, is he spinning his
web in the shadows?'

'I have absolutely no charges against him.'

'He must be either a loyal servant of His Majesty, or a
diabolical creature fully capable of resorting to crime in order
to sate his ambition. You do not have the means to act,
whereas I can observe him and prevent him from doing harm.
But I need your support.'

'We must request an audience with the king,' decided the
judge.

20

Despite a severe headache, Ahmose listened attentively to the reports from Judge Gem and Henat. Also present at this gathering of the king's inner circle were Queen Tanith, Udja and General Phanes.

'At Henat's request,' said the pharaoh, 'I did not summon Pefy to this meeting. You now know the reason for his absence.'

'It is Henat's job to suspect everything and everybody,' observed Udja, 'and I urge him to remain vigilant. However, despite Pefy's hostility towards the Greeks, I have heard nothing that proves he is party to the conspiracy. His ministry continues to be run in an exemplary way, and our economy is flourishing. Why would he be a murderer's accomplice?'

'Because of his hostility towards the Greeks,' replied Henat, 'he may have devised sinister plans.'

'Could Pefy have the pharaoh's helmet?' asked the queen.

'I do not know, Majesty. It is up to Judge Gem to arrest him and make him talk.'

'I have insufficient evidence,' objected the judge. 'Doing so would cause serious disturbances at the highest levels of government, especially in the event of an injustice being perpetrated, and I do not wish to act unless I am absolutely sure.'

'I agree,' said Ahmose.

'Allow me to urge you to be on guard, Majesty,' persisted Henat, 'and give me permission to keep a close watch on Pefy.'

'Granted.'

'Pefy has just left for his beloved Abydos, and while in Memphis he seemed very troubled by the arrival of a messenger from that town. Is Abydos at risk of becoming the seat of an insurrection?'

'I very much doubt it,' said Phanes. 'Abydos is merely a sleepy provincial town where old priests devote themselves to the Mysteries of Osiris, far from developments in the real world. And a barracks full of mercenaries ensures that order is maintained.'

'Double their numbers,' ordered Ahmose, 'and issue tougher security directives. If the priests of Osiris utter a single subversive word or commit a single suspicious act, I wish to be told.'

'As you command, Majesty.'

'Has the Interpreters' Secretariat succeeded in deciphering the code used in the hidden papyrus?' the king asked Judge Gem.

'I'm afraid not, Majesty. I have also shown it to several royal scribes and, despite their great learning, they have failed, too. The same disappointment applies regarding the equivalent document found in the shrine of Khufu. To my mind, only one man holds the key to reading it: the scribe Kel. The text probably serves him as a means of communication with the members of his network and, as he spoke several languages, he invented an indecipherable system which only looks like hieroglyphs.'

'When I met the murderer,' the queen recalled, filled with emotion as she relived the memory, 'he claimed to possess a coded papyrus which was the cause of the destruction of the Interpreters' Secretariat, and he swore that a conspiracy existed, while at the same time proclaiming his innocence.'

'I, too, have seen this man Kel,' went on the king, 'when he

82

tried to clear his reputation by handing me a fake copy of my helmet. Clearly, we shall always keep coming back to him. As both the mastermind and the perpetrator, he remains a dangerous enemy and will try to unite all possible opponents against me. To prevent a disaster, this is what I have decided: Judge Gem, you will continue to pursue the monster, using however many guards and soldiers you need. A royal decree authorizes you to inspect all the temples and imprison anyone who opposes you. I am now convinced that Kel is trying to reach the South. I am therefore placing at your disposal a flotilla of war-boats. Patrol our provinces and track down this savage beast.'

'I shall leave first thing tomorrow, Majesty.'

'You, General Phanes,' continued the king, 'are to go to Elephantine, whose garrison worries me. There are too many Nubians and not enough Greeks. Kel and his allies will be aware of that. Appoint a new fortress commander, establish iron discipline, dismiss the weak and indolent and hire elite mercenaries. Elephantine must continue to be a frontier which none can cross. Next, inspect all our garrisons in the South and do not tolerate any laxity.'

'You may rely upon me, Majesty.'

Ahmose turned to Henat. 'We ought to have resolved the Thebes problem a long time ago. The Divine Worshipper disapproves of my policies, and her very existence weakens my authority.'

'Do not think of resorting to . . . to the worst,' urged Queen Tanith anxiously. 'The High Priestess of Amun enjoys considerable popularity, and her integrity and respect for the ancient rituals have won her the people's highest esteem.'

Ahmose took his wife's hands gently. 'I am aware of that and, despite my annoyance, I believe it is necessary to preserve this outdated institution. However, the Divine Worshipper must be prevented from harming us. You, Henat, are to go to Thebes and set out the situation to her.'

'A delicate task, Majesty.'

'Inform her of the existence of a conspiracy and warn her
that its leader, Kel, is determined to contact her in order to
turn her against the legitimate authorities. She must not allow
herself to be deceived by him, and must remain loyal to the
crown. If she does so, she can retain her minuscule Theban
realm and continue to celebrate her ancestral rites.'

Henat bowed.

'I am entrusting the government of the state to you, Udja,'
Ahmose went on. 'You will remain here at my side in Sais,
and you will continue to strengthen our military forces,
notably our war-fleet. You will assemble the reports from the
members of this inner circle and will inform me of all incidents,
however small.'

'I shall not fail you, Majesty.'

The courtiers withdrew.

Wearily, Ahmose poured himself a cup of red wine.
'Leadership exhausts me,' he confided to his wife, 'but I have
no right to abandon my country.'

'Do not worry,' she said with a smile. 'You have just
strengthened your authority.'

'Every minister always ends up thinking he is a head of
state. It was time to remind them who governs. I am still
wondering about Pefy.'

'An elderly, wealthy man, preoccupied with the people's
well-being, hoping to retire to Abydos and devote himself to
the Mysteries of Osiris . . . I find it difficult to see him leading
a band of conspirators.'

'But is it a clever ruse? Kel needs people to support him, and
my finance minister could provide him with effective help
while pretending to serve me faithfully.'

The queen seemed puzzled. 'Wouldn't a man who sets such
store by tradition respect the office of pharaoh?'

'Ambition wipes away all restraint, my dear wife. Pefy knew
my predecessor; perhaps he misses him. And his opposition

84

to my foreign policy scarcely pleads in his favour. On the other hand, his sincerity is indicative of the behaviour of a courageous, honest official.'

'How is this problem to be resolved?'

'Henat will discover the truth.'

21

Bebon was under no illusions: if Kel, North Wind and he went anywhere near the Greek camp at Saqqara, they would be immediately arrested. Of course, Pefy would have alerted the soldiers and would boast that he had captured the murderer.

'I trust him,' declared Kel.

'Love has blinded you. That fine fellow is sending us into a trap. And this time North Wind's hooves won't get us out of it.'

'Pefy could easily have dealt with me on board his boat. He isn't one of the conspirators.'

'A clever trick, that's all. The minister won't dirty his own hands.'

'Saqqara is our only lead, Bebon, and—'

'Don't give me a lesson in morality! I never had any hope of holding you back, and all I want is to take a few precautions before foolishly dying.'

'Relax. I'm not suggesting that the three of us should attack an entire garrison.

'Oh, good! So what do you suggest?'

'Let's examine the surrounding area and capture the soldier whose job it is to deal with the refuse.'

'Suppose there are several?'

'Don't be such a pessimist.'

'And where will this get us? Assuming the fellow tells us Nitis is in the camp, we'll have to fight at odds of twenty against one.'

'The gods will help us.'

Bebon chose not to reply.

The two friends, looking for all the world like a pair of itinerant traders, headed for Saqqara, together with North Wind, who was laden with goatskin water-bags. As they got nearer, they came across other traders, greeted them and chatted to them.

When they reached the camp, they halted before a sentry.

'Greetings, soldier. Does the garrison need any fresh water?' asked Bebon jovially. 'It's excellent – and not at all expensive.'

'Sorry, my lad, the senior officers choose our suppliers for us.'

'Seeing as there are so many of you, surely little extra would be welcome?'

'There are only fifty of us here, and we have all we need.'

'It can't be much fun every day, though. Keeping watch on the burial ground – how boring! Wouldn't you rather live in Memphis? There's no lack of entertainment there.'

'Be off with you, friend. My superior doesn't permit me to talk to strangers.'

'But my water—'

'Go and sell it somewhere else.'

The trio spotted the mercenaries' rubbish dump. Part of the rubbish was burnt, the rest buried. Kel, Bebon and North Wind hid in a palm-grove, where the donkey found himself something to eat. The two men made do with dates.

As night was falling, a soldier appeared, carrying heavy baskets of refuse: it was the sentry. He was alone, and cursing this tedious duty.

When the point of Bebon's knife pricked his lower back, he dropped his baskets.

'Walk forward towards the palm-grove,' ordered the actor. 'If you call out, I'll skewer you.'

His nerves on edge, Kel forced the Greek to lie down on his back. North Wind placed a hoof on his chest.

'Our donkey is particularly aggressive,' explained Bebon. 'You won't be the first adversary he's torn to bits. But if you answer our questions we'll spare you.'

The soldier's eyes rolled in fear. 'If it's about the water, I'm not responsible. I just obey orders and—'

'We don't give a damn about the water. This camp has just witnessed an extraordinary event, hasn't it?'

'I didn't notice anything. I—'

Suddenly the donkey's hoof exerted more pressure, and the soldier let out a moan.

'Lying won't save you,' cut in Kel. 'Does protecting your superiors mean you have to die?'

On reflection, the soldier did not feel responsible for the orders he received. And he hadn't cared much for the latest ones.

'Despite the fact that it's absolutely forbidden in the rules,' he revealed, 'some men brought a woman into the camp. She was young, and very beautiful, even when gagged and bound. The commander spent a long time with them.'

'Was she hurt?' Kel asked anxiously.

'I don't think so.'

'Did you see her again?'

'Yes, when they came out of the commander's tent. They were arguing, and I listened. I didn't like seeing a beautiful girl like that being mistreated. I'd have handled her completely differently . . .'

Bebon feared that Kel might lose his temper. But the scribe managed to contain himself.

'What did you find out?'

'As the interrogation hadn't brought any results, the men wanted a secure place so that they could continue it. The commander pointed out the gallery that has just been dug out on the southern side of the Stepped Pyramid. Nobody will disturb them there.'

'How many torturers are there?'

'Three – and fearsome they are, too, in my opinion.'

'Does somebody take them food and drink?'

'At sunrise and sunset.'

Considering the interrogation over, North Wind stood aside.

'Undress,' ordered Kel. 'We need your uniform.'

'Are you . . . Are you going to kill me?'

'No, simply make sure you keep still and quiet. You'll be cool here, and someone's bound to find you eventually. Just one piece of advice: forget about us.'

The night was endless. Firmly bound and thanking the gods for saving his life, the soldier fell asleep.

Kel's only thought was to rush in headlong. Bebon advised him to rest a bit. Freeing Nitis was not going to be easy. This time, the scribe would have to kill.

22

The conspirators were so agitated that even the arrival of their leader did not quieten them down. Faced with this rebellious mob but completely unruffled, the leader looked at each of them in turn. And one by one they fell silent and sat down.

'We are assembled here before a long period of separation,' said the leader. 'So we must adopt a rigorous strategy, to which everyone will adhere.'

'The coded papyrus has fallen into the hands of the authorities,' pointed out the most anxious conspirator. 'And I don't mean the papyrus at Giza. Now the forces of order have two vital documents.'

The leader smiled. 'But they still have to decipher them. The only man capable of doing so was the late director of the Interpreters' Secretariat, whom we were obliged to kill. There is now no risk. Those papyri won't give up their secrets.'

'What about the scribe Kel?' another conspirator asked.

'He may perhaps have found the first key and read a few lines. But that's a minor success, with no serious consequences for us.'

'But suppose he manages to reach Thebes, where the second key is hidden? Then he will understand.'

'An absurd notion,' the leader retorted. 'All the same, we'll take it into consideration and place so many barriers between him and the Divine Worshipper that their meeting will be impossible.'

'The gods seem to be protecting this scribe.'

'The loss of his beloved Nitis will break him and send him mad. He'll forget all about being cautious, and he'll soon fall into the hands of his pursuers.'

'And if, in spite of everything—'

'We shall do what is necessary,' declared the leader. 'The Divine Worshipper will never heed the blandishments of a murderer.'

Their leader's calm demeanour and determination reassured the conspirators. In any case, they had no choice. It was too late to turn back.

As soon as he returned to Sais, Menk had been overwhelmed with work. The new High Priest was incompetent, and relied on him to ensure that the great rituals in honour of Neith proceeded without error.

At the sight of the Superior of the chantresses and weavers of Neith who had been appointed in Nitis's place, the urbane and courteous Menk almost flew into a rage. She was an old hag, sour-tempered and pernickety, with a shrill voice and jerky movements. Because of this dreadful woman, the chantresses would be sure to sing off-key and the weaving workshops would be a failure.

Disgusted, Menk avoided giving her instructions, which in any case she would not have followed. He, normally so adept at compromise and negotiation, was going to have to indicate his disapproval directly to the High Priest. Alas, the inevitable mistakes would be laid at his door and would ruin his reputation. Was someone trying to oust him?

At the height of his annoyance, Menk went to the court where Judge Gem presided. No longer able to bear Nitis's absence, he was determined to demand clear, precise explanations.

But another judge was presiding over the debates.

'I wish to see Judge Gem,' Menk told the assistant scribe.

'He is going on a journey. His boat is just about to sail.'

Menk ran to the official landing-stage, where he gave his particulars to the overseeing officer. The judge was informed, and he was given permission to come aboard.

Seated on the deck, the judge was drinking light beer and gazing at Egypt's capital.

'Judge Gem, I have come to ask for news of the investigation into Nitis's disappearance.'

'The law forbids me to answer you.'

'She was my principal colleague, and her absence is causing me serious problems.'

'Put her out of your mind, Menk.'

'Do you mean that . . .?'

'Nitis was not abducted; she ran away.'

'Ran away? Why?'

'She is no victim, but the accomplice of a murderer – and I shall arrest both of them. I repeat my advice to you: put her out of your mind.'

Deathly pale, Menk felt on the point of collapse. He almost fell as he descended the gangplank. So Kel had forced her to go with him. And she was in love with him, with a murderer . . . No, it was impossible!

Faced with such an appalling situation, he could not remain idle. Since the old judge was too set in his legal ways to find the monster, something else must be done.

Menk went to the palace and requested an audience with Henat, who was also on the point of leaving Sais.

'My time is limited,' said Henat. 'You look sad, dear friend. Do you have problems with your health?'

'It seems that Nitis has run away with Kel.'

Henat seemed embarrassed. 'That is indeed Judge Gem's opinion.'

'That evil monster forced her to go with him.'

'That is possible.'

'It isn't possible, it's certain! The judge is wrong, and his intervention is liable to be disastrous. Nitis will be injured, perhaps even killed. I must do something.'

'What do you mean?'

'I have worked for you before,' Menk reminded him, 'by watching and reporting on Wahibra's movements. Give me new orders: to find Nitis and free her. I need a small number of experienced soldiers, a fast boat and the beginnings of a lead. After that, I'll manage on my own. Officially I shall be on leave because of illness. My assistants will take my place, and the new temple officials will be principally in charge of organizing the next festivals.'

'Transforming you suddenly into a spy ... A delicate task, I would say.'

'Nitis was to become my wife,' revealed Menk. 'Now do you understand my determination?'

Henat nodded. 'I admire your courage, Menk. If I agree, will you promise not to take any risks? Kel is a formidable criminal.'

'I promise.'

'The killer has left Memphis and is heading for the South,' said Henat. 'He will try to reach Thebes, rally the Divine Worshipper to his cause, then foment an insurrection in Nubia. Finding him will be difficult, but perhaps luck will favour you. If you do find him, confine yourself to passing on the information to the authorities.'

'Understood.'

'My secretary will see to the necessary permits and other arrangements. They will be sorted out by this evening.'

'Thank you, Henat. I shall prove myself worthy of this mission.'

'I hope so.'

Menk omitted to mention that he had but one goal: to kill Kel and free Nitis in order to marry her on the spot.

Henat did not suspect his new spy's true intentions. But sometimes, he mused, an untrained man could succeed.

23

Bebon was not a happy man. There were persistent rumours that hostile spirits protected the Saqqara site and watched over Pharaoh Djoser's soul as it rested. The pharaoh's great Stepped Pyramid, a staircase joining the heavens to the earth, towered over the burial-ground. Nobody ventured here.

'You are a learned scribe,' he said to his friend. 'You ought to take account of the danger. The magic of the world beyond is all around us, and we are nothing but poor humans, incapable of fighting such a force.'

'Are you afraid?'

'Of course not! I would prefer to classify it as respect and caution.'

'Freeing Nitis won't displease the gods. Without their help we'd never have learnt the truth. Why would they abandon us?'

The actor gave up the argument. Kel's stubbornness meant that Bebon had lost before he began.

North Wind crossed the sacred domain of Djoser with great solemnity. Contemplatively, he trod in the footsteps of the ritual priests who celebrated the festival of the *ka*'s regeneration and of the union of the Two Lands, thus ensuring that Egypt possessed a never-changing foundation stone.

Kel remembered the intense moments he had experienced in the underground chambers of the Temple of Neith. Steeped in silence and darkness, surrounded by the divine powers, he had been stripped of his worldly skin. He saw things differently now, and felt ready to confront the demons who were seeking to destroy him.

Bebon, on the other hand, was covered in gooseflesh and would willingly have beaten a retreat. He could feel the presence of spirits prowling round the intruders, unsure whether or not to attack them. His ears down, North Wind moved with incredible lightness, as if he weighed no more than a bird. The actor was part of a strange procession in which the mortal world was touching the invisible.

At last, the trio reached the entrance to the Sais gallery. A wooden door barred entry to it.

The eastern sky was beginning to take on a rosy glow. Bebon breathed more easily. The demons of the night were returning to their caves, and now there were only the three Greek soldiers to confront.

Kel appeared suddenly downcast. 'If they've tortured and raped Nitis, she'll never recover. She would rather die.'

'Do you want to know or not? We can still abandon her.'

Kel's eyes flamed. 'Knock on that door, Bebon, and prepare to carry out the first part of our plan.'

The actor knocked firmly.

'Who goes there?' demanded a coarse voice in Greek.

'Delivery of water and hot flat-cakes.'

The door half opened, and a thickset, bearded soldier peered out. At first, the sight of Kel in his uniform and the donkey laden with food reassured him. Then his suspicions were aroused. 'You're new.'

'I've only just been taken on.'

'That's strange. This kind of job isn't generally given to novices.'

'I've had plenty of experience, and you won't escape me.'

'What does that mean?'

Bebon's palm-wood club smashed down on the soldier's

skull. 'One down,' he remarked, 'but my weapon has broken in two.'

Kel set down on the ground the hot coals he had taken from the waste depot at the military camp. With the aid of a piece of palm-wood, he got the flame going again. Soon smoke filled the gallery.

'Fire!' he shouted in Greek. 'Let's get out of here, comrades, or we'll suffocate!'

With perfect coordination, North Wind and Bebon charged at the next soldier to appear. He flew backwards and was put out of action by North Wind with a hoof-blow to the neck. The third was dragging Nitis, who was resisting him with all her might.

Mad with rage, Kel leapt at his throat, forced him to let go of Nitis, and rained down angry blows upon him. The torturer collapsed, unconscious. Never would the scribe have imagined himself capable of such violence.

'Nitis . . .'

Weeping with joy, she hugged him so tightly that she squeezed all the breath out of him.

'It's over,' he said. 'You're free.'

'It was terrible,' she confessed.

'Did they use violence?'

'No, just intimidation. But they destroyed everything I possessed, and I feared the worst might happen at any moment. The captain of the *Ibis* handed me over to three Greek soldiers, who took me to a large house and interrogated me.'

'Did you meet Minister Pefy?'

The question astonished the young woman. 'No. Why do you ask? Did he play some part in my abduction and imprisonment?'

'I don't think so. What did the torturers want?'

'To know exactly what our relationship is, and where you were hiding and who your friends are. I gave them vague and contradictory answers. They lost patience and decided to hand me over to experts.'

'We mustn't stay here,' cut in Bebon. 'This place worries me.'

'We must go to the far end of the gallery,'* urged Nitis. 'It contains a treasure.'

'I'll stand watch,' decided the actor. 'If I call out, run towards me.'

The horizontal passageway was about sixty paces long and was supported, in the middle, by a line of powerful columns. Carpenters had increased the gallery's strength and safety by installing wooden posts.

'We are right at the heart of the pyramid,' said Nitis. 'Can't you feel the energy emanating from it?'

It was having a profound impression upon Kel, who experienced an intense feeling of veneration. Far from feeling confined, this journey to the centre of the stone felt like a liberation.

'Look at these marvels.' He gazed admiringly at a group of Answerers.† Wearing wigs and short, long-sleeved tunics, they had their arms crossed upon their chests and carried two hoes. According to the writings they magically enacted, it was their task to sow seed on cultivable land, irrigate the riverbanks, and transport the fertilizer formed by the decomposition of the western silt to the east, and the eastern silt to the west. 'They're dedicated to Pharaoh Ahmose,' he observed.

'Probably stolen,' said Nitis.

---

* It was dug during the Saite era to remove the blockage in the central well of the pyramid of Djoser. Given the high quality of the pillars, which were formed from recycled blocks of stone, and of the wooden ceiling and posts, we can rule out any intent to loot the pyramid, and assume real archaeological concern, which is moreover characteristic of that era. This gallery is unfortunately not open to the public.

† *Ushebti*s or *Shauabti*s, blue porcelain figures placed inside tombs to carry out certain tasks in place of the reborn individual.

'More likely payment to the soldiers, who could sell them at a high price. Don't the Answerers confirm that the king is our main adversary?'

'We mustn't leap to conclusions. Let's take one Answerer and this amulet: two fingers made of obsidian, slipped by the embalmer into the incision made in the Osiran body during mummification. Separating the heavens from the earth, it enables the soul to pass through the clouds and reach paradise, and shields it from the evil eye.'

The young woman's self-control stunned Kel. After so many hours of anguish, she had recovered her energy and love of life with incredible speed.

'You and I have both lost our copies of the coded papyrus,' he said disconsolately.

She smiled. 'The copies, yes, but not our memories. I know that incomprehensible arrangement of hieroglyphs by heart. You, too, I imagine?'

One of North Wind's panniers contained a palette and writing materials. Although Bebon was impatient to leave the burial-ground, and protested furiously, the lovers separately re-wrote their own versions of the document from memory. They matched perfectly.

'We must leave,' insisted Bebon.

'Only the Divine Worshipper can save us,' Nitis reminded him.

24

The man who delivered water and flat-cakes to the Saite gallery knocked several times. Surprised when there was no response, he pushed the door. It creaked open, and acrid smoke assailed his eyes and nose.

'Anybody here?' he called nervously.

He advanced cautiously and almost tripped over the inert body of a soldier. The two others lay a little way off. In terror, he abandoned his jars and baskets, and ran to alert the camp commander, who came to the gallery immediately, accompanied by two soldiers.

One of the wounded men had just regained consciousness.

'What happened?' asked the commander.

'A surprise attack, sir.'

'How many attackers?'

'I don't know . . . We couldn't see because of the smoke, so defending ourselves was very difficult. Everything happened very quickly.'

The commander checked the gallery. The treasure seemed intact, but the girl had disappeared. He did not know who she was, and this secret mission displeased him so much that he had absolutely no wish to know. He merely carried out his orders to the letter, without seeking their origin or their ultimate destination. Mercenaries did not argue.

The three injured men would be treated and then transferred

to a far-off garrison, where they would forget about this incident and take care to hold their tongues. As for the commander, he would make haste to write a detailed report and send it to the authorities. The rest did not concern him.

The leader of the conspirators could not suppress a certain admiration for Kel on learning that Nitis had been freed. Kel truly was no ordinary man and had proven that he was madly in love: a love capable of moving mountains.

Judging by his record, he ought to have behaved like a typical petty official: nervous, over-cautious, incapable of taking a decision – in short, easy prey. Adversity had transformed him into a wild creature, both hunted and all-conquering. Escaping the authorities and following the trail of clues in order to free Nitis were both remarkable achievements. In the conspirators' service this brilliant man could have accomplished wonders.

Too late. In view of the circumstances, Kel and Nitis must be eliminated in one way or another. One of the hunters sent out to find them would eventually succeed.

They must have allies; all the evidence pointed that way. The most important had been Wahibra – it was fortunate that he had died – who must have provided Nitis with several contacts. The temples were probably serving as temporary shelters for the fugitives and should be closely watched.

Thebes and the Divine Worshipper were utterly inaccessible goals. The leader of the conspirators loathed the shrine-laden city and the old priestess, who was almost the equal of the pharaoh and who was wholly devoted to the service of the gods. The common people were stupid, and continued to venerate her, believing in her magic powers and her ability to protect them from misfortune. Many superstitions were becoming unbearable and would, when the conspirators succeeded in their aims, be swept away: Egypt deserved better. Despite his courage and his luck, Kel was not going to succeed in disrupting that process.

'Good Journey', Memphis's principal port, resembled an ants' nest. Goods were being loaded and unloaded, boats were coming into port and leaving, people were looking for the best positions for their market-stalls, checking that the boats were in good condition, selling goods, protesting against the strict security measures, and haggling over the cost of journeys. The Greeks, in their ever-increasing numbers, had proved to be formidable businessmen.

Bebon melted into the crowd and soon spotted the guards on patrol, accompanied by baboons whose task was to arrest thieves with a bite on the lower leg. The culprits were taken away to the central prison and severely punished.

Unshaven like a man in mourning, and dressed in a shabby Syrian tunic and cheap sandals, Bebon looked like an ordinary citizen of Memphis, neither rich nor poor, who was on the lookout for a good deal. Since the sweeping raids organized by Judge Gem, few dishonest traders had been seen, for they were wary of checkpoints and arrests. Shopkeepers and travelling merchants were delighted, because their businesses throve.

At the foot of the gangplank leading to a large and impressive trading-boat stood five soldiers and an officer.

Bebon approached them slowly, his head lowered. 'I'd like to speak to someone in charge,' he told the officer.

'In charge of what?'

'State security.'

'Be off with you, my friend. We have work to do.'

'This is very serious. Hear me out – you won't regret it.

The officer sighed. 'Has your wife left you? Have you lost your job? Don't worry, things will sort themselves out.'

'I have information which will interest the pharaoh himself.'

The officer smiled. 'You look tired, my lad, and it will soon be time for a nap.'

'Kel – that murderer – does he interest you?'

The smile vanished. 'I dislike bad jokes.'

'I want to know how much the reward is.'

'Don't move. I'll be back.'

Like all his colleagues, the officer had been given the order to pass on all information about Kel, even if it appeared to be pure fantasy.

He soon returned, together with a cleft-chinned senior officer.

'I must warn you, my lad,' said Cleft-Chin, 'I loathe people who make up stories.'

'How much is the reward?' repeated Bebon.

'A detached house, two servants, five donkeys and a fine array of food produce, not to mention the authorities' gratitude.'

'You could add some farming land.'

'We can talk about that if you're serious.'

'Of course I'm serious. When you're going to make a fortune, you don't joke about it.'

'I understand you said something about Kel the scribe?'

'He's preparing to leave Memphis to reach the city of Thebes, and I know how.'

Cleft-Chin held his breath.

'But I want guarantees,' Bebon went on. 'The state always promises a great deal but it seldom keeps its word.'

'What do you want?'

'A bag of gemstones.'

'Don't be ridiculous!'

'That's just on account,' explained Bebon. 'Then I want the rest of the reward. I shan't wait long – I'm sure other officers will be more interested.'

'Sit down and wait. We'll give you something to drink.'

Cleft-Chin hurried off, and when he returned he handed Bebon a bag of gems. 'Will these do?'

The actor examined them at length. 'They might.'

'Well, then, what is this information?'

'Kel has grown a small moustache and is wearing an old-fashioned wig. The day after tomorrow, he will embark on a trading-boat called the *Strong*, heading for Thebes. She's carrying fabrics, jars of wine and alabaster vases destined for the Divine Worshipper. I don't know the names of the crew-members he's bribed, or how many of them there are, but he'll pass himself off as a public scribe who can draw up administrative documents and thus pay the cost of his passage.'

Cleft-Chin tried to hide his excitement. 'Of course, my friend, you'll be our guest.'

'If I don't go back, Kel won't take that boat. He thinks I'm checking the final details, and I have to report to him. Above all don't try to follow me: lookouts will spot you and alert him. Tomorrow, after his arrest, I'll come and fetch the rest of my reward.'

25

Bebon was in no doubt: he was being followed. If the guards could capture Kel and his accomplices in his hideout, their feat would be even more enthusiastically received, and it would probably lead to promotion.

The actor headed down a twisting alleyway, in the middle of which the narrowest of passageways had been created, linking it to a broad main road. At the exit, he ran to a basket-seller's shop, walked through it and re-emerged from the back door. He had shaken them off.

Bebon fondled the bag of precious stones. A nice little fortune! And the remainder of the reward would have made him a wealthy man, whose life consisted solely of enjoying himself. His treachery had paid well . . .

Calmly he walked to the port and headed for the *Scarab*, a luxurious boat reserved for wealthy passengers, which was about to sail.

A sailor blocked the gangplank. 'Nobody comes on board, my lad. We've got a full crew – we aren't hiring.'

'I'm sandal-bearer to the wealthy landowner Neferet.'

The guard went to inform the lady, and then, having received her approval, allowed her servant to come aboard.

Bebon bowed to Nitis. 'We won the wager,' he told her, 'and here is the result. With these gems we'll be able to pay our way for quite some time.'

'Kel and I were desperately worried,' she said. 'The risks were enormous.'

'We've known worse – and the game isn't over yet. The authorities are so desperate for definite information that they're prepared to swallow anything.'

On Nitis's orders, Kel, who was playing the part of her steward, paid the captain, who immediately gave the order to weigh anchor. There was a good wind from the north so they would be able to leave Memphis quickly, while the authorities were still casting their net round the *Solid*, an entirely innocent vessel.

Judge Gem was searching for a couple forced to exercise extreme discretion, not a relaxed and smiling landowner accompanied by two of her servants. Officially, she was going downriver to Khemenu, the city of Thoth, in Middle Egypt, where she owned other large estates. She could have taken her own boat, of course, but journeying like this, in company with other wealthy folk, amused her.

Five comfortable cabins were reserved for four great ladies and one inspector of dykes. They all gathered at the ship's bow, chatting as they drank light beer and sampled plump dates, before enjoying an excellent meal, seated on low chairs with backs, in the shade of an awning. The dishes – grilled goose, dried and salted smoked beef soaked in honey, and fish prepared on board – were served in the broad-bean leaves, which were large, concave and strong.

The servants were less cosseted, and had to make do with preserved poultry, dried fish, lettuce from Memphis and dates. North Wind and two other donkeys enjoyed some fresh alfalfa.

'I'd love to play at being rich from time to time,' said Bebon ruefully. 'Still, at least the food's edible and the beer's passable.'

'Pefy hasn't betrayed us,' observed Kel. 'If he had, we'd already have been arrested. So he isn't one of the traitors.'

'To all appearances you're right. All the same, I'm worried that this is some kind of trick. Perhaps he wants to capture us himself, without the aid of the guards or soldiers, so that he can present himself as Egypt's saviour. That would be a good start for a future pharaoh, don't you think?'

'That would mean Judge Gem was manipulated, mis-informed and an honest man.'

'Impossible! He clothes his mission in a thick cloak of legality and obeys the orders of those in power.'

'In other words, Pharaoh Ahmose,' the scribe reminded him. 'Is he a future victim or the mastermind behind the conspiracy?'

Bebon scratched his head. 'The king organizing a con-spiracy in order to overthrow himself . . .? I must be missing something.'

'Suppose he's trying to get rid of certain ministers who have become a hindrance, by setting a trap for them? There's one thing we know is true: little by little, Ahmose is selling the country to the Greeks, and many influential men like Pefy disapprove of it. By dreaming up a conspiracy involving his opponents, the king can discredit and eliminate them.'

'There really is nothing worse than politics!'

'Yes there is: injustice.'

'It's the same thing. Well, I'm going to take a nap. The turpitude of the human soul exhausts me.'

Bebon could fall asleep anywhere in an instant. As for Kel, he did not much care for the little games being played by the inspector of dykes, who was quite obviously paying court to Nitis. One inappropriate move, and the scribe would take forceful action.

Fortunately, the meal ended and Nitis withdrew, on the pretext of working with her steward.

'I don't care for that fellow,' muttered Kel.

Nitis smiled. 'Are you jealous by any chance?

'Of course I am.'

'Unfortunately I can't kiss you, but I wish desperately that I could.'

Not being able to fall into each other's arms was unbearably frustrating. They had to be content with knowing looks, imbued with a love so vast and so deep that time, rather than damaging it, would strengthen it.

Together, they examined the coded text again, trying all sorts of combinations, including the most fantastical. Their efforts led nowhere.

'The key will probably be provided by symbols like the amulets in Khufu's shrine,' said Kel. 'And they, of course, are in Thebes, with the Divine Worshipper, so someone will try to stop us reaching it. I can't bear seeing you risk your life.'

'It's *our* life now,' she said firmly. 'The only chance of saving it is to uncover the truth, and the gods won't abandon us.'

'Such a slender chance . . .'

'We aren't without weapons. First there are Bebon's contacts in Upper Egypt. And then there are the places of Neith's power, which Wahibra told me about. We'll find valuable help in those places, and we'll soon be arriving at the first of them.'

As Nitis was obliged to rejoin her temporary friends and Bebon was still asleep, Kel leant on the boat's rail and gazed at the Nile, the earthly projection of the celestial river that carried energy to the heart of the universe. By irrigating the riverbanks, it provided human beings with what they needed to live happily and at peace. But if the king was unjust, no happiness was possible.

When the boat stopped to take on food and water at Faiyum,* the passengers ate their midday meal on dry land, and the crew cleaned the boat from top to bottom. The captain oversaw the delivery aboard of beer, wine, and both preserved and fresh

---

* About a hundred kilometres south of Cairo.

food; fish was caught on the boat every day. His guests must have everything they could wish for, and must declare themselves pleased with their trip.

To the captain's great surprise, the beautiful landowner's servant was equipping the donkey with leather bags as though preparing to set off on a journey, and her steward, with a bag on his back, was carrying a walker's staff. When she herself emerged from her cabin, she had exchanged her exquisite gown for a simple tunic.

'Lady Neferet, are you leaving us already? Are you unhappy with our service?'

'On the contrary, captain, everything was perfect. But my steward tells me that one of my farmers, whose land is near here, has submitted an unusual declaration. I wish to check it immediately, and we shall then head for Memphis once again after a short halt in a neighbouring village where I have lands. You have made us so comfortable that on my next trip to Khemenu I shall certainly choose the *Scarab*.'

'I must reimburse you and—'

'There's no need for that, captain. The quality of your service merits this small bonus.'

Ye gods, what a wonderful woman! Dreamily, the sailor turned his thoughts to the preparations for departure.

26

Alerted by the officer in charge of security at the port of Memphis, General Phanes immediately informed Udja, in accordance with procedure. Udja summoned Henat, and recalled Judge Gem, who had only just left the capital.

The four courtiers could scarcely believe it: were they at last about to arrest Kel the scribe, thanks to a reliable informant? Never had information been so precious.

'Shouldn't we inform the king?' asked Phanes.

'If we fail,' objected the judge, 'we would run the risk of disappointing him. I have lost count of the number of false rumours and fruitless checks relating to the Kel affair.'

'This one appears reliable,' Henat pointed out.

'We shall take it into consideration,' decided Gem, 'but we shall not boast about the result in advance.'

'According to the security officer's reports,' said Phanes, 'the *Strong* is an old boat, regularly checked, and capable of transporting heavy cargoes. Her current one, though, seems rather light: merely fabrics, jars of wine and precious metals.'

'And what is her destination?'

'The domain of the Divine Worshipper, in Thebes.'

Everyone held their breath.

'An important clue,' said Udja. 'What do we know about the captain?'

'He is aged around fifty, very experienced, the father of four children and enjoys good living.'

'Any vices?'

'He is a gambler.'

'So he has debts. Kel would have no difficulty in persuading him to accept a large sum for taking him secretly to Thebes. The problem of the informant himself remains, though.'

'I'm afraid we have very few details,' said Phanes. 'We don't know his name, we have only vague descriptions of him and, most annoyingly, we failed to follow him. After pocketing a bag of gemstones, an advance on his reward, he threw off the guards officer who was tailing him.'

'There is nothing surprising about that,' said Judge Gem. 'He did not want to lead your man to the murderer, for fear of being arrested with Kel and losing everything. His behaviour inclines me to believe that we are dealing with a professional, perhaps a renegade mercenary in Kel's service who, tired of living in hiding, has decided to sell the scribe to us in order to become rich.'

'What optimism!' said Henat sarcastically. 'I see experience has not made you sceptical.'

'There has never been any shortage of traitors and informers,' retorted Gem.

'This is a time for action, not talk,' cut in Udja. 'I assume the *Strong* is already being watched?'

'Naturally,' replied Phanes.

'Kel is a particularly cunning criminal, and must have planned an escape route in case of trouble. We must put in place around the boat a net from which no one can escape.'

'We could replace the sailors with guards,' suggested Henat.

'Too risky,' said the judge. 'Kel will watch carefully before he steps aboard, and if he doesn't see the usual crew he'll leave. We shan't alert the captain, but simply allow him to play his part. On the other hand, all exits must be covered, including the river. And we should also try to take the killer alive. His interrogation will be extremely interesting.'

'If he threatens the lives of our men,' Phanes reminded him, 'you have given the order to kill him.'

'That order is confirmed.'

Dawn had risen over Memphis, and the dock labourers were starting work. The coolness would not last, and it was best to take advantage of the early morning in order to load and unload the boats. Twenty were leaving and as many arriving, and the day looked set to be a busy one. The first traders were setting out fruit and vegetables, and early customers were examining the wares before beginning the haggling process.

At least a hundred guards in plain clothes were watching the *Strong*. The nerves of many were tensed to breaking-point, especially those of the action squad, who would have to intercept the killer. If he refused to lay down his arms, the archers hidden behind a stack of baskets would fire. And if he jumped into the water, several boats filled with soldiers would converge upon him.

'He won't come,' Henat told Judge Gem. 'This is a deception.'

'Have you learnt something new?'

'Unfortunately, no.'

'Kel must meet the Divine Worshipper,' the judge reminded him, 'and this boat is sailing for Thebes to deliver its cargo to her.'

'But what about the priestess Nitis? Would he really abandon her to her fate like this?'

'Kel will have realized that we were searching for a couple, so they have separated. I have no illusions: given the incessant activity at the port, it is impossible to check all the boats.'

At the far end of the quay there appeared a young man of average height and ponderous gait. Wearing an old-fashioned wig and a neatly trimmed moustache, he was heading towards the *Strong*.

'Our informant wasn't lying,' muttered Judge Gem.

The net tightened immediately.

The man, who appeared completely peaceable, started up the gangplank.

Five guards, each a good head taller than he was, threw themselves upon their prey, seizing him simultaneously by the shoulders, arms and legs.

'We've got him!' roared the group's leader, surprised by so little resistance.

The captain of the *Strong* and his crew had witnessed the scene and looked astonished.

'Don't move,' ordered an archer. 'You are under arrest.'

When Judge Gem arrived, the guards presented the killer to him, his hands and ankles shackled.

'Who are you?' demanded the judge.

The man was shaking so much that he could could scarcely get his words out. 'One of the accounting scribes at the food-preserving works in Memphis. I have come to check the number of jars loaded on board this boat in order to draw up an invoice, as I do for each trip.'

The captain confirmed that this was so.

'I'm leaving for Thebes,' announced Henat. 'We've wasted enough time here.'

Abandoning the hapless scribe, Judge Gem questioned the soldiers who had met the informer.

'He was a very good actor,' said one of them. 'He really convinced us.'

'Actor': the word set up strange echoes in Gem's mind. Hadn't he arrested an actor who was suspected of complicity with Kel but released because of lack of evidence? He went to his office, consulted his files and found the name of the likeable fellow: Bebon. Likeable, but wily. According to one report, he had evaded a guard who was following him. It was a delayed report, and Gem had neglected it. The judge had just taken an important step forward: he knew the name of one of the scribe's accomplices, perhaps his go-between or one of his principal henchmen.

An itinerant actor had many contacts, so Bebon could offer the killer a veritable network of helpers. At last the judge had an explanation for Kel's unexpectedly good luck: it was in fact a clever plan which had enabled him to escape from the authorities.

By scrutinizing Bebon's file, could the judge find the means of getting to Kel? From now on, he would be searching for two men and a woman.

27

Irrigated by a vast lake, almost an inland sea, Faiyum was a verdant region, set aside for hunting and fishing. Gigantic works undertaken in the Middle Kingdom had enabled the site to be transformed into a luxuriant paradise.

At the entrance to Faiyum, the pyramid of Pharaoh Amenemhat III kept a watchful guard to drive away evil spirits and guarantee the prosperity of this wealthy province. Overlooking the great canal that brought the waters from the Nile, it recalled the glory of a prosperous era which was also magnified by an immense temple dedicated to the pharaoh's *ka* and to Sobek, the crocodile-god. Inspired by Djoser's building projects at Saqqara, the temple complex comprised numerous courtyards bordered by shrines with vaulted roofs, zigzagged anterooms, sorts of cloisters and secret passageways in the stonework, and resembled a veritable 'labyrinth',* through which only the righteous soul of the pharaoh could find the correct route.

'This is the first place of power,' said Nitis. 'In the old days, great scholars from all the provinces assembled here in order to reconstitute the body of Osiris and thus enable the king to be resurrected.'

* This was the name given to it by the Greeks.

'Very praiseworthy,' commented Bebon, 'but the place looks abandoned now – not very reassuring.'

Kel stepped through the first door, suddenly moving from daylight to dusk. He collided with a wall, was obliged to head down a narrow passage and found an initial courtyard bordered with pillared walkways. A heavy silence hung over the place.

Nitis joined the scribe. 'The shrine seems empty,' she said.

'There, look!' cried Bebon.

At the foot of a column lay an ink-black cobra with a small, glistening head and the familiar terrible broad snout.

'Its bite is deadly,' said Nitis, 'and no incantation can immobilize it. Whatever you do, don't make any sudden movements.'

The predator fixed its gaze on its prey.

'This is no ordinary snake,' said Kel.

Indeed, the creature's eyes burned with a strange red glow. It looked at the intruders, one by one, as if it could not decide which victim to choose.

'We'd better go,' suggested Bebon.

'It is just waiting for us to try running away. Please, keep absolutely still.'

The cobra's tongue had begun flickering furiously. Entering the humans' minds, capturing their fear, the snake undulated towards them.

Nitis prayed to her dead master, Wahibra, for protection. Surely the gods could not abandon them here, inside a temple, and destroy their search for the truth?

Suddenly, a mongoose appeared from the colonnade and positioned itself between the three human beings and the snake. A great lover of cobras' eggs, 'Pharaoh's rat' had rolled in mud and allowed it to dry, in order to create a thick breastplate and so protect itself.

Recognizing its worst enemy, the cobra froze. Despite

its small size, the mongoose displayed extraordinary courage and relied upon its ability to move swiftly.

'It embodies the god Atum,' Nitis reminded her companions. 'At each moment he is born from the primeval ocean, at once a Being and a Non-Being.'

The mongoose walked round the cobra, looking for the best angle of attack. Both knew that they would only have one chance to bite, and that bite must be accurate and deadly.

The cobra relaxed, and Nitis closed her eyes. If it killed the mongoose, the gods would abandon them and falsehood would triumph.

'It's escaping,' said Bebon.

And the little animal launched its attack, taking advantage of the snake's momentary hesitation. With a huge leap, it caught the snake, and sank its teeth into the back of that glistening head.

A series of jerky movements, one final spasm, and the snake was dead. The mongoose had won. Dragging its victim, it left the temple.

'The gods are protecting you,' said a voice.

All three spun round, and saw an elderly priest, shaven-headed and wearing an old-fashioned white linen robe. Bebon could not work out where he had come from. Anxiously, he looked all around. There was nobody else there.

'Are you the temple guardian?' asked Nitis.

'I have that honour.'

'My name is Nitis, and I am the Superior of the chantresses and weavers of Neith in Sais. My master was the late High Priest Wahibra.'

The guardian seemed upset. 'So Wahibra has left us? A great, great loss. He was a wise and upright man, with a truly "just voice". He was well versed in all the sacred writings, and his learning was worthy of Imhotep. Why did he send you here?'

'I need Neith's help, linked to the power of Sobek the crocodile.'

The old priest's expression hardened. 'In this temple, the *ka* is expressed, and that is all. Human affairs do not concern it.'

'Atum destroyed the serpent of darkness,' Nitis reminded him. 'Would you ignore this sign from the heavens?'

The guardian of the labyrinth thought for a long time. 'I am no longer accustomed to receiving visitors. These places are dedicated to silence, meditation and memory.'

'My companions and I are searching for the truth. Without your help, we will fail.'

'Since the gods are helping you, I shall not turn you away. That which you seek may perhaps be found near Shedyet, the capital of Faiyum. Does Sobek still dwell in its lake? I do not know. If so, your adventure will end there, for none can escape the crocodile's jaws. Rising up from the subterranean waters, it fashions the new sun and devours all that is perishable. Farewell, priestess of Neith.'

28

Assisted by five hand-picked soldiers, who were experienced in all types of combat, Menk spent a long time questioning the Memphis port officials in charge of the rotation of boats. He had only one thought in his head: to find beautiful Nitis and kill Kel. The authorities would heap praise upon him, the pharaoh would offer him an important post at court, and he would marry a sublime woman who would soon learn to love him.

Egyptian scribes deserved their reputation. The administrative records were remarkably well kept and could be consulted swiftly. They contained the name of each boat, the destination, time of departure, names of the crew, the passengers and the guard whose task it was to check them, together with a detailed list of goods on board, and the ports of call.

Then something caught Menk's eye. A luxury boat, the *Scarab*, seemed to have been given preferential treatment. Nor was that all. 'The guard's name is missing,' he told the head of the department.

'Indeed,' agreed the scribe.

'A simple omission?'

'Not exactly.'

'What do you mean?'

'It is rather delicate . . .'

'I am investigating on the orders of the palace director,'

Menk reminded him, 'and I require your full cooperation.'

It was best not to annoy Henat's emissaries. 'The *Scarab*,' said the scribe, 'carries only people of quality, and the captain, an absolutely honest man, stands surety for their honourable character, so official checks did not seem necessary. Nevertheless, you have a list of the passengers: an inspector of dykes, and four grand ladies, one of them a landowner accompanied by her steward and sandal-bearer. There appears to be nothing amiss. Moreover, the *Scarab* wasn't going to Thebes.'

All the same, Menk felt a strong desire to question the captain of the *Scarab*.

Shedyet, the capital of Faiyum, was known as Krokodilopolis by the Greeks. It was a large agricultural town living peacefully according to the rhythm of the seasons and the harvests. People there ate well and drank excellent beer.

This stop heartened Bebon, who had not particularly enjoyed the encounter with the cobra and the guardian of the labyrinth. He preferred the atmosphere of a warm inn to that of a temple closed in on itself. Even so, it was difficult to relax, knowing that Judge Gem would never stop pursuing them.

'I'd like to see the Lake of Sobek,' he said to the innkeeper.

'It isn't far from here, my boy, but be careful. The god does not care to be disturbed, and he dislikes intruders and new faces. We in Shedyet are content with his protection, and we don't try to look at him close up.'

'Thank you for your advice.'

Armed with the necessary directions, and with North Wind in the lead, Nitis, Kel and Bebon easily found the way to the Lake of Sobek. Just as they spotted the lake, which was surrounded by sycamores, acacias and jujube trees, a priest barred their way.

'Who are you and what do you want?' he demanded.

'I am a priestess of the goddess Neith in Sais, and my

companions are ritual priests. We have come to render homage to Sobek, whom Neith suckled, so that he has access to primeval power.'

Still suspicious, the priest put to her a series of questions about the gods. The quality of her answers soon reassured him, but he said, 'You will have to wait. The god is resting, and we feed him only at the eighth hour of the day.'

The visitors sat down at the edge of the lake. North Wind browsed on the juicy grass.

Meanwhile, the priest hurriedly conferred with his colleagues. 'A priestess of Neith has arrived with two men. One of them might be Kel the scribe!'

'In their latest warning,' said the eldest priest, 'the guards say they are looking for a couple.'

'An acolyte must be helping them. This is a truly fearsome trio of criminals. We are in grave danger.'

'We must inform the authorities.'

'But if they see one of us making off, they'll kill us all.'

'Then what do you suggest?'

'Sobek will help us.'

'Are you thinking of . . .?'

'He'll rid us of at least one of them, and the other two will be so shaken that they'll be vulnerable. Then we can knock them out with staves.'

His colleagues agreed.

'Stay out of sight. I'll take care of our guests.'

The priest took meat, cakes, bread and wine down to the lakeside.

'The god will soon appear,' he told Nitis. 'Do you wish to feed the Beautiful-Faced One and pay homage to him in the name of Neith?'

She took the platter of offerings and stood in the place indicated by the servant of Sobek, who recited the ritual prayers.

At the last invocation, an enormous crocodile appeared. Its

size made a deep impression upon Bebon, and he was far from dazzled by the beauty of its hideous head and cruel eyes.

Suddenly, its jaws opened menacingly.

'Approach without fear,' the priest urged Nitis. 'Speak to him and pour the food into his mouth.'

There was one detail he did not mention: recognizing his benefactors by their voices, the huge creature did not eat them. Intruders, on the other hand, made an excellent meal.

The priest seemed impatient, in a hurry to finish. His behaviour made Kel suspicious.

'Wait, Nitis!'

Too late. She was within Sobek's reach.

'I have come to implore your help,' she said calmly. 'O you whom Neith suckled, give me the weapon I need to continue on my way.'

The god's mouth opened even wider, and was on the point of snapping shut on the stranger's legs. With elegant precision, Nitis slipped the food between his jaws. He began to eat.

Amazed, the priest staggered backwards and bumped into Bebon.

'Stay here,' he ordered. 'You weren't trying to trap us, by any chance, were you, you scoundrel?'

Sated, the crocodile dived below the water.

'What are you up to?' the actor asked his prisoner, who was having an attack of nerves.

'That's impossible . . . The crocodile ought to have—'

'Eaten the priestess, is that it? I'm going to break your neck, you villain!'

Armed with staves, the other priests came running up.

'And here is the rest of your band!'

'Surrender,' shouted the eldest priest, 'or you will die. You are outnumbered.'

In a great jet of water, the crocodile swam back to the surface, came towards Nitis, opened its mouth and deposited on the bank an acacia-wood bow and two arrows, symbols of Neith.

The priestess drew the bow and aimed an arrow at the priests.

Terrified, they fled.

29

'I am Menk, appointed as an investigator by Henat, the palace director. I have some questions to ask you.'

The aggressive attitude of this elegant and rather pleasant-looking man surprised the captain of the *Scarab*. Making a stopover two days' sail from Memphis, he had not expected this sudden check. After setting down all his passengers in Middle Egypt and taking on three senior officials who were in a hurry to get back to the country's economic centre, he was already thinking about his next voyage.

'I am listening, sir,' he said.

'During your latest journey, you had several important people on board.'

'That's right. An inspector of dykes and four noble ladies, one of them a wealthy landowner escorted by her steward and her sandal-bearer.'

'What was her name?'

'The lady Neferet.'

'Did you know her?'

'No, it was the first time I'd seen her. She owns her own boat, but wanted to enjoy travelling with pleasant company.'

'Were there any . . . incidents?'

'Not really.'

'Be specific.'

'Neferet and her servants left my boat when we stopped at Faiyum, even though they'd planned to go further.'

'What reason did she give?'

'Management problems in Memphis. The lady wanted to see one of her properties in the region again.'

Menk was convinced: Nitis was travelling under an assumed name, and was accompanied by Kel and one of his accomplices.

'In future, captain, submit to all the obligatory checks, otherwise you will have serious problems.'

Menk hoped to pick up the fugitives' trail in Shedyet. He was not disappointed. The inhabitants' only topic of conversation was the extraordinary events at the Lake of Sobek.

Menk went to the temple, where the High Priest, whose strange face resembled a reptile's, received him with much courtesy.

'I am in the service of the director of the royal palace,' said Menk, 'and I should like to help you. What happened?'

'The ritual priests charged with ensuring the wellbeing of the sacred crocodile were savagely attacked by a band of criminals. Only the priests' courage and the god's protection enabled them to escape death.'

'I should like to question them.'

'They are still very weak and—'

'Their testimony is vital. These bandits must be arrested with all speed, before they attack other innocent people.'

Menk listened to a painful litany of moans and complaints. Fortunately, the priest who had been in contact with the criminals recovered his composure and gave precise details.

'The woman was very beautiful and claimed to be a priestess of Neith. She wanted to ask Sobek for help.'

'Did you grant her permission?'

'Oh no, that would have been impossible. We are the only ones who can feed the great fish;* no outsider would be able to go near it.'

'A priestess of Neith is not an outsider.'

* The Egyptians regarded the crocodile as a fish.

'That's true, I suppose. But it would still have been impossible. When I flatly refused my permission, that diabolical woman ordered her servants to strike me with their staves.'

'Describe them to me.'

'Two giants – demons risen up from the darkness! Even if there had been twenty of us, we could not have defeated them.'

'That's curious. You don't seem to be wounded.'

'The god prevented them from harming us. When the crocodile came to my aid, the attackers fled.'

'Didn't your colleagues try to stop them?'

'Yes, but in vain. Despite their bravery, the two giants overwhelmed them. We are asking for considerable compensation from the palace. Our domain has been sacked, and several priests will suffer for a long time from their wounds. The High Priest of Shedyet will write a detailed report.'

'It will be studied very carefully,' promised Menk.

The story-teller continued to ramble, stressing his extraordinary courage and the amount of compensation necessary.

Menk was no longer listening. He was sure that this priestess of Neith was indeed Nitis, under the control of Kel the scribe. Had they taken refuge in Faiyum? It seemed unlikely, because they needed to reach Thebes as quickly as possible and contact the Divine Worshipper.

So he went to the port to question dock-workers, sailors and merchants. The men proved rather uncooperative, and he did not gather any useful information. The arrogance of one captain of a cargo-boat set his nerves on edge.

'You, sir, know a great deal. Soldiers, seize him,' Menk snapped.

'This is illegal! You have no right to—'

'I have every right.'

The sailor was bound and thrown to the ground.

'I want the truth,' demanded Menk with impressive coldness. 'If you refuse to talk, you will end your days at the bottom of the Nile.'

The captain took the threat seriously. 'Yes, I saw a woman with two men and a donkey.'

'Did they talk to you?'

'Not for long.'

'What did they say?'

'They wanted to travel south, but I never carry passengers. The conversation stopped there.'

Furious, Menk seized him by the throat. 'You're lying! You helped them, didn't you?'

'They . . . they offered me a piece of lapis-lazuli, so how could I refuse? I sold them a large boat, with a sail. Large, but rotten – they won't get very far. Now you know everything.'

The sailor was terrified and sweating profusely. Would this madman carry out his threat?

'If you have lied to me,' said Menk chillingly, 'I shall return. And then you will never have an opportunity to lie again.'

30

Judge Gem's renewed vitality astonished his subordinates. His weight of years, his painful joints, heavy limbs and hopes of a well-deserved retirement were forgotten. It was futile to talk to him of tiredness and limited hours of work. The only thing that mattered was tracking down the scribe and his accomplices.

Armed with a royal decree permitting him to arrest any suspect, even a provincial chief, the judge organized guards patrols on a previously unheard-of scale. Soon the whole of Upper Egypt would be permanently watched.

On board his boat, the two cabins had been transformed into offices and many scribes were hard at work. At each halt, information was brought to the judge and he issued new instructions.

A second reading of Bebon's file confirmed him in his opinion: the actor was a choice recruit for Kel's rebel network. A great traveller, who played several of the gods outside temples when the public part of the Mysteries was celebrated, Bebon must have built up a network of friends and acquaintances, who were now being used in the service of crime.

Unfortunately, the file contained no details concerning his friendship with the murderous scribe. Having no house of his own, Bebon lodged with his successive mistresses and, when not on his tours, lived by his wits. He must have been seduced by the prospect of belonging to a secret movement capable of overthrowing the royal throne.

Nitis, a priestess of Neith, had added her own stone to the edifice. Wahibra must have given her the names of ritual priests involved with the conspiracy and likely to help her. That was how Kel had escaped the forces of order for so long.

A terrifying thought crossed the judge's mind: was the Divine Worshipper the soul and the leader of the rebels? Unable to act openly, had she galvanized the conspirators' actions, spiritually as well as materially. Perhaps Ahmose was mistaken in believing that she was confined to Thebes and without any real influence. Perhaps she had succeeded in creating a secret army of supporters determined to offer her the full might of pharaonic office.'

An objective analysis of the situation rendered this theory unlikely. Ahmose controlled the army, the guards and all the secretariats of the state. The Divine Worshipper, on the other hand, celebrated rites in honour of Amun and reigned over only a few ritual priests and servants who took advantage of the Theban province's wealth.

Kel was deluding himself in seeking her help. She would be obliged to reject him and would probably hand him over to the authorities. Unless ... unless the coded papyri were an essential element of this tragedy and the immensely learned priestess possessed the key to deciphering them.

No one had succeeded in reading them. The great skill with which their contents had been hidden was proof of their great importance.

One of Judge Gem's assistants interrupted his thoughts. 'I have just received a large number of reports from the majority of the large towns in Upper Egypt.'

'Why are you wearing that expression? Have you been informed of a catastrophe?'

'The term does not seem excessive.'

'Explain yourself.'

'The provincial chiefs and mayors of Upper Egypt are in no hurry to apply your directives. They obey the pharaoh, it is true, but they do not share his love of Greece. Sais seems very far away to them and so oriented towards the Mediterranean that it has forgotten the far-away South and its traditions, which the Divine Worshipper defends.'

'Is this the start of a rebellion?'

'We must not exaggerate. The authorities are merely dragging their feet and moderating their efforts.'

'In other words, the checks and controls are not being exercised with the necessary thoroughness and the killer may slip through the net.'

'I fear so, Judge. As regards the temples, things are worse. They disapprove of the state's takeover of their management and possessions, and deplore the appointment of high priests by Sais without consulting the local men. The priests of the South feel scorned and shackled, and we can expect no help from them.'

'They might even hide the fugitives.'

'That is not impossible. Fortunately, we have a few informants in the region.'

The situation looked much worse than expected, and Kel would take full advantage of it. The judge wrote a long report for King Ahmose, describing this worrying underground reality. In these circumstances, the role of General Phanes at Elephantine seemed likely to prove decisive. If the garrison rebelled and made an alliance with the Nubians, the balance of the whole country would be threatened.'

Shortly after Gem's boat had docked at the principal port of Faiyum, an officer came aboard and requested an immediate meeting with him.

'There was a serious incident at the Lake of Sobek, Judge,' the officer said. 'Some priests were savagely attacked by three individuals, two men and a woman. The sacred crocodile was spared.'

130

'Bring me the witnesses.'

'Including the High Priest of Sobek?'

'*All* the witnesses – and quickly.'

The judge was met by a tide of moans and indignant protests. The priests were demanding substantial compensation from the state, on account of what they had suffered. As for their description of their attackers, it was positively fantastical. There was only one significant detail: the woman was a priestess of Neith who had come to seek Sobek's aid. And he had given her a monstrous bow and gigantic arrows.

Gem kept back the priest who had spent time with the trio. It was clear that he was hiding part of the truth.

'Did the woman speak to the crocodile?' asked Gem.

'No . . . Well, a little.'

'How did it behave?'

'Normally.'

'The incarnation of Sobek recognizes its servants by their voices, according to the High Priest. Now, this priestess of Neith was not one of those servants. If she approached the god, she was in mortal danger. Were you trying to get rid of her?'

'Our destiny belongs to the gods, and—'

'Attempted murder carries a severe penalty.'

'He promised me there'd be no trouble and I'd receive the compensation I deserve. Why are you torturing me like this?'

The judge's eyes flashed. 'Who is this "he"?'

'I promised not to tell.'

'Either you tell me or I shall send you to prison.'

The priest did not hesitate for long. 'A special agent appointed by the palace questioned me for a long time and ordered me not to mention his involvement or there would be reprisals.'

'What was his name?'

'He didn't tell me. He was accompanied by several soldiers, and they didn't look very accommodating.'

'Did you tell them anything you have forgotten to tell me?'

'No, nothing!'

'Soldiers will be appointed to keep watch on the region.'

The priest bowed, and was escorted outside.

The judge was perplexed. He could think of two possibilities: either Henat was conducting his own investigation, with the aid of a raiding-party, or else members of Kel's gang were spreading terror and intimidation. Either way, it was better not to come into conflict with Henat. The judge would get by on his own.

31

Thanks to a strong northerly wind, the boat was making swift progress. Comfortably bedded down, North Wind was enjoying a lengthy sleep. The Nile waters sparkled in the sun, their blue reflecting that of the sky above. A fairly good sailor, Bebon held the steering-oar and kept watch on the sail. Kel and Nitis stood hand in hand, savouring these moments of peace as they gazed at the verdant riverbanks of Middle Egypt.

'I never imagined I could be so happy,' he whispered. 'Your love drives away the darkness.'

'To live together as one life: is that not a gift from the gods?'

A sinister cracking noise startled them all.

'We're holed and taking on water,' observed Bebon. 'We'll have to bail.'

Kel set to work immediately but, despite his efforts, the hole in the hull grew larger and the boat became difficult to handle.

'That bandit sold us a rotting hulk!' roared Bebon. 'We'll have to berth.'

The two men furled the sail, then took to the oars together. They soon reached the riverbank. North Wind stepped reluctantly on to dry land again and shook himself; he much preferred sailing on the river to carrying all the baggage.

The trio looked around carefully. There was nobody in sight.

'I know where we are,' said Bebon. 'We'll cross the farmland and take the path that skirts the desert. I have friends in every village, and we'll easily find somewhere to eat and sleep.'

'That leak was fortunate for us,' said Kel. 'The boat-seller probably denounced us to the river-guards, and they'll have set out to catch us.'

'Our next objective is Khmun. I've acted in many Mysteries there, and the head ritual priest likes me. He will tell us where the guards are stationed, he'll help us escape.'

North Wind took the lead. Given the distance they had to travel, this was no time for idling.

Menk stamped his foot in rage. His boat ought to have caught up with Nitis's a long time ago, but it had overtaken nothing but fishermen and riverbank dwellers transporting goods.

'The fugitives may have hidden or scuttled their boat,' pointed out a soldier. 'If they have, it will be impossible to pick up their trail again on the river.'

'So they must have chosen a land route,' said Menk. 'But on which riverbank? Nitis has supporters among the priests who venerated Wahibra – after all, he studied at Khmun, at the great Temple of Thoth? It is the home of ancient rituals and trains scribes of the highest quality. Yes, Nitis will go to Khmun. And we shall be waiting for her there.'

The soldier thought Menk was celebrating prematurely, but he was accustomed to obedience, and he would carry out his orders.

The commander of the fortress of Henen-nesut was also the 'captain of boats', in charge of ensuring river travel in Middle and Upper Egypt. Close to Faiyum, the old town slumbered, and the commander's main concern was deducting the new taxes applying to people who had previously been exempt. A priest could now be arrested, even on temple land, if he refused to pay these general and obligatory taxes. This practice, imported from Greece, had enraged the local priests, but the last word went to the tax authorities, who had the support of the army.

Although he did not really approve of Ahmose's methods, the commander had to comply. Surely attacking the temples in this way was weakening the country's traditional base? Greek influence was constantly spreading, distancing the population from the gods and leading them towards ever-weightier materialism. Fortunately, in Thebes the Divine Worshipper celebrated the rites linking the earth to the heavens.

The arrival of Judge Gem disturbed the peace of the fortress. The judge's expression and tone of voice clearly conveyed his dissatisfaction.

'Commander, have you received the new security instructions from the capital?'

'Yes, sir.'

'You are not unaware of the fact that I am searching for a dangerous fugitive who is determined to reach the South?'

'The facts have been set out in detail.'

'Then why are you so lax? I have just seen a boat full of fishermen pass by without undergoing a single check!'

'You must understand the local situation, Judge. We cannot stop every single small vessel and poison people's lives. They pay heavy taxes and duties, and their work is hard. I am doing the best I can, but if the army is forever harassing them their hearts will sink even lower.'

'Your comments are irrelevant, Commander. How many boats have you neglected to check in the last few days?'

'It is difficult to say.'

'Are you aware of your lack of vigilance?

'I repeat, I am doing the best I can. I said the very same to the palace director's envoy, who came here on a fast boat, accompanied by five soldiers. He rushed off in pursuit of the fugitive. If the criminal has only one boat at his disposal, he will soon be caught.'

Gem was puzzled. Henat had sent a raiding-party in pursuit of Kel? It was possible but hardly likely, for Henat would not have permitted his men to show themselves so openly. The truth must be different. The raiding-party, which had used Henat's name to get past all the barriers, was helping Kel, gathering information on the army's and guards' operations against him, and protecting him most effectively. Kel, Nitis, Bebon, six loyal followers . . . The size of the enemy force was becoming clearer.

Judge Gem glared at the commander. 'I intend to dismiss you from office. Your attitude endangers Egypt's safety. You will be tried and punished.'

The officer was aghast. 'I don't understand! I—'

'You have only one chance of avoiding this well-deserved punishment. From this moment on, you will check everything that moves on the Nile – even people in reed boats – and you will send me a daily report.'

'Yes, sir,' agreed the officer, hanging his head.

32

After passing through several villages, where they received a warm welcome from Bebon's friends, Bebon, Nitis, Kel and North Wind neared a large town called Three Palms. Another two days of walking at a steady pace, and they would reach Khmun, which was inaccessible via the Nile because there were so many checks by the river-guards.

They passed a tall young peasant who was leading two donkeys bearing baskets filled with cloves of garlic.

Suddenly, he turned round. 'Bebon! Is it you? Is it really you?' And he grinned idiotically.

The actor stared at him. 'Head-in-the-Clouds! I didn't recognize you . . . You've grown into a man!'

The lad looked embarrassed. 'Not quite, but I have hopes. I very much like the baker's daughter, and she likes me, too.'

'That's wonderful news!'

'Have you come to see your friend, the maker of ritual sandals?'

'Yes, I have.'

'The poor fellow . . . The guards questioned him for hours and then took him away. They're everywhere and they have a really unpleasant look about them. We were living a quiet life, here in Three Palms. And it's the same in the villages near Khmun. They're questioning people and searching all the houses.'

'What about you? Did they bother you?'

'Oh, I obeyed my uncle and said I didn't know you. Then they left me in peace – and then I sold them my garlic at an extremely good price.'

'We've never met, all right?'

Head-in-the-Clouds agreed with a wink, and the four travellers retraced their footsteps.

'We must separate,' said Bebon. 'Nitis will play a peasant and, with North Wind, will take the path along the edge of the desert, well away from the villages. Kel and I will use the river – we'll swim. We'll join up again north of Khmun, at the start of the canal leading to the valley of the tamarisks.'

'I won't leave Nitis,' declared Kel.

'You must,' she said. 'If we stay together, we'll be arrested. Neith's bow and arrows will protect me. And you mustn't lose the amulet.'

'Nitis . . .'

She kissed him so tenderly that he could not help but give in.

'Come along,' ordered Bebon. 'This is our only chance of success.'

Torn in two, Kel watched Nitis disappear into the distance.

'North Wind will choose the shortest, safest way,' said Bebon. 'Now, my friend the endurance champion, to work! Don't worry, there are no crocodiles here. They don't like being disturbed, and there are a lot of boats in the area around Khmun.'

'What about the river's currents?'

'I know them by heart, thanks to a rather nice young lady who went swimming with me. We'll swim close to the bank, except for one place where we'll have to move further out.'

The water felt delicious, and swimming eased Kel's misery. He followed Bebon, who was determined and very much at

ease. The two men alternated periods of swimming overarm*
and resting, using the river's movements to carry them along at
a good speed.

Kel thought constantly of Nitis. Now that he was separated
from her, he appreciated just how vital her light was to him.
An otherworldly harmony existed between them, beyond
human love and physical desire.

Bebon headed for the middle of the river. The current
favoured swimmers, and an enormous perch brushed by them.
Swimming underwater, they increased their speed.

Returning to the surface to take a breath, Kel saw a guards'
boat with an archer at the prow, ready to fire.

The end of the journey, far from her, so far from her . . .

He smiled and waved a friendly hand.

The archer did likewise, and the boat continued on its way.

Bebon popped up beside him. 'By the gods, that was a close
shave!'

'You're not too tired?'

'Is that a joke?' The actor began swimming again.

The valley of the tamarisks appeared on the horizon. The trees
were full of pink blossom and created a magical landscape
framing the immense Temple of Thoth.† North Wind halted
and sniffed the scented air that bathed this magical place. Nitis
saw Kel swimming and overcoming the perils of the river.
Soon, they would be reunited.

Ten guards emerged from the trees.

'Where are you going, young woman?' asked their leader.

'I am delivering fresh vegetables to the temple.'

---

* Contrary to received ideas, this technique is not a recent invention.
A hieroglyph in the *Pyramid Texts* proves that the crawl was already being
used by the Egyptians as early as the Old Kingdom.
† Sometimes compared to Karnak, it was entirely destroyed by the *fellahin*,
who burnt its stones and used the residue as fertilizer.

'Isn't your husband with you?'

'I run my own farm.'

'A free woman . . .'

'That doesn't bother you, I hope?'

'I respect the law. What is your name?'

'Neferet.'

'I shall examine your donkey's load.'

'Be careful. He has an unpredictable temper.'

'If that animal attacks me, you will be responsible.'

'In that case, I shall open the baskets myself.'

The guards closed in around Nitis, as though worried that she might produce some fearsome weapon.

'Leeks, salad leaves and onions. Satisfied?'

'What about the bag on the donkey's flank? What's in that one?'

A simple peasant woman, owning a bow . . . The men were sure to arrest Nitis and take her to the guard-post.

'Personal items.'

'I have orders to examine everything. Show me or we will kill your donkey.'

Head and ears down, North Wind was careful to show no sign of hostility. In prison, Nitis would try to defend herself. Kel and Bebon would continue the quest for the truth.

Slowly, she took the bow from the linen bag.

Their eyes glued to the strange object, the guards all turned pale. Rooted to the spot, their arms hanging limply, they seemed unable to move or speak.

A brilliant light flashed from the acacia wood of the bow, as intense as the sun's radiance. Only Nitis was not dazzled by it.

'You may pass,' decreed the officer.

33

'Are you tired?' Kel asked.

'Absolutely not,' replied Bebon, who was exhausted.

As he fought to get his breath back, the actor wondered how he had managed to swim for so long. The riverbank seemed unreachable, and his body weighed heavy as lead. One more effort, just one, delving into a reserve of energy deep within him, and at last he was on dry land.

'You see,' he told Kel, 'it was no more arduous than a morning stroll.'

Kel helped his friend to his feet. 'We must hurry and join Nitis.'

'I'm sure she's succeeded, like us.'

Kel set such a punishing pace that it was torture for Bebon.

The shade of the first tamarisks was a relief. Suddenly Bebon's legs became lighter, and he recovered his usual cockiness.

They found Nitis and North Wind resting beside a well, and the lovers fell into each other's arms. They told each other of their ordeals, grateful yet again that they had gained the gods' protection.

'We haven't reached the temple yet,' Bebon reminded them. 'It would be dangerous for us all to be seen together. I'll contact the senior ritual priest, and come back to fetch you.'

'Thank you for being so courageous,' said Nitis.

The actor was so touched that he couldn't speak.

He was an unpleasant-looking fellow. 'I'm thirsty,' he grunted.

'The well doesn't belong to me,' replied Kel. 'Drink as much as you like.'

The thirsty man gave Kel a sidelong look. Nitis and North Wind were resting in the shade of a tamarisk. 'Are you from around these parts?'

The scribe nodded.

'Then you must know Three Palms?'

'I've come from there.'

'So you know the sandal-maker?'

'I took part in his arrest.'

The thirsty man stepped away from the well. 'You mean ... you're a guard?'

'I'd like to know why you're asking all these questions. Are you by any chance a friend of criminals on the run?'

'No, oh no! I'm one of the gardeners who take care of the valley of the tamarisks, and the guards ordered me to tell them about any new faces and suspicious people.'

'Continue to be vigilant, and you will be rewarded.'

'You can rely on me.' The fellow walked away.

'We ought to leave this place,' Kel told Nitis. 'But if Bebon can't find us, he'll think we've been caught. And we could be spotted by other informants. My play-acting won't always work.'

'Waiting is the only solution,' decided the young woman.

'Supposing Bebon's been arrested?'

'May the gods continue to protect us.'

North Wind seemed calm, and was showing no signs of anxiety. At nightfall he got to his feet and, pricking up his ears, alerted his friends. Someone was walking quickly towards them.

'Bebon!'

'We're safe. I met the senior priest and told him everything.'

'That was an enormous risk!' exclaimed Kel. 'He could have sent you to prison.'

'The fellow's much too intelligent to swallow nonsense.'

The quartet headed for the great temple of the god Thoth, the master of knowledge and patron of scribes. Kel had dreamt of visiting it one day, even of working there – but under rather different circumstances.

Bebon took them to an annexe, which contained a library, a dining-hall, a storehouse for sacred vases, a workshop and a stable.

The senior priest, a well-built man with a shaven head, was dressed in an immaculate white tunic. He greeted them at the doorway to a small official house.

'So this is Nitis! My very dear friend, the late Wahibra, told me so much about you.'

The young woman bowed.

'You were the main subject of his letters. He regarded you as his spiritual daughter and wanted to see you succeed him. But because of grave events, he feared sinister intervention by the authorities and asked me to help you if necessary. Today, I am happy to keep my promise.'

The priest looked long and hard at Kel. 'And this is the terrifying killer who is being sought by every guard and soldier in the Two Lands!'

'He is innocent,' declared Nitis.

'Bebon's explanation convinced me, and your testimony strengthens my opinion. You are mixed up in an affair of state, and the truth will not be easy to establish. Only the Divine Worshipper has the necessary authority. This house is to be renovated next week; so you may rest here for a few days. Bebon shall act the part of a stable-lad, while Nitis and Kel will be temporary pure priests in my service. And I shall try to find you a boat sailing for Thebes.'

'We are infinitely grateful to you,' said Nitis. 'Will you permit me to ask one more favour of you?'

'Go on.'

'Will you give us permission to work in the library? We might find information which would help us solve the mystery of a coded document central to this tragedy.'

'Granted. Speak to your colleagues as little as possible, and do not walk inside the enclosure. The priests have been ordered to indicate your presence, and several informants are constantly on the prowl.'

'In helping us,' observed Nitis, 'you are taking a great many risks.'

'I owe everything to Wahibra, and I disapprove of King Ahmose's policies. By imposing laws inspired by his beloved Greece, he is leading this country to ruin. Crushing people with duties and taxes will discourage them. Breaking the backs of the temples to the benefit of Greek mercenaries and traders is weakening the very spirit of the Two Lands. If the anger of the gods bursts forth, their vengeance will be terrifying.'

The prediction chilled Nitis's and Kel's blood.

The head priest took Bebon by the shoulders. 'I'm sorry, my friend, but you must sleep in the stables. This house is only for temporary priests. Don't worry, though: the straw won't disappoint you.'

At first grumpy, the actor thought of the young couple: they did indeed deserve a night of love.

34

'Filth!' snapped King Ahmose, upturning the cup of white
wine that his cup-bearer had just served him. 'Where did this
vile vinegar come from?'

'It is a fine oasis vintage reserved for the palace, Majesty.'

'Smash all the jars containing it. And get me the name
of the vine-grower responsible. His worthless career is at
an end.'

The cup-bearer slunk away.

Queen Tanith laid a gentle hand on her husband's arm.
'I don't think the wine merited quite such anger.'

'You are right, my dear. At the moment, my nerves are
completely on edge. Sometimes I have the unbearable feeling
that control of the country is slipping away from me.'

'Do you have any serious indications of that?'

'No, just a premonition, a sort of unease.'

'Henat occupies a vital position at the summit of the state.
One hears many acerbic criticisms of him. Should you not be
suspicious of his ambitions?'

'Henat informs me, he does not decide. He is a thoughtful,
methodical, hard-working and sly man. His job suits him
wonderfully, and he knows his limits.

'Would you say as much about Udja?'

'He is an excellent first minister, of rare probity and stature.
But . . .'

'But?'

'Does he dream of succeeding me? I can scarcely believe that he does. I would say the same of the Pefy. These men have spent their lives serving Egypt and know the heavy weight of the royal office.'

'Do not be too trusting,' urged the queen. 'According to an ancient text in *Wisdom*, the pharaoh has neither friend nor brother.'

Ahmose kissed Tanith on the brow. 'Don't worry, my dear: after listening to my advisers, I check what they have told me. And I alone govern.'

The arrival of Udja was announced.

'I shall leave you,' said the queen.

'No, stay. We may need your counsel.'

Udja's stature never failed to impress. He seemed to fill the audience chamber all by himself. He bowed respectfully to the royal couple.

'Majesties, I have the pleasure of announcing the launch of the new war-boat, the largest in our fleet. Having examined it minutely myself, I can assure you that no enemy can equal it. We still have to appoint a commander capable of manoeuvring it and using it to its best.'

'Do you have a name to propose?' Ahmose asked.

'Here is a list of experienced officers, Majesty. My two preferred candidates are marked with a red dot, those of General Phanes with a black dot. I have added full details of each candidate.'

Ahmose swiftly examined the list and personal details of the officers. He selected a forty-year-old captain whose name was not marked with a dot of either colour. 'He is to take up his post with all speed.'

'I shall inform him of his appointment immediately,' promised Udja. 'Within a month, two more of these new boats will be launched. Am I to continue the building programme?'

'Accelerate it and engage additional carpenters.'

Hands clasped behind his back, Ahmose strode up and down the audience chamber.

'Until the Interpreters' Secretariat is fully operational, I shall continue to be suspicious of the Persians. That race has war and intrigue in its blood. We must arm ourselves continually, in order to deter them.'

The queen agreed with a discreet nod.

'Is there any news from Kroisos?' she asked.

'Normal diplomatic correspondence, Majesty. I have brought you his last letter: he wishes you excellent health on behalf of Emperor Cambyses, who is very busy restoring the economy of his vast territories.'

'Write a conventional answer,' ordered Ahmose. 'Has Nitetis, Kroisos' wife, really forgiven me for overthrowing her father in order to succeed him?'

'It's impossible to say,' opined the queen. 'With maturity, she will see those painful times in a different light, unless an undying resentment is gnawing away at her. Whatever the case, has she any real influence on Persian policy?'

'Only Kroisos counts,' conceded the king.

'I have received a worrying report from Judge Gem,' said Udja in a grave voice. 'His investigation is progressing, and he is convinced that Kel heads a band of rebels who are both mobile and determined. So this is not simply a matter of murders but a conspiracy against the state and against you, in which Nitis the priestess is seemingly involved. There is also disappointing news: the various authorities in Upper Egypt are dragging their feet in applying the judge's directives. So the holes in the net are proving to be very substantial, enabling the insurgents to escape us.'

'The influence of the Divine Worshipper!' cursed Ahmose. 'She is opposed to the progress that the Greeks embody and she wants to keep Upper Egypt in its outmoded traditions. Has the judge any serious leads?'

'Yes, Majesty, for Kel has left traces of his movements,

notably at Faiyum. Thanks to the means at his disposal, Judge Gem is very hopeful of finding him. Nevertheless, he will come up against a lack of cooperation from the temples, which are discontented with your policies regarding them.'

'The temples ... I should raze a large number of them to the ground!'

'That would be a mistake,' said the queen. 'In the eyes of the population, even though they have no access to them, the temples are the dwelling-places of the gods and guarantee the survival of the Two Lands. The important thing was to bring the priests back to reason, and you have succeeded in so doing.'

'In appearance, only in appearance! Nitis undoubtedly has a network of accomplices who are sheltering them and providing them with the means of transport to Thebes.'

'We are pursuing the fugitives, Majesty,' Udja reminded him, 'and can rely on Judge Gem's pugnacity. And besides, the Divine Worshipper will not ignore Henat's solemn warning.'

'That old priestess is as stubborn as a mountain! Persuading her will not be easy.'

Udja looked shocked. 'The Divine Worshipper would never help a fugitive criminal and his band of rebels! As for her hostility towards the development of our society, she will not break the law. If she did, her reputation would be destroyed.'

'Have we received a report from General Phanes?'

'Not yet, Majesty. But Minister Pefy has arrived in Abydos, where he is supervising the reconstruction work and preparing for the celebration of the Mysteries of Osiris. He has left his files in perfect order, and his assistants are collaborating most thoroughly. Thanks to the efficiency of the taxation authorities, the new duties are a complete success, and the country's finances are flourishing.'

'You may withdraw, Udja.'

Ahmose sat down heavily on his throne. 'Power weighs heavy upon me,' he confided to his wife.

'But your reforms are very successful, aren't they? By applying them with a firm hand, you are increasing the wealth of the Two Lands.'

'That's enough talk of work, my dear. Now for a boat trip, some cool wine and lunch with some pretty musicians.'

35

Kel gazed at Nitis in wonder as she slept beside him. She had the most beautiful eyes in the world, a body worthy of a goddess, and the charm of a sorceress. Of course, this was nothing but a dream. She could not be here, right next to him, wantonly in love. He took the risk of destroying the fantasy, and dared to kiss her.

She awoke, as radiant as ever.

'Nitis, is it you? Is it really you?'

Her smile and her gaze overwhelmed him, and he hugged her until she could barely breathe.

'Gently,' she begged him.

'Forgive me. I'm so happy . . .'

'The gods will protect us Kel, as long as we fulfil our mission.'

Suddenly, harsh reality struck Kel with immense force. They were no ordinary married couple waking up in their own home in some peaceful village. Kel would not go to his office, Nitis would not carry out her duties as mistress of the house, and they would not talk about their future children.

This house was merely a temporary refuge, perhaps their last moment of grace.

'Don't lose hope,' she urged. 'Our allies will enable us to meet the Divine Worshipper, and we shall convince her that our cause is just. For now, we belong to the staff of this temple.'

Kel tried to forget that Pharaoh Ahmose's army and guards were searching for him. Alongside Nitis and other temporary priests, he purified himself in the sacred lake, then received his instructions from the head priest. His silence and contemplative mood did not surprise anyone. When you were serving the gods, you did not raise your voice. And Thoth detested gossips and chatterboxes.

Exploring the library was a wondrous experience. Thousands of manuscripts had been accumulated since the earliest times and carefully catalogued. This was a scribes' paradise! Kel concentrated on the mathematical papyri, but it would have taken him months, even years, to exhaust their content and discover any kind of decoding system. As for Nitis, she studied the ancient ritual of the creation of the world by the Odgoad, made up of four male and four female powers.

After breakfasting with the donkey-drivers who were working for the temple that morning, Bebon and North Wind received instructions from a steward, a friend of the head priest. They were to make several trips between the brewery and a boat whose destination was the South. The captain wanted plenty of jars of beer to combat thirst and, most especially, he would accept passengers who had not been declared to the authorities, in exchange for 'a suitable consideration'.

The initial contact was stormy, for the price asked was far above the acceptable level of dishonesty. As the beer deliveries progressed, negotiations became more and more amicable, and eventually an agreement was reached. Thanks to the bag of gemstones, Bebon could face up to future expenses.

Another two days of waiting; two more days of unbearable tedium.

The actor spent some agreeable moments in the company of

his colleagues, while North Wind imposed his calm demeanour upon the undisciplined donkeys. Strong beer was drunk and fresh onions eaten, and they all agreed that they were fortunate to serve a generous temple.

Bebon played his part well. In reality, he remained permanently on his guard, fearing the guards might turn up at any moment.

When he returned to the boat at dead of night, he did not notice anything unusual. Warily, he strode along the quayside.

'Are you looking for someone?' asked a coarse voice.

A burly fellow appeared, armed with a heavy staff.

The actor maintained his composure.

'A girl. I was told some of them ply their trade here.'

'You were told wrong.'

'A pity. I'll try my luck elsewhere.'

'Where are you from?'

'Go back to sleep, friend,' advised Bebon.

'I keep watch on the boats. And I punish anyone who's over-curious.'

'Good night, friend.'

The guards had men everywhere. Bebon would come back before the boat sailed, and check that they were not laying a trap.

In his investigations on land owned by the Temple of Thoth, Menk made great play of his two offices. Sometimes he introduced himself as the organizer of festivals in Sais, sometimes as the palace director's special envoy. According to whom he was dealing with, he used a gentle touch or menace. Despite this skilful strategy, he learnt nothing that led him to believe Nitis and Kel were hiding within the temple. All that had emerged was the hostility of several priests to Ahmose's policies, hence their possible complicity with the fugitives.

As he was resting beside a well in the valley of the tamarisks, he noticed a strange fellow hiding behind a tree-trunk and watching him.

'Go and fetch him,' Menk ordered two soldiers.

The man was detained with a certain amount of brute force.

'I'm an honest gardener,' he yelped, 'and you have no right to arrest me!'

'The palace has granted me full powers,' said Menk icily. 'One lie, one refusal to answer me, and you will die. Why were you spying on me?'

The gardener's voice quavered. 'Because of the other man, the guards officer . . . I was wondering if it was starting again, if you were his colleague. I help the guards, you know. I tell them about suspicious strangers, and they reward me.'

'Did you tell them about that one?'

'No, because he was one of them.'

'Was he alone?'

'No – at least I don't think so. Near the well there was also a very pretty woman and a donkey. I expect she was with the stranger.'

Kel and Nitis! thought Menk. So the Temple of Thoth *was* sheltering them!

'Did my colleague question you?' he asked in a friendly voice.

'No, he just told me that he was from Three Palms, where he had taken part in the arrest of a criminal. I didn't ask any more.'

'You did right, my friend. This investigation does not concern you. Hold your tongue, and nothing bad will happen to you.'

Under the soldiers' menacing gaze, the gardener scuttled away.

Menk ought to have alerted Henat and arranged for guards to arrive in force, but he did not want anyone else to kill Kel and save Nitis. The young woman would understand the meaning of what he had done, and would be grateful to him for it. So he must use a subtle strategy in order to lure his rival into a deadly snare.

36

The High Priest of the Temple of Thoth was very old, and rarely left his modest official house near the sacred lake. Nevertheless, he continued to direct the ritual life of the immense temple and closely oversaw the administrators whose task it was to maintain the prosperity of the vast domain. Each morning, he rejoiced at the sight of the sun lighting up the buildings, and thanked the god of knowledge for granting him a beautiful and long life in his service.

His closest colleague, the head ritual priest, performed his many duties impeccably. He belonged to that exceptional category of Servants of the God who were wholly free of ambition and were concerned only for the perfection of the ceremonies. His latest actions were surprising, but his arguments had persuaded the High Priest, who was greatly attached to the right of refuge that the current regime was demolishing. And the law of Maat must be applied to human justice. If they became distanced from each other, the world would become impossible to live in.

Having to receive Judge Gem annoyed him. Faced with the judge's insistence, the High Priest had, however, agreed to meet him so as not to provoke King Ahmose's anger towards Khmun.

'Thank you for seeing me, High Priest,' said the judge, equally annoyed at having had to wait so long.

'I have little furniture. Will this three-legged stool be sufficient for you?'

'Certainly.'

'What good wind brings you here, Judge Gem?'

'The pharaoh has given me full powers to arrest or even execute a killer of the worst kind, the scribe Kel. He is the leader of a band of dangerous conspirators to which Nitis, a priestess of Neith, and an actor called Bebon belong. Bebon has often played parts here, during the presentation of the sacred Mysteries on the temple forecourt.'

'Bebon? He's an excellent lad, a little whimsical, perhaps, but liked by everyone.'

'I must remind you, High Priest, that he is aiding and abetting a merciless criminal accused of many murders.'

'Why should the scribe have done such terrible things?'

'That is a state secret.'

'Ah. So he has displeased the king.'

The judge forced himself to remain calm. 'Do not believe that, High Priest. Since the state is threatened, we must act at once to prevent a gang of rebels from overturning the throne.'

'The pharaoh is the foremost servant of Maat. As a temple-builder, he provides the gods with their earthly dwellings and, through this offering, attracts their benevolence. It is therefore a grave error to attack the temples and regard them as ordinary estates. Tell the king that respect for tradition preserves harmony and that unbridled adulation of progress leads to misfortune.'

'High Priest, I have not come here to talk about a policy for which I am not responsible.'

'And yet you apply it, since the law of the temples is no longer recognized.'

Gem was at boiling-point. 'At this moment, only one question matters: are the murderous scribe and his accomplices hiding in this temple?'

The old man reflected for a long time. 'First, you would have to bring irrefutable proof of their guilt – knowing Bebon, I find it hard to see him taking part in a criminal conspiracy against the king. Second, how are all comings and goings to be controlled? I rarely leave this house and must trust the reports of my subordinates. At my age, so close to the Beautiful West, I am less and less involved with worldly problems and more concerned with attempting to perceive the words of the gods.'

'Who checks the temple's employees?'

'At least twenty scribes and priests.'

'I wish to see a list of them.'

'Very well. But please be tactful, because your actions will displease them.'

'A strict order from you would make my task easier.'

'Since I disapprove of your task, I will not give it. Advise your king to re-establish the financial and legal autonomy of the temples. By forcing them to submit to ordinary law and imposing a disastrous egalitarianism, he will arouse the wrath of the gods. Now I must rest. I wish you a good journey back to Sais, Judge Gem.'

Faced with the authority of this obstinate, widely revered old man, the judge felt powerless. Demanding the necessary documents from the priests would probably lead nowhere. The absence of the people responsible, poor filing, the inexplicable disappearance of certain papyri: a hundred wily ruses would be used to prevent his investigation from making progress. Ahmose had broken the backs of the temples only in appearance, and their submission was nothing but artifice. Now compelled to pay heavy taxes, they fabricated their declarations and obstructed the state's investigations.

However, it was for Udja and Pefy to resolve this difficult problem. What Judge Gem had to do was arrest the killer and his accomplices. Judging by the High Priest's embarrassed declarations, one thing was certain: they were indeed hiding in Khmun, where Nitis and Bebon had strong support.

Gem was certain of something else, too: the temple was only a stage on their journey, not their final destination, which was Thebes. Fearing indiscretion and denunciation, the fugitives were unlikely to stay here long. So what would be their best means of moving on? Probably one of the temple's boats.

Sending soldiers and guards to the quay to question the captains and crews would be stupid – the sailors would lie and then warn their clandestine passengers. The judge must obtain one crucial piece of information: the list of vessels ready to leave for the South. These would all be closely watched and he would await the arrival of Kel, Nitis, Bebon and the rest of the band.

They would be intercepted not in Khmun itself but a good distance away, so as to avoid the anger of the High Priest and exonerate him. If he benefited from the law's clemency, perhaps he would prove less hostile to the new laws.

Judge Gem summoned ten officers and set out his plan to them. It was decided to use only local informants and dock-workers capable of providing good information. If offered enough, they would make every effort to earn their reward. Every officer was aware of the importance of his mission. This time, the manhunt was on the point of succeeding.

37

It was the first time General Phanes had been to Elephantine, capital of the first province of Upper Egypt, and he found the whole area delightful. There were flower-covered islets in the middle of the Nile, the age-old temple of the ram-god Khnum, cliffs housing the houses of eternity belonging to important personages from the Old Kingdom, and a bustling town where merchants traded in items from Nubia, such as ivory and cat-skins.

The beauty of the place did not capture the soldier's attention for long. He was more interested in the imposing fortress that safeguarded the region's security and prevented access to Egypt by the fearsome black tribes, which were forever ready to rebel, tempted by the wealth of the land of the pharaohs. However, for many years the disturbances had been only minor, and at present there were no alarming signs to arouse the authorities' anxiety.

Two sentries were dozing at their posts at the entrance to the fortress.

With the side of his hand, Phanes dealt the first man a blow to the neck. The soldier instantly collapsed. His comrade woke up and pointed his spear at the general, but Phanes tore it from his grasp, snapped it in two and fractured his skull with a single punch.

'Defend yourselves, you band of cowards!' roared the Greek.

When about ten men appeared, Phanes brandished his heavy sword. The soldiers were rooted to the spot in fear, incapable of attacking their huge assailant.

'You miserable wretches! I ought to slit your throats.'

When he spat at them, they beat a retreat into the interior of the building. Followed by his personal bodyguard, made up of unquestioningly loyal men, the general strode into the first courtyard.

Eventually an officer appeared. He was unshaven and had clearly been enjoying a long nap. 'Who are you?' he enquired.

'Phanes of Halikarnassos.'

'The ... the ...?'

'The commander-in-chief of the Egyptian armies.'

'But we ... we weren't told that you were coming.'

'All the fortresses in Egypt are my domain, this one included, and I have no need to announce my arrival. At any moment, the entire garrison must be ready to repulse an attack. Given your state and that of your men, you would undoubtedly fail.'

'But, sir, nobody's threatening us.'

'Go and find the commander.'

Four at a time, the officer dashed up the stairs to the commander's quarters.

A paunchy man afflicted with a treble chin and shortness of breath, the commander descended slowly from his perch. 'What is this nonsense?' he said testily. 'I am the only authority around here.'

Phanes' slap knocked the protesting commander off his feet.

'I dismiss you from your post, you incompetent fool! You shame my army and you will end your career in some far-flung oasis, guarding prisoners. Get out of my sight immediately.'

His face scarlet, the fat man slunk away.

'Immediate roll-call of all soldiers!' thundered the general.

The order was carried out posthaste.

'Effective today, I am appointing a Greek to the command of this fortress. First he will teach you discipline, then you will learn the art of war. Exercise three times a day. The slow and the lazy will be sentenced to solitary confinement. We shall begin by cleaning this pigsty. By this evening, I want a clean fortress, with washed and shaven soldiers. Do it. Now.'

Phanes summoned the officer responsible for submitting reports on the state of the fortress. They had been reassuring, repetitive documents.

'Why did you not inform me about this disaster?'

'General, the situation appeared normal to me. Here, in Elephantine, the climate is not conducive to excessive work, the region is calm and—'

The general stove in the man's chest with a head-butt. 'Get rid of that,' he ordered two frightened Egyptian soldiers.

At the double, Phanes explored every room in the fortress. He spent some time in the former commander's office, where the military correspondence was kept. To all appearances, there was nothing here but banal administrative documentation. And then, suddenly, he found a wooden tablet bearing two different kinds of writing, one Egyptian and the other foreign.

The senior local interpreter was summoned.

'It's Nubian, sir,' he said.

'Translate it.'

Stammering, the interpreter read out a request from a tribal chief for privileges and reductions in taxation in return for his maintaining the peace. The former commander had agreed.

A second item revealed that food, bows, arrows and shields had been misappropriated by the officers checking trade.

'You are to keep absolutely silent about this,' demanded Phanes. 'One word, and you will be executed for high treason.'

The interpreter swore in the names of Pharaoh and all the gods.

So the reality was much more worrying than the general had thought. The fortress was dilapidated, the troops in a lamentable condition, there was corruption and collusion with the enemy ... In the event of an attack, Elephantine would be unable to offer any resistance.

'Bring me the scoundrel who claimed to command this garrison.'

But the Greek soldiers sought him in vain. He had fled.

'We shall interrogate all the officers,' decided Phanes. '*Really* interrogate them. I want to know the nature of the conspiracy and its extent.'

The sessions of torture began that same night. Although it was forbidden by the law of Maat, the general carried on regardless. State security required it.

The results were even worse than he had feared. The former commander of the fortress, priests from the Temple of Khnum and some chiefs of Nubian tribes wanted to create an autonomous region, hostile to King Ahmose's reforms. Kel's name was not mentioned, but he was undoubtedly involved in this all-encompassing conspiracy.

38

'Your boat will be ready to leave at nightfall,' the head ritual priest told Nitis. 'Normally river travel at night is forbidden. But because of the extreme heat I have obtained special dispensation.'

'Will the captain not betray us?'

'He is venal, but correct in his behaviour. Failure to honour a contract would destroy his reputation. You can trust him; he will get you to your destination.'

'What about the river-guards?'

'I know the times when they patrol. As for the watchman, he will be deeply asleep – the temple workshops contain effective potions. At the opportune moment, a sailor will come to fetch you from your official dwelling.'

'How can I thank you?'

'By enabling the truth to triumph, and by asking the Divine Worshipper to consolidate her power. Otherwise, Ahmose will lead the country to ruin. Your struggle goes far beyond justice for you, Kel and Bebon. The fate of the entire country depends upon its outcome.'

The young woman returned to the library, where Kel was reading yet more mathematical papyri. Alas, none had provided him with a key to deciphering the code.

'We're leaving Khmun tonight,' she whispered, and she told him what the priest had said.

'I'll go and tell Bebon.'

Although their numbers had been strengthened, the guards behaved with discretion – the High Priest had flatly refused to see his domain invaded by armed men. Given his authority, his directives were respected.

Wisely, Kel made a large detour and stopped several times before approaching the stables.

North Wind was lying down, and Bebon was dozing. The scribe stroked the donkey, which was calm and relaxed.

'Any news?' enquired Bebon anxiously.

'We're leaving for Thebes tonight. A sailor will take us to the boat.'

'I'll follow you at a good distance. If there's danger, North Wind will warn us. I've just been for a stroll along the quay.'

'Was there anything out of place?'

'Not that I saw. But there's still the night watchman.'

'He'll be neutralized.'

'It's almost too perfect.'

'Don't you trust the ritual priest?

Bebon nodded. 'He's neither a liar nor a thief, and he has strict morals . . . I can't see him setting a trap for us. Besides, we can't stay here long. The guards and the army will search the temple sooner or later.'

'Soon we'll be in Thebes and we'll talk to the Divine Worshipper.'

'You're a real optimist, aren't you?'

'What's this, my friend? Are you having doubts?'

Bebon looked awkward. 'That's not my style. And we haven't any choice. So let's take the plunge. One thing, though: no moralizing speeches about the risks you're making me run, or I might well turn violent.'

Kel sat down beside North Wind. 'How strange fate is. I love a sublime woman who grants me her love, I have a friend whom no danger can deter, and yet injustice and misfortune may strike at any moment.'

'Stop asking yourself pointless questions and look to the future. Asking yourself about yourself only leads to ... yourself – deadly boredom guaranteed. Real life begins tomorrow.'

North Wind's ears pricked up. Unhurriedly, Kel walked away.

An inquisitive donkey driver appeared at the stable door and asked Bebon, 'What did that priest want with you?'

'He asked me why I wasn't working. Because of this heat, we're entitled to extra rest periods, so I sent him off with a flea in his ear.'

'He must have been a guard – they're everywhere at the moment.'

'Why?'

'Haven't you heard about the murderous scribe who killed hundreds of unfortunate people? He's a bloodthirsty monster, quite capable of attacking an entire army.'

'Surely he's not hiding here in the temple?'

'No, but the guards are looking for him everywhere. I say, there are some jars to deliver to the port. Could you do it?'

Bebon stood up slowly. This was an excellent opportunity to examine the area once more. 'Well, just to help you.'

'I owe you a favour, friend.'

Bebon and North Wind collected the jars from the brewery and took them to the quay. One boat was leaving and another arriving. The dock-workers were preparing to unload its cargo as soldiers patrolled the area.

There were no additional guards at the storehouse, just the usual one, who noted down how many jars North Wind was carrying.

'It feels safe around here,' commented Bebon.

'We were even honoured with a visit from Judge Gem, head of all the judges in Egypt, accompanied by a whole swarm of officers. Apparently he was looking for assassins.'

'Did he find them?'

'No, he left empty-handed. Rumour has it that the High

Priest wouldn't give him permission to disturb the peace of
the temple – the High Priest may be old, but he isn't afraid
of anyone! So, back to routine. The patrols try to spot petty
crooks trying to steal goods. Anyone who's caught gets a good
beating and loses the taste for doing it again. How hot it is . . .
Would you care for a swig of beer?'

'Indeed I would.'

His thirst slaked, Bebon walked off very slowly, carefully
scanning his surroundings. He saw nothing out of the
ordinary.

39

Night had long since fallen when the sailor knocked at the door of the house where Nitis and Kel were staying. The scribe leapt to open it.

'Follow me,' said the sailor quietly.

Kel and Nitis exchanged looks. What if this was an ambush?

The young woman stepped outside first. Kel followed, carrying the bag containing the bow and arrows of Neith that Sobek's crocodile had given Nitis.

The domain of Thoth seemed to be asleep; the heat was still oppressive. The new moon provided only a feeble glimmer of light, but their guide, a stocky man with a low forehead and powerful limbs, hurried them along. Not hesitating for a moment over which way to go, he set off towards the port.

From one moment to the next, Kel expected to see a horde of guards or soldiers bearing down on them, delighted to have captured their prey so easily. Bebon and North Wind would have no time to do anything, and would be overwhelmed by force of numbers. Would the attackers at least spare Nitis? He would shield her with his body and give his life to defend her, but how could she escape a mob hell-bent on killing?

At last they reached the quay.

This was the most dangerous place; the guards were bound to be waiting there.

The sailor halted. Kel put his arm round Nitis. Long,

never-ending seconds elapsed. Then, with a wave of his hand, their guide directed them towards a large boat with twin cabins.

The quay still seemed deserted.

At the foot of the gangplank, Kel turned round. 'We'll wait for Bebon and North Wind,' he said.

'You can't,' replied the sailor. 'The captain wants to leave Khmun immediately.'

'Tell him to go, then.'

'As you wish. I've done my job.' He climbed the gangplank.

The rowers were in place, ready to set to work.

'Come aboard!' called the captain angrily.

'There will be four of us,' said Kel.

'Too bad for you. I'm going to give the order to leave.'

'There will be four of us,' repeated Kel.

Peering into the darkness, Nitis hoped to see their two friends arrive – the forces of order might intervene brutally at any moment.

This delay translated into a horrible reality: the donkey and the actor had been arrested.

Suddenly, she heard a strange moaning sound.

And then Bebon's irritated voice: 'Get a move on, for pity's sake! We're almost there.'

He and North Wind appeared on the quay, but it was obvious that North Wind didn't want to go aboard.

Nitis stroked his head. 'We must hurry.'

The donkey opened large, sad eyes. Despite his reluctance, he consented to follow her on to the boat. The gangplank was pulled up, and the oars plunged into the water. The manoeuvre was executed perfectly, and the heavy boat moved quickly away from the quay.

'Go in here,' the captain ordered his clandestine passengers, opening the door of one of the cabins. 'The donkey will be tethered to the mast. Now, go to sleep. I'll wake you at dawn.' The door closed behind him.

'I don't like this,' said Bebon. 'It feels like a prison.'

'It's carrying us to freedom,' Kel reminded him. 'Did you spot anyone following you?'

'No, nobody. Let's rest in turns. I'm not sleepy.'

'North Wind's attitude worries me,' said Nitis. 'Why was he so unwilling to come aboard?'

'He likes his nights to be long and peaceful,' explained Bebon. 'He doesn't care for this nocturnal trip.'

'If the captain had sold us to the guards,' said Kel, 'they wouldn't have let us embark.'

Bebon lay down on the floor. 'Well, let's enjoy sweet dreams. Let's imagine that we're in Thebes, in a sumptuous palace, with the Divine Worshipper listening eagerly to us and assuring us of her unconditional support. What a wonderful future!'

Nitis smiled. If such were the will of the gods, it would come to pass.

The door flew open.

Greek soldiers pinned Kel and Bebon to the floor, threatening to slit their throats.

An elegant, softly spoken man took Nitis gently by the hand and said, 'Nitis, I have come to free you.'

'Menk! What are you doing here?'

He led her out on to the deck. 'I am on a special mission, on Henat's orders. I was instructed to find you and prise you free from the claws of the monstrous scribe Kel.'

'You're mistaken. He is neither a criminal nor a monster.'

'Dear, credulous Nitis, he has deceived you. The proof of his guilt is irrefutable.'

'The evidence was fabricated. In reality, Kel is the victim of a plot devised at the highest levels of the government.'

'Dearest Nitis, don't believe that tale.'

'It's the truth, and we shall prove it.'

'The Divine Worshipper would never have received you. Despite her hostility to Ahmose's policies she obeys the law,

and you are fugitives and criminals. Come, let us leave here.'
He turned to the soldiers' commander. 'Ensure that the
prisoners are watched at all times.'

Reluctantly, Nitis agreed to go with him.

'I can have all accusations against you dropped, Nitis.
Of course you aren't this vicious killer's accomplice, you're
his hostage. My testimony will be decisive, Judge Gem will
exonerate you, and we shall be married.'

'I do not wish to marry you, Menk. I love Kel.'

'A fleeting illusion, dear, sweet Nitis, a mere aberration, due
to the circumstances. We shall experience perfect happiness
together, you and I, and you'll forget these painful events.'

'I shall never leave Kel, and I shall fight with all my strength
to prove his innocence.'

'That fight is futile, for it is lost before it has even begun.
I forgive you your mistakes and promise that I shall make
you one of Sais's most celebrated ladies. Given what I have
achieved, the king will grant me a ministerial post and you
will be appointed High Priestess of Neith.'

'I am sorry to disappoint you, Menk. But those fine plans
will not come true.'

'This is your only chance of escaping disaster, Nitis.'

'I am not afraid of death. Only the truth matters.'

'I shall defend you against yourself and prevent you from
speaking. Little by little, you will recover your reason.'

'But Kel will speak.'

Menk's voice hardened. 'He certainly will not, my future
wife. For I am going to kill him.'

40

Nitis shuddered. Once so elegant and worldly, so full of empty compliments, Menk had suddenly turned into a fierce animal.

'Spare Kel, I beg you!' she pleaded.

'Impossible, my dear. That dog must die. That is the price of my triumph and our happiness.'

'Then kill me, too!'

Menk looked astounded. 'But I don't wish you any harm, Nitis. On the contrary, I'm going to free you from his spell.'

She fixed her eyes on him. 'You are going to commit murder.'

'I am on an official mission, and the authorities will congratulate me on dealing with the killer who has evaded them for so long. Finding you took a great deal of thought and good luck. Since the High Priest of Khmun was hiding you, I knew he would find you the means to reach Thebes. When I learnt that a boat had been granted special dispensation to travel by night, I knew you'd be on board. The captain didn't really betray you; he bowed before the higher interest of the state.'

'Why have you become so cynical?'

'The end justifies the means.'

'How can I convince you that you're wrong? Kel has

committed no crime. Become yourself again, Menk. Help us to defeat injustice.'

'I don't care about justice and truth. Kel will die and you will belong to me.'

'Has your heart really grown so hard?'

'My men will keep guard over you all. Don't try anything, or they'll bind and gag you.'

Turning away from her, Menk told a couple of soldiers, 'Fetch the other two prisoners.'

When they appeared, Menk looked Kel up and down. 'A sorry end for such a famous criminal. You are going to die like a dog, and no one will miss you.'

Kel was surprisingly calm. 'I assume it is pointless to tell you the true facts?'

'Absolutely pointless. Sentence has been passed, and I am carrying it out.'

'Why are you so intent on killing us?' Bebon protested. 'We haven't done anything wrong.'

Menk's eyes blazed with hatred. 'This damned scribe tried to steal away the woman destined to be mine. Nothing else matters.' He brandished a knife. 'I shall cut your throat myself, and your corpse will feed the fishes.'

Two of the soldiers gripped Kel firmly, two others held Bebon, and a fifth restrained Nitis.

The knife-blade touched the scribe's neck.

'Stop, Menk!' Nitis cried. 'Don't become the worst kind of murderer!'

'Deliverance, Nitis, deliverance – and the prospect of a long, happy life as soon as this miserable scribe is dead.'

Kel's eyes met Nitis's one last time.

'Ship to starboard!' shouted the captain. 'We're under attack!'

The soldier holding Nitis threw her against the rail, seized a bow and fired. His arrow hit the man standing in the bows of the attacking ship.

172

Unknown to him, she was commanded by Judge Gem, who had decided upon the attack. When their comrade was killed, his elite archers responded in kind. Despite the poor light, they proved deadly accurate.

Menk, a Greek soldier, the captain and two sailors were hit. An arrow grazed Bebon's shoulder, leaving a bloody furrow.

Under the impression that he was attacking the entire band of conspirators, the judge gave the order for a full assault. This time he would capture Kel and his accomplices dead or alive. In view of their initial reaction, they would not surrender without a hard fight.

North Wind snapped the rope tying him to the mast and butted one of the Greeks who was trying to strangle Bebon. The actor managed to pull himself free, and two arrows plunged into his attacker's back.

Nitis ran to the cabin and took the bow of Neith out of its bag. As she drew it, a trail of fire lit up the darkness. The soldiers let go of Kel and Bebon, who found themselves abruptly free – but for how long? A rain of arrows was falling on the deck, finding more victims, and the war-boat was bearing down on them. If they escaped death, they would fall into the hands of Judge Gem.

'We must dive into the river,' cried Nitis. 'It's our only chance.'

She suited action to words, and North Wind followed her.

'The river's full of crocodiles!' protested Bebon.

Kel gave his friend a push. This was no time to think.

'They're escaping!' yelled the lookout on the war-boat.

A dozen soldiers hurled themselves into the water, which was indeed infested with crocodiles. Jolted out of their torpor, several enormous crocodiles rushed towards this large and un-expected quantity of food. Their furious somersaults whipped up the waters of the Nile while the soldiers took control of the trading boat, on which all resistance had ceased.

By the light of torches, Judge Gem strode along the deck. One of the corpses astonished him: it was that of Menk, the organizer of festivals in Sais! So this elegant courtier had belonged to Kel's armed band, which had also included several soldiers and a boat captain.

A good number of criminals had been eliminated! However, the main culprit, Kel the scribe, was still missing, together with his closest accomplices, Nitis the priestess and Bebon the actor.

Of the swimmers who had sped off in pursuit of them, only three returned to the boat alive.

'The fugitives can't have escaped the crocodiles,' said an officer.

The judge said nothing. He waited impatiently for morning, when he could inspect the Nile and its banks.

When day broke, his men searched for hours but they found nothing.

'The great fish have left nothing of the criminals for us to find,' confirmed the officer. 'When they're really hungry, they are incredibly voracious. The three criminals would have been their first victims.'

Judge Gem was still unconvinced. 'A guard-boat is to sail slowly south, and try to identify any human remains. We shall re-examine the riverbanks, and question the fishermen and peasants in the area. And we shall search the houses in all the nearby villages.'

'A waste of time,' said the officer. 'The fugitives cannot possibly have survived.'

'I am the one who is conducting this investigation,' the judge reminded him coldly.

Gem thought about the strange flash of lightning that had appeared just as the vessel was being boarded. There had been no signs of a storm, so it must have been a sign from the gods. How was he to interpret it? Doubtless as their righteous anger, striking the assassin and ending his deplorable life.

One final check would put an end to this sinister affair, and the kingdom could once again breathe freely.

41

General Phanes worked night and day, and achieved excellent results in record time. Afraid of his brutality, the Elephantine garrison had been transformed overnight. They had developed a sense of discipline, were impeccably dressed, their weapons were properly maintained and their quarters spotlessly clean, and they followed orders to the letter. And the arrival of Greek instructors would put the finishing touches to the transformation of second-rate, lazy soldiers into fierce fighters capable of repelling an attack by Nubian tribes and denying them access to Egyptian territory.

The charm of the languid Southern town and the beauty of the landscape now made no impression on the general. He saw only the effectiveness of the troops and their ability to cut the enemy to pieces. And they were still a long way from that.

'Immediate roll-call!' he shouted.

The soldiers promptly came running from all directions and formed ranks in the centre of the great courtyard.

Phanes waited for complete silence. Some of the soldiers went as far as holding their breath.

'Soldiers,' he roared, 'I am displeased with you. The officer training you in hand-to-hand combat tells me that several of you cowards have only been pretending to fight. This behaviour is unacceptable. Fatalities are a part of training, and nobody must interfere with the rules.' He pointed at a thirty-year-old with a furrowed brow. 'You, step forward.'

The man obeyed.

'Bare-knuckle fight.'

'General . . .'

'I am your opponent. Destroy me – or I'll destroy you.'

Phanes punched him in his unprotected belly. Angry at being caught off guard, the soldier charged forward, head first. Phanes dodged aside and, with the edge of his hand, broke the soldier's neck.

'Clumsy and incompetent,' he declared, spitting on the body. 'Tomorrow, if your instructors' reports are bad, there will be another duel. Dismissed.'

The general had brought in ten Greek soldiers from the North. They would train the Egyptians and give them a hard time.

He still had to carry out a profound reform of trade control at Elephantine, which was lax and corrupt. When examining the reports and accounts, he had found many false declarations, deliberate omissions and the doctoring of documents, some of it crude and amateurish.

A senior state official would have proceeded with the greatest caution, taken an infinite number of precautions and consulted his superiors, in order to avoid any procedural errors. But the general had not been trained to behave that way.

Leading a detachment of thirty footsoldiers, he raided the trade-control offices, which housed around twenty scribes.

'You are all under arrest!' thundered Phanes. 'Anyone who tries to resist will be killed.'

The head scribe stood up very slowly, absolutely stunned. 'I don't understand. I—'

'Theft of public property and damage to national security. The courts will sentence you to many years of forced labour.'

'You are mistaken! You—'

Phanes seized him by the throat. 'Tell me the whole truth – now. Or I'll break your neck.'

The scribe talked non-stop and provided all the details the general needed in order to draw up a full report for King Ahmose. That same day a trade-control department was created, composed of soldiers under the command of a civilian overseer, a specialist in imports from Nubia. He would give a daily account of his activities to the governor of the fortress.

Phanes explored the First Cataract, made up of rocks which were partially covered during the Nile's annual flood, and set off along the canal used by war-boats and trading-vessels.

The lack of watch-posts worried him, so he ordered the construction of forts overlooking the site, to strengthen the natural frontier and seal it completely. Within a short time, the danger of a Nubian attack would be past.

He must also purge the senior administrators in Elephantine, who were guilty of having allowed the situation to degenerate. A meeting was arranged at the mayor's house in the town, the last stage in this reconquest in the name of King Ahmose.

As was his custom, the general intended to strike hard. The mayor, who was suspected of secretly supporting the Divine Worshipper, might well be preparing to intervene in favour of Kel and his rebels. Once that hypocrite had been eliminated, Elephantine would become a secure town, loyal to its king.

A Greek soldier provided his leader with proof of the mayor's corruption. The man was also accused of stealing weapons intended for the fortress.

Furious, Phanes strode towards the large white, two-storey building that housed the mayor's offices.

A cry of pain rang out behind him. Someone had stabbed a member of his personal bodyguard, from which he was suddenly cut off by a band of ten attackers, led by the former commander of the fortress.

Maddened with rage, the general seized two of the spears pointed towards him, tore them from the hands of his adversaries and turned them against them, piercing right through their chests. Dumbstruck, the others drew back. With his heavy, double-edged sword, Phanes proceeded to carry out a massacre, cutting off heads and arms.

His bodyguard finished off the work.

The last survivor was the former commander. He was mortally wounded and in his death throes.

'Who ordered you to kill me?' Phanes demanded.

'The . . . mayor . . .' And he died.

'Throw that rubbish out with the rest,' the general ordered his men.

The mayor's offices had emptied of their officials, who had fled in terror. Their employer had gone to ground in his luxurious private office, hoping that the general had been killed.

When he appeared, alive and well, the mayor poured out a flood of prayers and entreaties.

'High treason deserves death,' decreed the general. 'However, you still have one chance left to save your life.'

'I'll do whatever you say!'

'I want the truth. You and the former commander of the fortress were running an illegal weapons trade and were party to a conspiracy, weren't you?'

'It was mostly him! I just made his task easier.'

'Your goal was to assassinate the pharaoh.'

'Oh no! We just wanted to get rich and—'

Phanes brandished his sword. 'I repeat: your goal was to assassinate the pharaoh.'

'Yes, but I was opposed to it and—'

'And your leader was Kel the scribe.'

The mayor hesitated for a brief moment. 'Indeed, Kel the scribe! He devised everything and organized it all. He terrorized us and threatened us with death if we disobeyed him.'

'Write that out for me clearly, then sign it and affix your seal to it.'

His hand trembling, the mayor did so.

Phanes checked what he had written. 'Excellent. Now I can complete the cleansing of this town.'

With a single sweep of his sword, the general slit the mayor's throat. The official report would show that the mayor had been guilty of attacking the general.

Phanes rolled up the papyrus, which he would send to Judge Gem, who would thus have a new piece of firm evidence at his disposal. Meanwhile Phanes, having cleansed Elephantine and rendered the southern border impregnable, could return to Sais to take his troops in hand. Despite his many good qualities, Udja was still an Egyptian and a civilian. Only a Greek soldier, hardened by the demands of war, could command an army capable of striking down any aggressor, in particular the Persians.

42

North Wind's patience was inexhaustible. He licked and licked Kel's forehead as he lay in the middle of the reeds. Several times the donkey had to kick away water-snakes which grew a little too curious. Ibis and egrets, on the other hand, presented no danger.

At last, the scribe's eyes opened.

The sight of that friendly muzzle was a great comfort to him. 'North Wind! So you're alive, too!' He checked himself: two arms, two legs, the ability to stand up, no pain ... he seemed to be intact, like the donkey.

'It's impossible,' muttered Kel. 'I saw those enormous mouths gape open, ready to crush us ... Nitis! Bebon! Where are you hiding?'

No one answered his call, so he began to force his way through the reeds, which stood far higher than his head. If he could not find Nitis and Bebon, having escaped from an appalling death would be an unbearable punishment. What was the good of surviving if he had lost the woman he loved, along with his faithful friend?

As it emerged from the thick clump of reeds, the bank sloped sharply upwards towards an earthen road. Pricking up his ears, North Wind invited Kel to follow him and trotted along to a copse of young tamarisk trees, a little way away from the road.

'Just be patient!' cried an easily recognizable voice. 'I'll do it.'

'Bebon!' Kel exclaimed.

Nitis emerged from the copse.

'My love, you're alive! They embraced passionately.

To Bebon their kiss seemed to go on for ever. 'I say,' he grumbled, 'I'm hungry and I'd really love some grilled perch. Come and help me.'

They collected some twigs and arranged them in a small pile. After hollowing out a piece of soft wood to make a base, Bebon made an indentation into which he inserted a very hard piece of acacia wood, splayed out at its base. He twirled it back and forth repeatedly, and eventually a flame sprang to life.

'Success! Dinner will be hot and tasty.'

'How did we manage to escape from the crocodiles?' Kel wondered.

'They are the sons of Neith,' replied Nitis. 'I swam in front, holding the goddess's bow. It lit up the water, and the great fish recognized the light that enveloped all four of us. We were neither enemies nor prey. They merely brushed past us and attacked our pursuers.'

'I've told hundreds of unlikely tales in my time,' admitted Bebon, 'but that one beats them all.'

'Yet you're perfectly all right, apart from that dressing on your left shoulder.'

'At last, you condescend to take an interest in me. I was hit by an arrow.'

'It's only a flesh wound, isn't it?'

'"Only a flesh wound"? That's easy for you to say. You haven't got any injuries.'

'I have found the herbs we need,' said Nitis with a smile. 'The wound won't become infected, and I think Bebon's well enough to continue the journey.'

'As long as I'm properly fed. Just taste this, it's wonderful.

All in all, what could be more enjoyable than an escapade in the countryside? You have to catch your food and prepare it yourself, using nature's resources. Inns are just too easy. Living in towns leads to softness and decadence. A return to life in the wild, that's the future.'

'But we must go to Thebes,' pointed out Kel. 'Judge Gem was aboard that war-boat – I saw him standing near the prow. He'll never give up trying to capture us.'

'Perhaps he believes we're dead,' ventured Bebon. 'Escaping from those crocodiles did seem impossible.'

'But without one shred of flesh from a corpse he won't be sure, and he'll continue his investigation.'

'I agree with Kel,' said Nitis. 'The judge knows the power of the gods and takes account of it. He is aware that Wahibra taught me magical incantations and how to use them to fight adversity.'

'Have you any idea where we are, Bebon?' asked Kel.

'The boat covered a good distance, and we swam for a long time. I shouldn't think we're far from Djawty.* As soon as we pass through the first village, I'll know for certain.'

'Do you have friends in the area?'

'The temple isn't as hospitable as the one in Khmun, but we'll get by. Enjoy your food.'

The grilled perch was delicious, but Kel had no appetite.

'After a miracle like that,' said Bebon, 'you ought to be ravenous.'

'Menk was there, and he wanted to kill me . . .'

'And marry me,' said Nitis. 'The truth didn't matter to him. In killing you, he would be carrying out a deed worthy of great rewards. He thought that, once he became a minister he would have me appointed High Priestess of the temple in Sais, and he and I would lead a life of luxury.'

---

* The ancient city of the jackal-god Wepwawet, the 'Opener of the Ways', linked to the symbolism of Anubis. Its modern name is Asyut.

'And you gave up that paradise for a scribe on the run, accused of murder?' enquired Bebon in astonishment. 'In your place, I would have taken some time to think it over.'

Kel chose not to hear that.

'Menk was like a madman,' added Nitis. 'It was impossible to reason with him.'

'It's too easy to say he was mad,' objected Bebon. 'Several Greek soldiers were serving under his command, and he had been given a specific mission: to kill us.'

'Who could have made him play such a grim role?' Kel wondered. 'Henat? Udja? Judge Gem? The king himself?'

'The coded papyrus probably contains the answer,' said Nitis. 'Menk was being used by someone, and he almost succeeded.'

Bebon's eyes lighted on the bow of Neith, though he dared not touch it.

'We seemed certain to die,' he recalled, 'and then I saw a line of fire cross the sky. The soldiers were blinded by the light and let us go.'

'The bow itself fired the goddess's two arrows,' revealed Nitis. 'Now we must find them again, or we'll be vulnerable.'

'I still have the obsidian amulet,' said Kel. 'It will protect us against the evil eye. And don't forget the Answerer.'

'What use can that statuette be? A flying boat would be of more use to us.'

'Perhaps somewhere near here there's a Temple of Neith where they keep arrows originating from the flame of the lion-goddess Sekhmet,' suggested Nitis. 'We must ask the priests in Djawty and hope they give us a positive answer.'

'Djawty?' said Bebon. 'Will we really be able to reach it?'

'Surely you of all people aren't being pessimistic?' exclaimed Kel. 'Isn't the gods' protection enough for you?'

'Eat your fish,' retorted the actor, 'and then we'll rest before we set off again. Staying here too long would be dangerous, especially if that stubborn judge keeps chasing us.'

North Wind was dozing, his belly filled with good grass and succulent reeds.

'Yes, the gods,' conceded Bebon. 'That's quite something. When I wore their masks, I had no idea of their power. Friendly crocodiles, arrows of fire, freedom ... Life seems more and more mysterious.'

43

There were three of them: repulsive-looking, dirty and wicked. Driven from their village by the council of elders, they lived by crime and sought out travellers to rob. Now they had seen signs of some foolish people who were clearly unaware of the dangers of this place: smoke rising up from the tamarisk copse near the river. Nobody ever ventured there.

'Guards, do you think?' Twisted-Mouth wondered anxiously.

'I doubt it,' replied Broken-Nose. 'We'd have seen them arrive by boat. Besides, these people are hiding.'

'If they're hiding,' said Pockmarked, 'they're not honest folk. And personally I hate dishonest people.'

'On the other hand, stealing from thieves isn't a crime,' said Twisted-Mouth, 'especially if they're not armed. Because armed thieves are too much of a risk.'

After mature reflection, Broken-Nose nodded. 'Go and take a look, and come back and tell us.'

'Why don't you go?'

A long deliberation ensued. As this was a failure, the three vile characters resorted to drawing straws. Twisted-Mouth was the disappointed loser. If anything happened, his companions had no intention of rushing to his aid.

'It would be better not to bother,' he said.

'Fate chose you,' Pockmarked said firmly. 'The travellers

must be carrying enough to pay for what they buy. We'll kill them, rob them and then leave.'

The simplicity of the plan, plus his own greed, won over Twisted-Mouth, who eventually agreed to act as scout.

When he returned, he was drooling with excitement. 'There are three of them and they're all fast asleep.'

'Three strong men?' asked Broken-Nose.

Twisted-Mouth salivated even more. 'Two men, not very strong-looking – and a woman! She's young and really beautiful, I can tell you. We won't kill her right away. And I saw her first, so I'm going to have her first.'

Pockmarked looked dubious. 'Rape carries the death penalty.'

'So does murder,' retorted Twisted-Mouth. 'And as we're going to kill her afterwards, she won't tell on us.'

This logic dispelled all fears.

'They've got a donkey,' added the scout. 'We'll keep it to carry the booty.'

'It might raise the alarm,' warned Broken-Nose.

'Not if we sneak up by way of the bank, and keep downwind of it.'

'Is it tied up?'

'No, it's lying down next to one of the men.'

'Well, hobble it with this rope. I'll threaten to strangle the girl, and Pockmarked will threaten to strangle one of the men.'

'What about the other one?'

'You can deal with him after you've hobbled the donkey.'

The thought of the woman dispelled Twisted-Mouth's worries. Never had the three companions enjoyed such good fortune.

Suddenly overcome by feverish enthusiasm, they immediately put their plan into action.

North Wind got to his feet just before the attack. Braying loudly to sound the alarm, he lashed out so fiercely that his front hooves crushed in Twisted-Mouth's forehead. But Broken-Nose already had his dirty hands around Nitis's neck, and Pockmarked was preparing to cut Bebon's throat with his flint knife.

'Stop!' Kel shouted. 'Or I won't tell you where we hid our precious stones.'

The two thieves stopped dead. Treasure *and* a woman!

'Get on with it,' demanded Broken-Nose. 'We're in a hurry. Let's take the gems and go.'

Pockmarked chuckled, his eyes fixed on Nitis. He was going to have fun tonight.

North Wind scratched the ground with his rear hoof. He didn't dare do anything: if he charged forward, he would spark off a massacre.

Kel went towards the burning coals. 'Let go of the woman and I'll give you the gems,' he said to Broken-Nose.

'Forget it.'

'If you kill us, you won't have the treasure.'

The choice was too much for the thief's reasoning abilities. An idea came to him. He said, 'Throw me the rope poor old Twisted-Mouth is still holding. Gently.'

Kel did so, avoiding any sudden movements.

Broken-Nose forced Nitis down on to the ground and bound her wrists and ankles. This gorgeous woman wouldn't lose any of her appeal by waiting.

Brandishing his flint knife, he walked towards Kel. 'The precious stones – now!'

Scooping up burning coals in both hands, Kel flung them in Broken-Nose's face. With a howl of pain, he dropped his weapon and staggered backwards. North Wind bounded forward and snapped his spine with one kick.

Dumbfounded, Pockmarked forgot Bebon and tried to hit Kel. Bebon tripped him up and kicked him until he lost consciousness.

Kel was already freeing Nitis.

'Your hands are burnt,' she said. 'I must treat them quickly to prevent infection.'

'You're alive and unharmed; that's what matters.'

'Phew! We had a lucky escape there,' said Bebon. 'We must leave here immediately.'

'I know how to treat Kel's wound,' said Nitis, 'but I need the right herbs. We'll find them at the temple in Djawty.'

'Given the urgency of the situation, we really need a boat. But that's an enormous risk. And imagine us turning up at the workshop with the murderer being hunted by Judge Gem, whose men may well be searching Djawty from top to bottom right now!'

'I can cool the burning with the aid of a few herbs and an invocation to fiery Sekhmet,' said Nitis. 'But that won't be enough.'

Bebon faced the facts: a scribe could not afford to lose his hands. But in trying to save them, he, Nitis and Bebon would be heading for their downfall.

The young woman was distraught. 'There must be a solution, mustn't there?'

'I've got an idea, but it's completely mad.'

'We'll do it,' decided Kel.

44

A special messenger delivered General Phanes' long and detailed report to Judge Gem. As he read it, the judge realized the sheer extent of the conspiracy. Kel really was no ordinary murderer. Determined to seize power, he had had strong support in Upper Egypt, notably from the mayor of Elephantine and the fortress commander. At long last his plan had been revealed: to bring rebels together; to seize King Ahmose's helmet; to kill his colleagues at the Interpreters' Secretariat in order to render Egypt deaf and blind; to launch a rebellion from the South, probably with the aid of Nubian tribes; to conquer the North and then, after a bloody civil war, to become pharaoh.

It was true madness, which could have set the Two Lands aflame! The danger had not completely disappeared. Given the temples' attitude, Kel and his allies were still dangerous. While he lived, the scribe would never abandon his devastating plans.

Soon Ahmose would be informed of the results of the investigation and of the general effective action. By bringing Elephantine and the country's southern border back under control, Phanes had ruined the conspirators' strategy.

They now had only one last hope: the Divine Worshipper. Although she had no army, the old priestess was capable of raising one. Many temples would answer her call, and peasants would turn themselves into soldiers. True, the Greek mercenaries would make easy meat of them; but how much slaughter there would be, and how much suffering!

Kel, assuming he had survived the crocodiles' attack, still had to reach Thebes, meet the Divine Worshipper and convince her. But Henat would get there before him and give good advice to the illustrious priestess.

'I have brought you the guards' latest reports, sir,' said the judge's secretary, handing him wooden tablets covered with the section chiefs' handwriting.

Gem read them attentively. No trace of the bodies of Kel, Nitis or Bebon, and the general opinion was that the crocodiles had eaten them.

The judge piled up the tablets, sank into his armchair and gazed at the Nile.

It was a very, very reassuring theory. But the guards had forgotten one vital detail: Nitis was the pupil of Wahibra, who had been one of the most remarkable sages in Egypt, worthy of the 'great seers' of the age of the pyramids. Despite her youth, Nitis had received exceptional teaching. She knew the incantation for enchanting crocodiles, the sons of Neith, so she had thrown herself into the water with Kel and Bebon, certain that they would escape both the great fish and their pursuers.

All three were alive. And they were continuing their journey towards Thebes.

Their next stop might well be the temple at Djawty. Rumour had it that its High Priest was an alarming man. Authoritarian and pernickety, he applied rules to the letter and would tolerate neither idleness nor indiscipline. His temple housed important writings relating to the geography of the world beyond, for the jackal-god Wepwawet, the Opener of the Ways, guided the souls of the righteous to paradise.

Would the old man be hostile or friendly to the fugitives if they asked his help? Since a guards' raid inside the temple was impossible, the judge would apply his new tactics, which had just brought such good results: keeping watch on the port, the boats and the area around the sacred domain.

The captain of one of the numerous river-guards boats was the first to spot a man waving frantically. He was standing on the bank, to starboard, and seemed very agitated.

'Stop rowing!' the captain ordered his crew.

They obeyed immediately, and archers took up position.

'What do you want?' called the captain.

'To speak to you.'

'About what?'

'A special mission. Apart from you, no one must hear what I say.'

Interested, the captain allowed the man to come aboard. He drew his sword from its scabbard and took the man to his cabin, watched by the archers.

'Explain yourself, and no sudden movements.'

'I am under orders from Henat, director of the royal palace and head of Egypt's spy network,' said Bebon. 'I belong to a raiding-party of five mercenaries, and we are in pursuit of a murderer, Kel the scribe. We fell into an ambush. Three of us are dead and one, our officer, is badly wounded. If he isn't treated soon, he'll die.'

'Do you have any documents proving what you say?'

Bebon smiled sarcastically. 'That's not usual on this type of mission.' The actor bent his head. 'Confidentially,' he whispered, 'I'll tell you that even Judge Gem doesn't know about this. We were hoping to be the first to spot the criminal but we made a serious mistake.'

'Where is the wounded man?'

'In the middle of that clump of reeds.'

'I must check.'

'As you wish, captain. But by the time a message has been sent to Sais and an answer has come back, my officer will be long dead. I'll make my report and you can explain everything to Henat. The temple at Djawty is very near here. Its doctors can save the wounded man, and you will earn yourself promotion. My officer is an elite fighter, well liked by Henat.'

On reflection, the captain was not risking anything. Transporting a seriously injured man and keeping one soldier prisoner would be no problem. As soon as they arrived in Djawty, he would request confirmation and further orders.'

'Go and fetch your officer.'

'I need a stretcher and three men.'

Kel was so heavily bandaged with leaves and reeds that he looked like a mummy. His eyes were scarcely visible.

'Be careful,' warned Bebon. 'The slightest jolt could kill him.'

Immobile, apparently unconscious, the scribe played his role to perfection. He was thinking about Nitis and North Wind. It was impossible to include them in this insane attempt to reach Djawty by using a river-guard boat, so, pretending to be a simple peasant woman delivering vegetables to the temple, she would take one of the boats linking the villages to the city. Judge Gem was searching for three people, not a woman on her own.

Concerned at the condition of the wounded man, the captain ordered his crew to make for Djawty as fast as possible.

45

The wall of the temple in Djawty marked the frontier between the outside world and the sacred domain of the jackal-god Wepwawet. At the main gate, several guards were checking the pure priests and the craftsmen authorized to work in the temple workshops.

'I'd like to go with my officer,' Bebon told the guards captain.

'That's out of the question. We shall hand him over to the doctors, who will know what to do with him. You're staying with us.'

'Am I your prisoner?'

'Let's not use such harsh words.'

'Then I'm staying with my officer.'

'You're coming back to the boat, and I shan't take my eyes off you.'

'Don't you trust me?'

'The rules require me to verify what you've said. It won't take that long. Have a rest and some good food, and you'll soon be off on another mission.'

To insist would have looked suspicious, so Bebon gave in and watched the stretcher carried past the guard-post.

This was a disaster. The first doctor to arrive would see the true state of the wounded man and would alert the forces of law. In an instant, Kel would lose his hands, his freedom and his life, and Bebon's life would be worth less than a pair of papyrus sandals.

The guards summoned four pure priests. They carried the litter to the temple hospital, where experienced doctors worked.

Kel wondered what to do. Should he try to run away, tell the truth, make up a story? His hands were becoming agonizingly painful, and he needed urgent treatment. No doctor would believe his story, and he would be flung into the clutches of Judge Gem.

The litter was set down inside a small, cool room, and the bearers withdrew. Kel was still wondering what to do when two people entered the room.

'An emergency,' said an irritated voice, 'and I'm swamped with work. Can you deal with it?'

'I hope so.'

'If you have any difficulty, tell me. Those wooden chests contain everything you need.'

'I shall do my best.'

That sweet, measured voice – Nitis's voice!

She took the leaf-bandages from his eyes, and he opened them.

'Nitis, how—'

'Nobody would refuse hospitality to a doctor from the prestigious school in Sais, who is on the way to the capital after a stay in Dendera. Now it is time to deal properly with your hands.'

She applied a salve composed of sea salt, bull's fat, wax, cooked leather, virgin papyrus, barley and the rhizomes of the edible chufa papyrus.

'You will heal quickly,' she promised him. 'Thanks to the incantation used to conjure the devouring flame, there will be no scars. The head doctor won't return before this evening, but we're leaving at once and I'll take all of salve we need. Where is Bebon?'

'He wasn't allowed to accompany me. I hope he's been able to escape from the guards. What about North Wind?'

'He's in the temple stables. As he carries my medical bags, he will be well treated.'

'It's a wretched story,' Bebon told the captain, as they were rowed towards the boat, along with ten archers. 'There we were, pursuing a criminal on the run, and suddenly we were confronted by a veritable army! That Kel is a fearsome warlord.'

'You're not exaggerating?'

'There are serious problems in store for the authorities. Me, I'd like to go back to Sais and not bother with the affair any more. A post in the archives would suit me fine. When you've seen death close to, all you can think about is living peacefully.'

'Have you undertaken many dangerous missions for Henat?'

'Nothing comparable to this one. Be on your guard, captain. Kel could attack anywhere.'

'Don't worry. Judge Gem has trebled the number of guard-boats. That bandit won't escape us.'

As they were climbing the gangplank, Bebon stopped dead. 'Did you see that?'

'See what?

'The hull . . . Look at the hull, just by the prow.'

'It looks normal to me.'

'Not to me. My father was a carpenter, and I know what I'm talking about in boatbuilding. Look again: the colour of the wood has darkened slightly.'

'And that worries you?'

'There's a risk of transshipment, and if that happens the boat will go down in seconds. I'm going to examine that hull.'

Without waiting for the captain's permission, Bebon dived in.

The captain had never heard of transshipment, but he was

no naval carpenter. The difference in colour was very slight. Only an expert eye could have spotted it.

Seconds passed, then minutes. The secret agent did not resurface. Had he had an accident? The captain ordered two sailors to dive in, too.

There was no trace of Bebon.

'That rogue tricked me!' exclaimed the captain. 'Seal off the port and bring him back to me. I'm going back to the temple.'

The captain could argue all he liked, but the guards respected the High Priest's instructions: no unknown guards were to be allowed inside the enclosure, despite the new law promulgated by Ahmose. Faced with the officer's insistence and the threat of force, the High Priest's assistant was sent for.

'I want to question a wounded man who was brought to you today – he is almost certainly a criminal.'

'Only the head doctor can give you permission to do that.'

He had to wait again, until a highly unpleasant individual arrived. The captain explained what had happened.

'I entrusted that man to a young female colleague from Sais, the best medical school in the land.'

'A woman,' murmured the officer.

'Indeed so, captain. Are you unaware that they make excellent doctors?'

The false secret agent, the false casualty, the priestess from Sais playing at being a doctor ... It was the trio of terrorists sought by every guard and soldier in the country!

'I demand to see this so-called patient immediately.'

'Given his condition, you will not learn anything. He is incapable of speech.'

'Take me to him.'

'The High Priest's instructions—'

'In view of the urgency of the situation, my archers will force their way through, and Judge Gem will uphold their behaviour.'

Since the captain did not look as if he was joking, the doctor yielded and took him to the small room where the young doctor was treating the wounded man.

The small, empty room.

46

Bebon was grateful for the long hours he had spent with Kel, swimming underwater until they were both exhausted. The two boys had become just like two fish, rarely needing to take a breath and able to cover long distances. Today that intensive training was saving his life.

Bebon emerged at the far end of the quay, took a deep breath and swam further away from the guard-boat. Once he was a good distance away, he scaled the bank.

A peal of laughter made him jump. A little boy was sitting on the bank, watching him.

'What's so funny, youngster?'

'You're all red!'

Bebon was covered in silt. Silt from the great South, churned up by the Nile. In other words, the arrival of the annual flood. For several days, because of the flood's power it would be impossible to travel by water, and the water itself, laden with this fertile mud, from which the Two Lands derived their prosperity, would not be drinkable.

This would make the travellers' task much more difficult, and the guards' much easier – all they had to do was keep watch on the land routes.

Had Nitis and Kel managed to get out of the temple? Despite the risks, Bebon walked towards the encircling wall. At the main guard-post, the sentries were deep in discussion.

The actor went up to one of them and said, 'I'd like to offer my leeks to whoever's in charge of buying vegetables.'

'You've picked the wrong day, my lad.'

'I've come a long way.'

'The temple's sealed off indefinitely.'

'Why? What's happening?'

'Some brigands have escaped, apparently. Don't stay here, go home.'

Excellent news! But when Kel and Nitis realized that the flood was coming, they would not know what to do. There was only one solution: to find a caravan passing through the desert and join it as traders. North Wind's presence would help them do so. But would this good idea occur to the priestess and the scribe?

Bebon headed for the centre of town. He had to be constantly on his guard, because if he was identified he'd instantly be arrested. Humiliated and furious, the captain must have sent a horde of men to track him down.

He easily gained the information he needed: the location where caravans rested between stages of their journey.

Standing rigidly to attention in front of Judge Gem, the river-guards captain was visibly losing his composure.

The judge said, 'A scandal at the temple, a woman doctor and a seriously wounded man who disappears and whom you apparently brought to Djawty ... I should like an explanation.

'It's simple ... and complicated.'

'Try to resolve this contradiction, captain.'

'It's simple and—'

'Complicated, you have just said so. Now, simplify it.

The captain took the plunge. 'I must provide you with some unwelcome information.'

'Do not hold anything back.'

'A special agent, acting on Henat's orders, asked me to take him to Djawty along with his senior officer, who had been seriously wounded when they were ambushed by Kel the scribe and his gang.'

'Henat . . . His name was definitely mentioned?'

'Yes, sir.'

'In reality, this man deceived you.'

The captain looked down. 'I'm afraid so.'

'And you did not check what he had said?'

'I sent a messenger to Sais, but the deceiver gave me the slip.'

'Deplorable,' grumbled Judge Gem.

'Deplorable,' agreed the captain. 'But I didn't think saving an officer's life was a fault.'

'In the current circumstances, your credulity certainly was a fault. In future, be more vigilant.'

'You . . . you're not dismissing me?'

'Yes, I am – back to your post. And don't make any more of these foolish mistakes.'

The captain's stupidity was no great matter. Kel, Nitis and Bebon were indeed alive and proving remarkably skilful.

A strange idea came into the judge's mind. Had the clever 'agent' – undoubtedly Bebon – made up the story, or was he really in Henat's service? An infiltrated spy, controlled by Henat, he might be remaining with Kel in order to discover the identities of all his accomplices and the extent of his network. That twist bore all the hallmarks of Henat, who was accustomed to scheming alone and reluctant to collaborate with the law.

Perhaps Gem could derive some advantage from the situation. In any event, he would not pass on any information to Henat; he would plough his own furrow.

Kel and North Wind hung back, while Nitis walked on to the quay. She was planning to identify the river-guards boats and try to find out if Bebon had been detained aboard one of them. Many tense-looking soldiers were coming and going.

She went up to a haughty-faced officer.

'I was supposed to deliver some vegetables, but I was told that a prisoner had just escaped and nobody could go into the buildings during the search.'

'Correct, young lady. Go home and don't move until further orders, or you'll be in trouble.'

Nitis walked meekly away and rejoined Kel. 'Bebon's escaped,' she told him. 'And I noticed a lot of insects jumping on the surface of the water, making a distinctive sound: they're dedicated to Neith, and they announce the imminent arrival of the annual flood.*

'So the river won't be navigable any more. But there are still the land routes.'

'The guards and the police are barring all access to Thebes,' Nitis replied. 'It's becoming impossible to take a normal route.'

Only North Wind did not seem downcast. Ears pricked up, he was anxious to leave this place.

'We should follow him,' advised Nitis.

The donkey walked round the outside of the city, taking paths which skirted the edges of the fields, then came back towards the eastern outlying districts. In a palm-grove, a hundred or so donkeys were gathered, along with numerous traders in coloured tunics.

'A caravan!' Kel exclaimed. 'That's almost the only way of evading the security checks. But is it going south?'

The trio approached one of the watchmen.

'We would like to see the man in charge,' said Kel.

He was a Syrian called Hassad, aged around forty with a small moustache.

'May we know where you are headed?' asked Kel.

'We're going to Coptos by way of the desert. From there, we'll make for the Red Sea.'

---

* A species of beetle, *Agrypnus notodanta*.

Coptos was north of Thebes, and not far from it.

'May we join you?'

Hassad seemed less than enthusiastic. 'My caravan is made up only of professional traders. They share the profits – and the expenses.'

Nitis showed him a magnificent lapis-lazuli. 'Will this be enough?'

The caravan-leader's eyes almost popped out of his head. 'It should. We're leaving as soon as we've had our midday meal. You and your donkey are to travel at the back, just in front of the overseer.'

'Very well.'

Kel and Nitis sat down at the edge of the encampment. They were brought flat-cakes filled with beans and salad.

'Will Bebon have time to join us?' said Kel worriedly.

'If he doesn't, he'll catch up with us on the way,' Nitis assured him.

For several hours, Bebon had been slipping from one hiding-place to another in order to escape the soldiers. Judge Gem had ordered a systematic search of Djawty and had not even spared the temple. At nightfall, the searches stopped and the actor was at last able to reach the oasis where the caravans halted. It was deserted.

An old man was leaning against a well, eating an onion.

'Did a caravan leave today?' asked Bebon.

'Yes. It was heading for Coptos.'

'Did you notice a young couple and a donkey?'

The old man gave an odd smile. 'What a beautiful girl! In her place, I'd have avoided that caravan. The leader, Hassad, is a twisted character. And he hates women.'

47

Impressive, very impressive. Even Sais, though it was an extremely beautiful city, could not compare with Thebes, the city sacred to Amun; its Egyptian name, Waset, meant 'City of the Power Sceptre'. Henat had not expected such grandeur.

During his journey, he had met many of his agents, whom he had asked to comment on the local people's state of mind and the temples' attitude. Ahmose's policy, imposed as it was by force, was not winning support. True, people appreciated security; however, the omnipresence of the Greek soldiers, the creation of the tax on each inhabitant's income and the suppression of the temples' traditional privileges had met with opposition.

Fortunately, the Divine Worshipper preserved the ancestral values, rejecting decadence and celebrating the rites that maintained the divine presence.

And Thebes was not some small, somnolent community far from the capital. The vast domain of Amun reigned at the heart of Egypt's wealthiest province. From the prow of his boat, Henat saw broad, well-cultivated plains on either side of the Nile. The Thebans enjoyed an abundance of fruit and vegetables, the numerous herds of cattle benefited from luxuriant pastures, and the fishermen never returned home empty-handed.

Pretty villages in the shade of palm-groves, strong dykes,

perfectly maintained pools for retaining water, channels irrigating the countryside, hundreds of donkeys delivering produce to the temple and the city: the management of the province seemed excellent. Clearly the Divine Worshipper was not bogged down in a mysticism far removed from daily realities and economic imperatives. And the sheer extent of her wealth was no legend.

When he neared Karnak, the greatest of all temples, known as Ipet-Sut, 'The Census-taker of Places' – in other words, the temple that gives each divinity his or her rightful place and welcomes them all into its bosom – Henat could not believe his eyes. From the landing-stage, he saw a forest of monuments whose roofs were visible above the brick curtain-wall, and obelisks whose tips pierced the sky. Here, the Senusrets, Mentuhoteps, Amenhoteps, Thutmosids, Sety I and Ramses II had all carried out work. Each pharaoh had embellished the domain of Amun, god of victories and guarantor of the power of the Two Lands.

The Divine Worshipper was the inheritor and guardian of this fabulous treasure, and was initiated into her office according to the royal rites. At her enthronement, a ritual priest came to fetch her from the House of Morning, where she had been purified. Nine pure priests dressed her in the garments, jewellery and amulets associated with her office, and the scribe of the divine book revealed its secrets to her. Proclaimed sovereign of the sun-disc's entire celestial route, she presided over the survival of all living beings. Like the pharaohs, she received coronation names inscribed inside a cartouche,* and carried out rites formerly reserved for monarchs.

Seeing Karnak enabled Henat to appreciate the true power

---

* An oval, elongated according to the number of hieroglyphs making up the royal name. It symbolized both the magical cord linking together all the diverse elements of life, and the order of the universe.

of the Divine Worshipper. As the head of this vast sacred domain, employer of thousands of peasants and artisans, surrounded with immense prestige, the old priestess had considerable power at her disposal. How many provincial chiefs would obey her if she decided to secede and no longer recognized Ahmose's authority?

True, there was nothing to suggest that this might happen, and Henat's spies had not informed him of any desire for rebellion on the part of the Theban administration. But were their reports reliable? The Divine Worshippers formed a sort of purely religious dynasty, limited to the province of Thebes and the Temple of Amun, and perfectly loyal to the reigning pharaoh. Up to now, they had confined themselves to that role. That was a reassuring fact. Perhaps too reassuring.

The boat docked. Henat could not take his eyes off Karnak where, clearly, an imposing number of divine forces were concentrated. Under the aegis of Amun, all the divinities of the sky and the earth were housed here. Beyond the enclosure wall, the temporal and worldly had no place. How far this world seemed from the Delta, especially from the Greek town of Naukratis. With its face firmly towards the past and tradition, Karnak rejected the future and progress.

Henat had expected worn-out glory, buildings eaten away by time, an outdated museum of derisory customs. He had been sorely mistaken. Before him there stood an immense magic vessel, in perfect working order. He was in a hurry to find out more and to meet the elderly ritual priestess in charge of commanding that vessel's crew. Had the years really any hold on her? Was she succumbing to them, or had she retained a dynamism comparable to that of these thousand-year-old stones, nourished by the rites practised here?

If the latter were the case, their meeting was likely to be a difficult one. But it was essential that the Divine Worshipper should submit and obey Pharaoh's orders. Otherwise, Henat would plan a radical solution, in agreement with the king.

Optimism suggested that a single meeting would be sufficient. Henat would explain the situation to her, provide the illustrious priestess with the necessary details, and indicate what she was to do. She would never receive Kel and his accomplices. And if, by chance, they managed to reach Thebes, they would be arrested there and taken back to Sais.

A shaven-headed priest asked and was given permission to come aboard.

'Welcome to Karnak,' he said. 'May I know your name, your titles and the reason for your visit?'

'I am Henat, director of the palace in Sais, and Pharaoh Ahmose's special envoy. Did you not receive the official message announcing my arrival?'

'Forgive me, my lord, I am merely the official in charge of boat traffic on the canal leading to the temple. Because of the annual flood, we must make special arrangements.'

'Take me to my official accommodation.'

The priest looked horribly embarrassed. 'As I said, I deal only with boats and—'

'Did you not hear my name and my title?'

'I am sorry, my lord, but my duties are strictly limited.'

'Then fetch someone in a position of authority.'

The priest thought for a long time. 'I shall try to give you satisfaction, but I cannot do so before the end of my service or I will be reprimanded.'

Henat dismissed the useless man with a wave of his hand.

An official message had been lost? Impossible! This was some grotesque joke. Emerging from his cabin, he descended the gangplank and walked straight into two men armed with swords and clubs.

'You have not been authorized to leave your boat,' said one of them. 'The formalities are still being dealt with.'

'My name is Henat, I am the director of the royal palace, and I order you to let me pass.'

'I'm sorry, my lord, but High Steward Sheshonq's instructions are very strict.'

Although furious, Henat did not initiate a trial of strength. 'Advise him to come here quickly – very quickly.'

48

The caravan was an ideal refuge. Despite the heat, it moved forward at a good pace, while allowing sufficient time for rest so as not to exhaust the people or the animals. Hassad had taken care to bring a large quantity of flasks of new water,* talismans against thirst. And he knew the location of the wells that dotted the route.

Radishes, garlic, onions, dried fish, cheese, bread and beer featured on the menu for the meals.

'I don't like that Syrian,' Nitis confided to Kel as she smoothed the healing salve over his hands. 'He has untrustworthy eyes.'

'We've paid him handsomely, and he seems content.'

'He'll soon want more.'

'We have enough to satisfy him, and we'll be leaving the caravan at Coptos.'

'I'm worried, Kel.'

Suddenly, the donkeys came to a halt. North Wind pawed the ground in irritation.

'Stay calm,' ordered the overseer at the rear. 'Wait for instructions from Hassad.'

Before long, Hassad came over to the couple. 'It's a security check. You'll have to separate.'

---

* The Nile's water became drinkable again after the first week of the annual flood.

'Certainly not,' retorted Kel.

'If you stay together, they'll arrest you. You, young woman, I'll introduce as my cousin's wife; you, my boy, are the cook; and your donkey can mix in with the others.'

Nitis and Kel did not even have time to embrace. And the priestess had to persuade North Wind to obey.

Hassad went back to the front of the caravan, where his younger brother was trying to answer questions from an officer in the desert patrol. The officer's men, who were armed with bows and slingshots, did not look very accommodating.

'Everything's in order,' declared Hassad. 'You can search all the bags and baskets.'

'We're looking for a woman doctor and an injured man. Have they asked you to hide them?'

'Officer, I've travelled this desert for many years, and the patrols have never had any reason to criticize me. I have no wish whatsoever to ruin my reputation and lose my caravan. If those people had contacted me, I'd have refused to bring them. The only people travelling are my employees and their families.'

'We shall check.'

'As you wish.'

The officer stared hard at the women and men alike. Hassad gave him their names and specified their duties. Nitis's beauty caught the officer's attention for a never-ending moment, but he accepted the Syrian's explanation and before long the caravan set off again.

Soon the patrol was out of sight, and Kel moved to rejoin Nitis. Four men seized him and bound him.

Hassad contemplated his prisoner mockingly. 'You aren't so proud now, my boy.'

'My wife . . . Don't hurt her!'

'Don't worry, I'll take care of her myself. But first, I want to know who you are.'

'Simple traders.'

'You wanted to leave Djawty and escape the forces of order. And the patrols are searching for a woman doctor and a wounded man.'

'I'm in perfect health, and my wife isn't a doctor.'

Hassad fingered his moustache. 'I have heard talk of a fearsome assassin, Kel the scribe, accompanied by a beautiful priestess and an actor. At Khmun, they escaped from Judge Gem, who has recently arrived in Djawty. And I, a mere caravan-leader, have the good fortune to have both of these fugitives in my hands.'

'You're completely mistaken.'

'You will talk, believe me. I already have the bag of gemstones, and I'm delighted to have accepted you and your pretty wife.'

'You dared to—'

'Don't worry, she's unharmed. I gave her a choice: either she gave me the gems or I killed your donkey. Since she has a sensitive heart, she didn't hesitate. It's a magnificent treasure, I must say, but I'm hoping for better – a great deal better. Delivering Kel the scribe to the authorities will earn me a fortune. So you are going to do me the courtesy of confessing.'

Kel met the Syrian's gaze without flinching.

'Oh, I wasn't expecting you'd cooperate immediately. Fortunately, the sun's rays are merciless. While we eat and drink in the shade of the tents, you will be exposed to it, lying on your back with your wrists and ankles tied to stakes. As you'll see, it soon becomes unbearable. Confess, and your ordeal will come to an end.'

Bebon had tracked down the caravan. When the detachment of desert-guards approached, he just had time to hide behind a pile of rocks. The snoopers must have searched the traders and discovered Kel and Nitis. But he could not see either of them with the patrol.

There was only one explanation: the leader of the caravan

was protecting them, probably by introducing them as members of his family. But what price was he asking for his protection?

He quickened his pace, taking only occasional small sips from his water-skin. It would soon be empty, and then he would be done for. Refusing to be overcome by fatigue, he saw his efforts rewarded two hours later: the caravan's tents had been pitched near a well.

Exhausted and gasping for breath, Bebon shivered with horror when he saw the torture Kel was being subjected to. It was impossible to help him. Bebon could not defeat twenty men single-handed.

And what about Nitis? Crawling on his belly, Bebon made a circuit of the encampment. She was tied to a stake nearby, and was being watched by two Syrian women in gaudy tunics; they were dozing as they sat beside her.

He never normally used violence against women, but this was an emergency. Picking up a round stone, he approached slowly, sprang up at the last moment and struck each of the Syrians sharply on the base of the neck. Neither even had the chance to cry out. Bebon tore up their tunics to make gags, and bound the women hand and foot.

Then he freed Nitis, who collapsed, motionless. She had clearly been drugged.

'Wake up, please!' he hissed.

Bebon sensed someone behind him. He was caught, and had no chance of escaping.

But the expected attack did not come.

He turned round. 'North Wind!'

The big donkey licked Nitis's forehead gently, and she slowly regained consciousness. 'Bebon!' she whispered.

'We must get away from the camp,' he said.

'Have you freed Kel?'

'It's impossible.'

'I won't leave without him.'

212

This was exactly what he had feared she'd say.

'There are too many people in the caravan. Let's find somewhere safe for the moment and then come up with a plan.'

North Wind laid a hoof lightly on Nitis's forearm.

'He already has one.'

49

Hassad counted and re-counted the precious stones. His favourites were the lapis-lazuli from Afghanistan. Obtaining them involved a long and dangerous journey, during which many traders died, victims of the climate and the local tribes. That far-off country had always been devoted to pillage and killing. But it was also home to this wondrous stone, which was analogous to the starry sky.

Once he had added the value of these gems to the enormous reward he would receive when he handed over the two rebels, Hassad would be in possession of an immense fortune. He would buy a luxurious house in Coptos, surrounded by a garden, and be the master of an army of servants. As the owner of ten caravans he would be acknowledged as supreme trader in the eastern desert, and would even be able to buy himself one or two boats for crossing the Red Sea.

Several times he had accepted clandestine travellers, in exchange for a large fee. Not one had reached his or her destination. Hassad robbed them, then cut their throats, and the vultures, hyenas, jackals and insects took care of making their corpses disappear. Nobody missed them, anyway.

This time the prize went beyond his wildest dreams. Soon he would have a harem of beautiful and totally submissive women, who would satisfy his every whim. When he tired of one of them, he would hand her over to his servants.

One thing puzzled him: the bow he had taken from one of the leather bags carried by the prisoners' donkey. It was a sizeable weapon, made of acacia wood. When his cousin had handled it, he had cried out in pain, and all at once his hands were covered in blisters. And the same thing had just happened to his brother.

The bow was now lying near a fire where flat-cakes were cooking.

'That thing is cursed,' Hassan's brother told him. 'It will bring us bad luck. Let those two go, and we can continue on our way.'

'Have you gone mad? Because of them, we're going to be rich.'

'Your greed is leading you astray, Hassad. The bow proves that they have dangerous magic powers.'

'Don't be ridiculous.'

'If you mock magic and the gods, you'll arouse the gods' anger.'

'Those are tales for imbeciles.'

'Then pick up the bow.'

Hassad hesitated. His mind was on raping the beautiful young woman, but he was afraid of damaging her so that he would have to sell her at a lower price. But she was only one woman, and he'd soon have dozens at his feet. And he couldn't afford to lose face.

So he seized the bow with a firm hand. Immediately his flesh sizzled, and a terrible stench filled the camp. Hassad howled and dropped the bow.

'Look,' his brother warned him, 'the donkeys are threatening us!'

To the amazement of the caravan-leader, the animals were forming a circle and pawing the ground with their hooves, visibly hostile.

'Filthy beasts! They're going to have a taste of the whip.'

The cousin tried to strike one, but North Wind broke ranks

and butted him in the lower back. The man's broken body crumpled to the ground.

Terrified, the caravan traders clustered round their leader.

Nitis appeared, looking calm and determined.

'Don't move,' she ordered, 'or the donkeys will obey their leader and kill you.'

The anger in North Wind's eyes dissuaded the few who were tempted to resist.

Nitis went over to Hassad, who was twisted with pain; the palms of his hands were bleeding. She picked up the bow and said, 'See, the goddess Neith gives me permission to hold her symbol. Whosoever outrages her and is ignorant of the words for appeasing fire is justly punished. Free the man you are torturing, and bring him here immediately.'

Two of the traders hurried to obey.

Although in a bad way, Kel managed to walk. And seeing Nitis again gave him a strength he did not realize he had.

Bebon sprang up behind Hassad and pressed the blade of the Greek knife to his throat. 'Pick up the gemstones and put them back in the bag.'

'I'm in pain, I—'

'Do it.'

Despite his pain, the Syrian obeyed.

'Now, my friends and I are leaving. Load our donkey with baskets of food and water-skins. Quickly!'

Nitis moistened Kel's lips. There was so much love in her eyes that he forgot his ordeal.

'You're coming with us,' Bebon told Hassad.

'I can't! You have to let me go. I'm the leader of this caravan, my family need me.'

'You'll join them later – they'll wait for you. Now move.'

North Wind set off first, followed by Nitis, Kel and Bebon, who was pricking the point of his knife into the Syrian's back.

Still forming a circle, the donkeys continued to exude

menace. They did not open the circle until North Wind was satisfied that his group was safe. He led them out of the camp. The salve was already soothing Kel's burns, and many-coloured tunics protected the travellers from the sun.

'Show us the way to Coptos,' Bebon ordered Hassad.

'It's that way,' replied Hassad, pointing to a path between the sand dunes.

North Wind headed in the opposite direction.

'You filth, you're still lying!'

The Syrian fell to his knees. 'Don't kill me, I beg you!'

'We'll see about that when we reach the next watering-place.'

The sunset brought with it a little coolness. The travellers stopped for the night. They drank some water, ate sparingly and then slept – Bebon tied Hassad up.

At the end of a restorative night, they recommenced their journey.

Suddenly, North Wind halted, staring fixedly at the Syrian.

'Don't let that creature attack me!'

'You may go,' said Nitis.

'I . . . I'm free?'

'Can a criminal like you ever truly be free?'

At first hesitant, the Syrian walked backwards. Then he turned and ran.

'Good riddance,' said Bebon. 'Now, in my opinion we should cut across in the direction of the valley and try to reach Abydos.'

'Abydos is Minister Pefy's domain,' said Nitis.

'Is he a friend or an enemy?'

'We'll soon find out,' replied Kel.

A series of howls interrupted them. Then there was profound silence: the entire desert held its breath.

Then deep growling echoed around and a lioness appeared atop a dune, her jaws dripping blood. Nitis raised the Bow of

Christian Jacq

Neith as a sign of offering and, appeased, the lioness walked away.

Hassad would never return to his caravan.

50

Henat paced the deck of his boat. Ordinarily so calm, he could not stand still. The humiliation he had suffered deserved a violent response, but he had chosen instead to continue analysing this surprising situation.

In showing her hostility so openly, the Divine Worshipper was taking great risks. Her attitude would displease Ahmose and he was bound to impose heavy penalties. In Sais, Henat would have encouraged him to do so, but his better knowledge of Upper Egypt and his discovery of Karnak – however brief – inclined him to hold back.

Was this mere intimidation or a real determination to oppose the will of one of the most senior members of the government? It was too soon to answer.

The sun was setting, and the stones of the temple were covered in golden tints. Above the sacred lake, the swallows were dancing. The peace of this place was nourished by centuries of wisdom. Here, time had no place and human affairs seemed derisory.

Refusing to allow himself to be captivated by this magic, Henat thought of his mission. He decided to step down on to dry land. No soldier would prevent him doing so.

As he was about to descend the gangplank, a procession of people carrying torches arrived on the quay. Several priests surrounded an imposing man who moved heavily.

The guards bowed and made way for him.

He climbed the short gangplank slowly and with great difficulty.

'Will you pardon me for this most unfortunate incident, Director Henat? I am High Steward Sheshonq, servant of the Divine Worshipper, in charge of governing her temporal domain. As such, I ought to have arranged a great reception in order to welcome you fittingly, but . . .'

'But?'

'I was not informed of your arrival.'

'An official message was sent to you.'

'Alas, it did not reach me, which explains this deplorable situation. As soon as I was told that you were here, I stopped everything – and here I am!'

'An official message went astray? That's impossible.'

'The messenger services between the North and the South have not been working well recently. I was in fact intending to inform Sais about a number of mishaps. A close study of the errors and shortcomings will enable them to be remedied, particularly since you are a victim of one of them. My detailed file is at your disposal.'

The High Steward was a very round man, and looked eminently likeable. Jovial, warm and courteous, he seemed sincere and pleaded his cause convincingly.

'As your boat was not announced, the guards observed their instructions to the letter. At this time of year, when the annual flood is beginning, boat manoeuvres present serious difficulties. There have already been accidents.'

'Why was I prevented from leaving my boat?'

'For simple reasons of security. Unknown visitors are kept at the landing-stage for as long as it takes to process the administrative formalities. I repeat, the unfortunate loss of your message is the sole reason for this miserable welcome. In the name of the Divine Worshipper, I offer you a thousand apologies.'

Sheshonq had cleared up the misunderstanding. His explanation was perfectly credible, because Henat had himself experienced the difficulties of communication between Upper and Lower Egypt.

'Thebes rejoices and is honoured by the presence of the royal palace director,' continued Sheshonq. 'We all too rarely receive visits from senior figures of state and are anxious to treat them with all the consideration befitting their rank. Our beautiful province serves King Ahmose faithfully.'

'I don't doubt it.'

Sheshonq seemed troubled. 'Unfortunately, I have other apologies to make.'

Henat's expression hardened. After so many civilities, now they were dealing with the delicate subjects.

'Because of the circumstances, your official apartments will not be ready until tomorrow. I should like to offer you my hospitality tonight.'

Henat was caught unawares. 'My boat is perfectly comfortable, and—'

'Ah, you haven't forgiven my mistake. I understand, and I accept your anger. Nevertheless, permit me to insist and to crave your indulgence.'

'Very well.'

A broad smile spread across Sheshonq's ample face. 'The gods be praised! I promise you a tasty meal, accompanied by excellent wine.'

The High Steward was not idly boasting. His house near the Temple of Karnak was a veritable palace. It had about twenty rooms, with two reception halls, several bedchambers, each with its own washroom, a vast library, outbuildings for the servants, a kitchen presided over by a cook of genius, and a wonderful wine-cellar.

'Would you care for a massage before dinner?' suggested Sheshonq. 'I know no better way of dispelling fatigue after a long day's work. Do try it – you won't regret it.'

Although reluctant, Henat agreed. The massage soothed away his tensions, and it was followed by a warm shower, perfumed soap, a tunic of royal linen and brand-new sandals ... The High Steward knew how to live and appreciated comfort.

The dinner was sumptuous. Henat had never tasted such delicious quails in wine, and the flesh of a Nile perch, served on a bed of onions and leeks, was pure perfection. As for the red wine from Imau, it would have delighted King Ahmose himself.

Henat's doubts were dispelled: the Theban administration had in no way sought to humiliate him, and its head had provided him with a welcome beyond his hopes.

'I visited Sais more than thirty years ago,' revealed Sheshonq, 'and I very much appreciated the charm of our capital. But I confess that I do prefer that of the Theban province, which is so rich in memories. So many illustrious pharaohs lie at rest on the western bank, and so many magnificent temples have been built to keep their *ka* alive. Wonderful discoveries lie in store for you. I am not only talking about Karnak, which is a world unto itself. Thebes will win you over, I am sure.'

'I am no ordinary visitor,' Henat reminded him. 'The pharaoh has entrusted me with a mission, and I intend to carry it out swiftly.'

'In what way can I help you?'

'By arranging a private audience for me with the Divine Worshipper.'

'I shall request it as soon as possible. And while you are here, perhaps you would care to see a little more of our way of life. Tomorrow I am to receive the officials in charge of the dykes and ensure that they have followed my instructions. According to the experts, the annual flood will reach a good level, neither too high nor too low. However, despite their skills at prediction, I'm cautious. Over-optimism can lead to negligence, and the level of the water-storage pools concerns me. The hot season is harsher here than in Sais, and our prosperity depends on thoroughness and hard work. But enough of that. Would you like some cakes?'

'No, thank you.'

'A little date wine to aid your digestion?'

'I have already drunk a great deal, High Steward. Permit me to retire for the night.'

A servant took Henat to his room. He was tired, and glad of the soft sheets and cushion. His stay in Thebes seemed likely to be both brief and enjoyable.

51

'We have arrested ten suspects,' Judge Gem was informed by the officer in charge of the checkpoints in Djawty. 'Eight men and two women.'

'Bring them to me immediately.'

He was in for a cruel disappointment. They were all just petty criminals, guilty of minor offences.

So Kel, Nitis and Bebon had succeeded in leaving the city. Not by river, because the ferocity of the first few days of the flood made the Nile impassable. And a multitude of soldiers was keeping watch on the roads and paths heading south – officials sent the judge daily reports and brought all suspects to him. But here again he had met with total failure.

That left only one possibility: the desert. But how could the fugitives survive its dangers? Thirst, wild animals, snakes and scorpions would prevent them getting far. Only experienced professionals, such as patrols and caravan-leaders, could survive in that hell.

A caravan . . . Perhaps that was the key to the riddle!

The judge summoned the scribe whose task it was to register the arrival and departure of nomads, and to tax them according to the length of their stay in Djawty.

'How may caravans have taken the southern trail in the last few days?'

'Only one,' replied the scribe, 'the one belonging to the Syrian, Hassad.'

'What is its destination?'

'Coptos.'

'This man Hassad, is he honest and serious-minded?'

'He knows the trails and watering-places well. His honesty, on the other hand . . .'

'Would he agree to take along travellers whose situation was irregular?'

The scribe hesitated. 'There have been rumours about that, but I have no proof.'

'Has the patrol watching the area around Djawty returned yet?'

'It won't be back until the day after tomorrow.'

The judge resigned himself to the delay. But the time of the patrol's return came, and there was no sign of them. At the end of the fourth day, certain that something terrible had happened, the judge decided to send out a rescue team. It was about to leave when the patrol appeared at the city gates.

Their leader was taken to Gem immediately.

'Extraordinary things have been happening, Judge,' he said. 'We checked Hassad's caravan and found nothing amiss. But then we were joined by his family, who were distraught. They said that all the donkeys rebelled to free a man and a woman whom their employer was planning to hand over to the authorities in Coptos in exchange for a large reward. A second man apparently took Hassad hostage, and the four all disappeared. Two of my men are leading the caravan to Coptos, and we've found no sign either of Hassad or of his abductors.'

'Kel, Nitis and Bebon!' concluded the judge.

Their hostage would guide them across the desert and then, once they had reached their destination, they would get rid of him. But what was that destination? It could not be Coptos because the guards were waiting for them there.

Trying to put himself in the rebels' place, Judge Gem consulted a map, One name stood out: Abydos. Abydos, favourite city of Pefy, the finance minister. A strange coincidence that he was in residence there just when Kel and his allies were trying to reach Thebes.

Abydos was an obligatory stop. There, the assassin would join up with an accomplice, one of Egypt's highest dignitaries, who would provide him with a secure refuge and help him to contact the Divine Worshipper.

Pefy, the close friend of Wahibra, Nitis's spiritual master. Pefy, the mind behind the conspiracy. Using Kel the scribe to do his dirty work, he had helped him at every stage.

Abydos would be the conspirators' tomb.

North Wind hated the furnace-heat of the desert, and was overjoyed to rejoin the Nile valley. Striking the ground with their staves, the travellers created vibrations that deterred snakes from attacking them. At night, a fire kept predators away.

Suddenly, the quality of the air changed and the heat seemed less unbearable.

'The river isn't far away now,' said Kel.

'We must be especially careful,' warned Bebon. 'If we meet a desert patrol, we're done for.'

Each sand-dune, littered with fragments of stone, served as their observation post. Between the little mountains they ran, and North Wind galloped.

After a night spent at the summit of a dune, Nitis spotted monuments in the distance.

'Abydos, the kingdom of Osiris,' said Bebon. 'I've often played the part of Seth there during the celebration of the ritual drama on the temple forecourt. It's very effective, believe me! The mask is terrifying, and Osiris's final victory doesn't seem like a foregone conclusion. What wonderful memories . . . One of my finest roles.'

'The fire of Seth enabled us to cross the desert,' Nitis pointed out.

'We did very well,' agreed the actor, 'but I haven't the slightest desire to go back there! All the same, we mustn't count our chickens before they're hatched. Abydos is protected by a barracks full of Greek soldiers from Milet. Assuming they obey Minister Pefy's orders, we are walking right into the jackal's mouth.'

'Pefy was Wahibra's friend,' objected Nitis. 'He listened to his advice and took account of his opinions. Although he knew nothing about the affair of state we are unjustly caught up in, Pefy tried to defend us. Faced with the king's blindness, he has chosen to withdraw to Abydos and devote himself to the cult of Osiris.'

'That's real optimism!' Bebon exclaimed. 'I'm more inclined to believe we'll encounter a well-laid trap. Pefy's an experienced courtier, and he likes his privileges. To prevent suspicion falling on him, he'll be plotting our downfall. We won't get out of Abydos alive.'

What were they to do?

'We've run out of water,' said Kel, 'and we need more food, too.'

The argument was decisive.

'I know a farm where we will be received kindly,' said Bebon.

'Is the farmer's wife one of your conquests, by any chance?' enquired Kel.

'No, but her daughter is. Not much intelligence and a limited vocabulary, but the sort of breasts a man dreams about.'

'Did you part on good terms?'

'I've known worse.'

North Wind was famished, and dreaming of fresh alfalfa and thistle-shoots, so he put an end to the discussions and set off towards the fields.

Leaving the desert was an immense relief. At last: trees, vegetation and the gentle quivering of the water in the irrigation channels.

'Halt!' ordered a rough voice.

Five Greek soldiers.

North Wind stopped, and his companions followed suit.

'Who are you?'

'Itinerant traders.'

'Where have you come from?'

'The North.'

'With only one donkey? That doesn't ring true! We know all the traders around here, and we've never seen you before. Follow us. We're going to question you at the barracks.'

We won't get out of Abydos alive, Bebon told himself again. We'll never be able to beat five strong men.

'You are to take us to Minister Pefy,' demanded Nitis.

The soldier's eyes opened wide. 'He doesn't receive mere traders!'

'I am the daughter of his closest friend, the High Priest of Sais, and the minister is expecting me.'

52

Henat had spent a delightful day. His official accommodation was a large detached house half an hour from the palace of High Steward Sheshonq. A cohort of servants answered his every whim, a cook served him his favourite dishes, and a barber, manicurist and masseur were constantly at his disposal.

A lake purified by lotus-flowers had given him an opportunity to swim, and he had fallen asleep in the shade of a pergola. When he woke, he was greeted by cool, light beer.

'Does Your Excellency desire anything else?' asked a beautiful brown-haired girl dressed in a small kilt.

'Not for the moment.'

With a mischievous smile, she withdrew. Probably another gift from the High Steward!

These moments of unhoped-for relaxation had shown Henat just how tired he was. For several years he had taken no rest, so overcome was he with work and cares. This sudden break had unsettled him, revealing aspects of life he had not previously thought about. Thebes the temptress ... No, he would not yield to that mirage! Sheshonq, himself a lover of good living, was very skilful but would not make Henat forget his mission.

When night fell, a messenger from the High Steward invited him to dine at the palace belonging to the head of the Theban government.

Brightly lit and perfumed, the dining-chamber housed a dozen guests. They all rose to their feet when Henat entered.

'Director of the Royal Palace,' declared Sheshonq, smiling delightedly, 'allow me to introduce you to my principal colleagues and their wives. We are enchanted to receive Pharaoh Ahmose's envoy and are anxious to do him every honour.'

Beside this official banquet, the previous evening's dinner resembled a cold collation! There were three appetizers, four main dishes and two desserts, and wines were of exceptionally high quality – though Henat took care not to drink too much. These pleasures were enhanced by exquisitely sensual dances performed by three young girls. Dressed only in amethyst belts, they described graceful figures, accompanied by women musicians playing the harp, the lute and the flute.

Ahmose would have appreciated this reception, thought Henat; it is worthy of a king!

Sheshonq asked the Scribe of the Treasury to explain to their guest the manner in which he managed the Theban province's finances. Then it was the turn of the Scribe of the Fields to detail his policy, stressing the vital need for grain reserves in case of an inadequate annual flood. As for the Overseer of Craftsmen, he praised their professionalism and their dedication to the domain of Amun. And the official in charge of trading exchanges congratulated himself on the number of boats moving between the North and the South, and the speed of deliveries. In short, everything was for the best in the best of all worlds, and Thebes was thriving under the rule of Ahmose.

At the end of this highly successful evening, the dignitaries of the Theban administration bade him goodnight and thanked him for coming.

'Is the house satisfactory?' Sheshonq asked.

'It seems perfect,' replied Henat.

'You're quite sure?'

'Quite sure.'

'Are the servants giving complete satisfaction, too?'

'They, too, seem perfect.'

'Don't hesitate to tell me if there's the slightest problem. I'll resolve it immediately.'

'Many thanks, Sheshonq. However, though this stay in Thebes is enchanting, I have a mission to fulfil: an audience with the Divine Worshipper.'

'I have not forgotten, dear Henat.'

'Good night, High Steward.'

Henat rose early. He was immediately served warm milk and flat-cakes with honey, a rare and costly food. The first hour of the morning was exquisite. Then came the burdensome heat, forcing people and animals to protect themselves from the burning sun.

'What would you like for your midday meal?' asked the cook.

'Rib of beef and salad.'

The washer-man brought a fresh tunic, the barber shaved him delicately and the perfumer asked him to select his preferred scent.

Henat settled beside the lake and waited for Sheshonq. Late in the morning or that afternoon, Henat would speak to the Divine Worshipper and pass on Ahmose's instructions. If the old priestess's welcome was as warm as that of her High Steward, the conversation would be cordial and fruitful.

Hours passed. Henat ate his lunch, then strode around the garden.

At last Sheshonq appeared.

'I should like to invite you to a banquet with the principal scribes in charge of offerings,' he said. 'They will explain to you in detail how the economy of Karnak and the temples of the west bank functions.'

'Delightful. When can I see the Divine Worshipper?'

Christian Jacq

Sheshonq appeared embarrassed. 'Let us go and sit in the shade.'

A servant hurried up with some beer.

'Did the Divine Worshipper refuse to receive me?' Henat asked.

'Of course not! This is a mere hitch. And I owe you the truth: I myself have not been able to see her today, even though we had planned to deal with many subjects relating to the management of her domain.'

'Has this happened before?'

'Not often.'

'What was the reason?'

The High Steward looked even more embarrassed. 'The Divine Worshipper attaches more importance to ritual tasks than to material concerns. Moreover, it is my duty to free her from them, provided I obtain her agreement regarding the major decisions.'

Henat did not hide his scepticism. 'Are you telling me *all* the truth, Sheshonq?'

The High Steward lowered his eyes. 'You must understand the situation, Henat. The Divine Worshipper is a very old lady in frail health. Fulfilling all her obligations is becoming difficult, and I cannot permit myself to rush her.'

'I understand.'

'I have submitted, in writing, your request for an audience. When I receive a reply I'll tell you immediately. In the meantime, I shall place a litter with bearers at your disposal. Thebes offers so many marvels that your days to come will be well filled. Until this evening, my friend. My subordinates are anxious to get to know you.'

Henat felt strangely calm. Either Sheshonq was lying, and the Divine Worshipper was refusing to see Pharaoh's envoy, or else he was telling the truth and the old lady really was ill, perhaps even on her deathbed. If the latter were the case, she would no longer be of any help to Kel.

232

Henat decided he would continue to play the role of the satisfied guest, so as not to arouse the High Steward's suspicions. But there was one thing he must do urgently: contact his Theban agents and verify what Sheshonq had said.

53

Since the earliest days of the pharaohs, many kings had built at Abydos, and certain of them had built their houses of eternity of the *ka*, being reborn in the company of the god who had vanquished death. Minister Pefy's house stood near the great Temple of Osiris, the work of Sety I, father of Ramses II.

The leader of the Greek soldiers who had caught the fugitives went up to the door-keeper. 'A young woman wants to see the minister. She claims he's expecting her.'

'What is her name?'

'She refuses to tell me. Apparently, she's the daughter of the minister's closest friend, the High Priest of Sais.'

'I shall go and inform my master.'

Kel was calm, but Bebon was downcast. The soldiers were alert, and had given them no chance to escape. If Pefy refused to see them, they would be brutally interrogated and then handed over to Egyptian guards. And if the guards considered them guilty, they would inform Judge Gem.

'On reflection,' said Bebon, 'Nitis's plan seems bound to fail.'

The door-keeper reappeared. 'She may enter.'

A soldier seized the priestess's arm.

'Let her go,' said the door-keeper. 'I will take charge of her.'

He led Nitis through a small anteroom containing an altar

dedicated to the ancestors, and down a corridor lit by a high window, at the end of which they came to an office cluttered with papyri and tablets.

'Here she is, my lord.'

Pefy was seated on the ground. He looked up. 'Nitis! So it really is you.'

'I am not alone: Kel's with me. He loves me and I love him. And his friend Bebon has saved us from many dangers. And I mustn't forget our donkey, North Wind, who's intelligent and brave.'

'And you are going to declare the innocence of a scribe who is being hunted by all the forces in the kingdom! The evidence against Kel is overwhelming; no one doubts his guilt. And now you yourself are accused of complicity with him. Judge Gem regards you as dangerous conspirators, whose progress is littered with corpses.'

'It is all false,' she declared calmly, 'and the true conspirators are continuing to act in the shadows.'

'Who are they and what do they want?'

'We still don't know, but a coded text probably includes their names and their goal.'

'How am I to believe such a tale?'

'By accepting the truth. A young scribe, a priestess and an actor threatening the throne of Ahmose: is that tale any more believable?'

'Kel murdered his colleagues and fled. By helping him, you have associated yourself with those murders.'

'The Divine Worshipper will give us the key to the code and will enable us to prove our innocence. Help us to reach Thebes and obtain an audience.'

Pefy turned his head away.

Nitis awaited his verdict. With one word he could have them arrested and condemned to death.

'I have just sent my resignation to King Ahmose,' he said. 'Managing the country's economy no longer interests me, and I do not approve of the policy favouring Greece, so I have decided to settle here and devote myself to the cult of Osiris.'

Nitis felt new hope. 'Will you help us?'

'I have only limited authority over the garrison of soldiers. Their commander will inform his superior of your presence, and he in turn will inform Judge Gem. On the pretext of interrogating you, I will shelter you and obtain food for you. Do not ask more of me.'

'Then you believe me?'

'Go and fetch Kel and Bebon.'

Only North Wind remained outside. A servant brought him water and fodder, and the donkey ate gratefully.

Pefy looked long and hard at the scribe who was at the centre of an affair of state. The ordeal had matured him; his face had become that of a man determined to fight to the end. He seemed neither defeated nor exhausted. And he asked a question which surprised the minister: 'Did you write the coded papyrus?

'No. Certainly not.'

'Do you know who did?'

'I do not. Now, I shall entrust you to my steward. I must send away the patrol.'

Bebon displayed an enormous appetite and an un-quenchable thirst, and promised himself that he would never again cross the desert. Nitis and Kel could not eat until Pefy returned – it seemed a long time before he did.

'The soldiers have gone back to their barracks,' said the minister, 'but they want an account of the interrogation and are astonished at my intervention. In view of my eminent position they gave in, but their commander will soon show his disapproval, for it is not my job to meddle in military or security matters.'

'How long may we stay?' Kel asked.

'Two days at most. I fear the soldiers' reaction may be rough. Now, eat and then rest.'

'Is your private boat at the port of Abydos?'

'Indeed.'

'Would you permit us to steal it to get to Thebes?'

'The Divine Worshipper will not receive you. Despite her spiritual radiance, she must obey the king. Henat will describe you as the worst of criminals and convince her that she must keep her distance from this sinister affair.'

'We shall see. Do we have your permission?'

'I was not planning to use that boat any more. Once the theft has been noticed, I shall lodge a complaint.'

Leaving the lovers to their happiness, Bebon left Pefy's house by way of the terrace. He felt an irresistible desire to see once again the workshop where craftsmen made the gods' masks used in the celebration of the Mysteries. Situated not far away, it would give him the opportunity to dream of his recent past as a strolling actor and of the happy hours he had spent in the company of the delicious expert in painted cartonnage.

Abydos was already asleep. A reliquary of a city, devoid of economic activity, it was devoted entirely to Osiris and saw its small number of inhabitants diminishing each year.

The main door of the workshop was closed, but Bebon knew how to open a window at the rear of the building. His eyes soon grew accustomed to the darkness, and he could make out the faces of the falcon Horus and the terrifying animal of Seth, a sort of okapi with large, pricked-up ears.

Suddenly, a sound alerted him. Risking a glance at the window, he saw soldiers taking up positions outside. Pefy had betrayed his guests.

54

General Phanes bowed before King Ahmose.

'My mission has been accomplished, Majesty. Elephantine is now a true fortress and our southern border has been firmly established. Experienced officers head a properly trained garrison, ready to repel any attack. The new commander and the new mayor are loyal servants of the kingdom, who will obey your every command.'

'Have the Nubians been informed of these changes?'

'I sent messengers to the principal tribal chiefs. If any desire for rebellion existed, it will have been extinguished.'

'Excellent work, Phanes.'

'I am not completely satisfied, Majesty. Some Southern provinces still have a rebellious attitude and are not applying the laws rigorously enough. It seems to me that they need taking in hand.'

'What do you suggest?'

'We should establish more barracks near the main cities and large towns. The soldiers' presence will quell any disputes.'

'I shall think about it, Phanes. For the moment, I am going to entrust you with an important mission.'

The Greek drew himself up straight, his arms stiffly at his sides. 'I am at your command, Majesty.'

'Do you know my son, Psamtek?'

'I have seen the prince at official ceremonies.'

'What do you think of him?'

'Majesty, I cannot allow myself to—'

'Allow yourself.'

'He is an elegant and level-headed young man.'

'Too elegant and too level-headed! At his age, I wielded the sword and the spear. He spends time with scribes and in high society, and neglects the army. It is time to give him a rigorous military training. One day he will be at the head of our troops and will have to defend the Two Lands.'

'Majesty, my methods . . .'

'They are perfectly acceptable to me. Do not kill him, but do not treat him gently, either. That boy must swiftly become a first-rate warrior. I shall send him to you this very day.'

'I shall train your son, Majesty, and he will prove worthy of his father. As I was planning to undertake large-scale manoeuvres in order to maintain the army of the North at its highest level, I shall involve him in them.'

'To work, Phanes.'

There was determination in the general's stride as he withdrew. He was succeeded by Udja, as imposing as ever.

'Have your headaches gone, Majesty?'

'Your remedy was highly effective. I don't have the slightest pain any more, and my energy has returned. I trust the war-fleet is taking part in the great manoeuvres?'

'Most assuredly. I feel that the coordination between war-fleet, footsoldiers and cavalry is vital. We have just received diplomatic mail from Kroisos: he assures us of the Persian emperor's friendship and hopes to pay us a visit with his wife, Nitetis. Nitetis sends her best wishes for the health of Queen Tanith.'

'That is very good news indeed, First Minister! The Persians really do seem to be growing calmer and renouncing their policy of conquest. Nevertheless, we must not lower our guard. Has the Interpreters' Secretariat been re-formed?'

'In Henat's absence, recruitment has been marking time,

Majesty. It is better to take time and engage only professionals of a very high level, who are familiar with their duties. The current number of employees is sufficient to handle most of the diplomatic mail.'

'Has Henat met the Divine Worshipper?'

'Not yet, Majesty.'

'Would she dare refuse to see the palace director?'

'That is unimaginable,' said Udja. 'Moreover, Henat's latest letter does not voice that accusation. No doubt he is strengthening his control of his Theban network and gathering information before his audience.'

Ahmose nodded. That was indeed Henat's style. 'Any reports from Judge Gem?'

'He is closing in on his prey, Majesty. At Djawty, the murderous scribe and his accomplices only just escaped him.'

'Djawty . . . So the fugitive is getting near Thebes.'

'His base in Elephantine has been destroyed, and he is being hunted down.'

Ahmose glimpsed a sombre prospect. 'And what if Kel were to go not to Thebes but to Abydos, home of my finance minister, Pefy?'

'Your former minister, Majesty: I have just received his resignation.'

'So Pefy has resigned in order to fight me! Pefy, the soul of the conspiracy . . . Inform Judge Gem immediately.'

'Have no fear, Majesty. The judge followed an identical line of reasoning and is planning to surround Abydos in the hope of arresting the conspirators there.'

'So is Pefy their leader, and Kel the one who carries out his evil plans?'

'We must await the judge's conclusions.'

'Do you still have doubts?'

'Pefy was an excellent minister, was he not? Our finances are wonderfully sound, the country is wealthy, and agriculture is prospering.'

'A perfect conspirator, honest and hard-working ...
Admirable Pefy! Why did he want to take power? It is absolute
madness at his age! The ideal of wisdom is vanishing, Udja.
But that is enough work for today.'

Ahmose left the palace and joined his wife, who was resting
in the shade of an old sycamore tree.

'Would you like to go boating, Tanith?'

'Actually, I do need to talk to you.'

Four oarsmen, a man at the prow, a man at the steering-oar,
some cool white wine and a sunshade. Ahmose stretched out
on a pile of cushions and looked up at the sky.

'Sometimes, my dear, human beings bore me. I should think
more of the gods and be less concerned with the happiness of
my subjects. But I cannot escape my destiny, so I continue to
bear the duties of my office, and you alone know their true
weight. This sky is so beautiful, so pure and so ... mysterious.
Egypt must not doubt her king, and I must not have doubts
about the direction to take.'

'I am worried,' confessed the queen.

Ahmose sat up. 'What concerns you, Tanith?'

'It is about our son, Psamtek. Has he not just left the palace
with General Phanes?'

'Correct, my dear. The time has come to harden him in the
arts of war.'

'But Phanes is so brutal, and our son so fragile ...'

'He will succeed me, Tanith, and must learn to understand
the rigours of life. Confining him to the palace would be a
grave mistake.'

'Couldn't you wait?'

'The years pass quickly, and Psamtek is no longer an
adolescent boy. One day he will have to give orders to soldiers.
I neglected his upbringing by abandoning him to learned men
who were bogged down in their own good manners. On a
battlefield, their erudition will count for nothing.'

'But we are not under threat of war,' objected the queen.

'We are soon to receive a visit from Kroisos and his wife,' revealed Ahmose, 'and we shall provide them with a warm welcome. Thanks to him, Persia knows of our military capabilities and will therefore be wary of attacking us. Nevertheless, I am still suspicious of that warlike race. One day Psamtek may have to fight them.'

55

About fifty soldiers were moving silently towards Pefy's house. They would soon meet the men sent by Judge Gem, who was coordinating the operation. The judge had arrived in Abydos that day and, learning of the three suspects' presence in the house, had decided to take immediate action. This time, the conspirators would not escape him.

The full moon came out and lit up the sleeping town.

One of the soldiers turned round. What he saw shocked him so much that he cried out in fear. His comrades stopped and, in their turn, saw the horrible spectacle: the god Seth had sprung forth from the darkness to threaten them.

Those men who were superstitious took flight, bumping into those who had not quite made up their minds what to do, and knocking some of them over. The fine, subtle plan collapsed in ruins.

Satisfied with the result, Bebon beat a retreat, took off his mask and ran to the port. It was too late for him to warn Kel and Nitis; North Wind would take care of that. He could not possibly fight this army alone. There was only one way out: to seize Pefy's boat and prepare to set sail, in the hope that the young couple would be able to join him.

Knowing Abydos very well, Bebon took a succession of narrow alleys down to the port. Several war-boats and river-guard vessels were moored there, including the one belonging to Judge Gem. Sentries were keeping watch on them.

At the end of the quay a large boat was berthed. Little by little, dark clouds hid the moon. Taking advantage of the darkness, Bebon clambered up on to the deck. He almost collided with a sleeping sailor, and woke him by pricking the point of his knife into his lower back.

'Help me, or I'll kill you.'

Kel started up as North Wind's loud braying shattered the calm of the night.

'Nitis, get dressed quickly.'

Looking tired, Pefy emerged from his bedchamber.

'You are in danger,' he told his guests. 'We will leave the house by the back entrance and go to the temple. The soldiers won't dare enter it.'

'North Wind—'

'I am sorry,' cut in Pefy. 'Donkeys are the creatures of Seth, and cannot be admitted to the Temple of Osiris.'

'He'll wait for us,' Nitis assured Kel.

'Hurry,' urged Pefy. 'My door-keeper cannot hold them back for long.'

He was right. The door-keeper, afraid of being beaten, informed the soldiers that the occupants of the house had taken refuge in the shrine of Sety I. Finally regrouping, the men hurried off after their commander.

When they reached the shrine, a priest emerged from it. 'Do not violate the peace of this sacred space,' he said.

'You are sheltering criminals,' retorted the commander. 'Hand them over to us.'

'That is out of the question.'

'You are breaking the law!'

'The only law I know is that of the gods.'

Inside the temple, Pefy showed the young couple the

passageway leading to the Osireion, the partially underground temple reserved for the celebration of the great Mysteries. A vaulted corridor would lead them to the edge of the divine domain, not far from the port.

'My boat is at the far end of the quay. If your friend has managed to reach it, you may succeed in leaving Abydos.'

'What about you?' Kel asked anxiously.

'I have nothing to lose,' said Pefy. 'Now go, and may the gods protect you.'

A flash of lightning zig-zagged across the sky, thunder rumbled and heavy drops of hot rain began to fall.

The priests had gathered together to prevent the soldiers from invading the temple.

Pefy joined them and his deep voice rose above theirs. 'Leave,' he ordered. 'I am the finance minister of the Two Lands, and I speak in the name of Pharaoh.'

'Do not listen to him,' shouted Judge Gem, pushing his way through the soldiers. 'This man is a traitor and is sheltering murderers.'

'You are wrong, Gem, and you are hounding innocent people.'

'No temple is outside the law. Ahmose's soldiers are going to enter and seize the criminals who are conspiring against him.'

'I forbid them to profane the Temple of Osiris!'

'Stand aside, Pefy.'

'Never.'

'Death to the traitor!' shouted the soldiers' commander, and he hurled his spear deep into Pefy's chest.

Pefy collapsed, the priests fled and the soldiers charged into the temple.

I would have preferred a trial, thought Gem, to this tragedy. But at least the mastermind behind the rebels has been eliminated.

*

The violent wind and rain hindered Kel's and Nitis's progress. Nevertheless they eventually reached the port, where a stoical North Wind was waiting for them. Forgetting the wild weather for a moment, they stroked him and the trio headed for the far end of the quay.

On this terrible day of the great battle between Horus and Seth,* people were meant to stay at home, not swim, not climb aboard a boat and definitely not travel. The Nile was in full spate, enormous waves were assailing the boats and threatening to sink them. Abandoning their posts, the sentries sought places to shelter.

'Quick!' yelled Bebon. 'Let's cast off the last mooring rope and leave!'

'This is madness,' said Kel. 'The boat will sink and we'll drown.'

'Seth's creature, the donkey, will protect us,' said Nitis. 'He knows the secret of the storm and he isn't afraid of it.'

The trio managed to get aboard.

'The sailor on guard has run away,' said a dripping-wet Bebon, 'and we won't be able to handle the boat.'

'We must leave,' decreed Nitis.

New flashes of lightning cleaved an ink-black sky. Kel clasped his amulet very tightly and wrapped his arms round Nitis.

Driven by the current, tossed around by the tempestuous winds, the murdered minister's boat disappeared into the night.

* The twenty-sixth day of the first month of the *akhet* (Nile flood) season, approximately 14 August.

56

The sun dispelled the last clouds. The terrifying storm, which had not eased until daybreak, had caused considerable damage, and an exceptionally strong east wind was still blowing.

Emerging from the Temple of Osiris, where the soldiers had found only priests, Judge Gem stopped by Pefy's corpse. Why had that exemplary minister erred in such a way?

'Bury him,' he ordered the soldiers.

The garrison commander would be suspended for a few days for indiscipline, and Gem would write a detailed report for King Ahmose.

Part of the quay had been destroyed, and all the boats were seriously damaged.

'Two sank,' said a sailor, 'and the minister's boat is missing.'

'Did anyone see it leave?' asked the judge.

A still-shocked witness was found. 'Because of the driving rain I couldn't see very well. But I'm sure I made out a couple boarding the boat with a donkey. Then the boat suddenly moved away from the quay and the current carried it away at incredible speed.'

'It must have been knocked to pieces,' ventured the sailor, 'and the passengers drowned.'

'We shall carry out searches,' decided Judge Gem.

'But the repairs will take a long time!'

'Other river-guard vessels will soon be here.'

'With respect, Judge, searching is pointless. Even an experienced sailor couldn't survive a storm like that, and the crocodiles and other fish will leave no trace of the bodies.'

Henat visited several temples of a million years on the west bank, notably those of Ramses II and Ramses III,* gigantic edifices surrounded by annexes. Storehouses, workshops and libraries were still in operation.

Four servants satisfied his every wish and made sure he was comfortable. Henat talked to a large number of officials, taking an interest in their working methods and their ways of resolving difficulties.

At the temple of Ramses II, he had many questions for the craftsman who made high-quality papyri, the only ones used for writing down rituals. The craftsman delivered them notably to the Divine Worshipper and often went to Karnak. He was also the head of Henat's network of spies.

'It's an honour to welcome you to Thebes, my lord.'

'Let us dispense with the polite formalities. I need detailed information.'

'The situation here is entirely calm. The province is tranquil, the temples manage the economy to everyone's satisfaction and people's main preoccupation is worshipping the gods.'

'Tell me about High Steward Sheshonq.'

'He is both a scholar of religion and an administrator, and is held in high esteem both by dignitaries and by ordinary folk. Despite his lumpish appearance and his love of good food, he is meticulous and a hard worker. He is uncompromising, and cannot bear laziness or incompetence. The Divine Worshipper chose well when she appointed him High Steward.'

'Have you seen her recently?'

'She has been invisible for two months. According to close

* Respectively, the Ramesseum and Medinet Habu.

248

servants, her health is failing rapidly. She still celebrates certain rites, but she never leaves the Karnak enclosure and stays in her palace most of the time.'

'Does Sheshonq visit her?'

'At least three times a week. He has to consult her before taking important decisions regarding the governing of the province. Lately, though, she has refused to receive him. Some people think that she is on her deathbed.'

So Sheshonq was telling the truth. But Henat was not a trusting man, and he wanted to be absolutely certain.

'Do you know the Divine Worshipper's doctor?'

'He has treated me, too. He is a likeable and very competent man.'

'Tell him that I am ill and send him to my official residence. Has the High Steward financed a secret military force?'

'You need have no fear of that, my lord. The security forces have been reduced to the minimum and are a long way from forming an army. The guards at Karnak confine themselves to keeping watch on the approaches to the temple. The Divine Worshipper's spiritual radiance remains considerable, but she is in no way a warrior chief.'

The wreck of Pefy's boat was found between Abydos and Thebes, near Dendera. There was nothing left of it but a scattering of debris. It had been strongly built, but the Nile's fury had pulled it apart.

'Were any human remains found?' Judge Gem asked the officers who had inspected the wreck.

'The river and its habitants have cleansed everything.'

Kel, Nitis and Bebon, all drowned ... It was indeed probable. But the judge was sceptical and continued his investigations further south. Again with no result.

Given the ferocity of the storm, which had lasted several hours, the chances of the fugitives having survived were non-existent. Should he not face the facts, conclude that they were dead and lift the security controls? But those three had already escaped from so many dangers . . . There was still doubt.

Judge Gem summoned a small detachment of soldiers and gave them their orders.

Carrying a heavy leather satchel full of remedies, the doctor entered Henat's bedchamber. Henat was reading a report from the head of his network.

'I came as quickly as possible,' said the doctor. 'What is the trouble?'

'I am wonderfully well.'

The doctor frowned. 'I don't understand. I was told—'

'I wished to see you, Doctor. Officially, you are treating a patient. In reality, I need some information.'

'I am at your service.'

'Are you the Divine Worshipper's personal doctor?'

'I am.'

'I want to know everything about her state of health.'

'I am sorry, that is impossible. Respect for professional secrecy is part of my duties.'

'Forget it!'

'I repeat, that is impossible.'

'We do not quite understand each other, Doctor. I want a detailed answer. Or else . . .'

'Are you threatening me?'

'You and your family. The king has entrusted me with a mission and I am going to carry it out.'

'You wouldn't dare—'

'I have full powers, and in my eyes all that matters is the service of the state. I strongly advise you to answer me.'

'Betraying a patient's confidence is a terrible thing and—'

'Needs must.'

The doctor swallowed hard. 'You are asking a great deal of me.'

'Only you and I will know that you have spoken. You will hold your tongue, and I shall hold mine.'

The doctor took a deep breath. 'The Divine Worshipper suffers from several incurable conditions: a worn-out heart, tired lungs, shrunken energy channels. Because of her great age, no medicine works. I can only ease her suffering.'

'Does she still grant audiences?'

'She has not the strength to do so and even refuses to see her principal colleague, High Steward Sheshonq.'

'Do you consider the Divine Worshipper ... doomed to die?'

'Unfortunately I do. Her exceptional resilience may enable her to survive for a few weeks. If the pain became unbearable, I would be forced to administer powerful drugs that would render her deeply unconscious. And there could be a fatal heart attack. Her death will be an immense loss.'

'We shall all mourn it,' declared Henat, delighted with this excellent news.

Sheshonq had told the truth, and the Divine Worshipper no longer represented the slightest danger.

As he left the house, the doctor felt immense relief. His hands moist, his back soaked with sweat, and terrified by Henat's icy coldness, he had behaved like a tightrope-walker. Managing to control himself, he had followed the directives of his august patient: to persuade this formidable man that she was at the threshold of death, powerless and unable to do anything. He had also confirmed the High Steward's testimony, and dispelled Henat's fears once and for all.

57

For a moment, one brief moment, the leader of the conspirators doubted the success of their plan. The gods seemed to
be protecting a young scribe whom he had selected as an ideal
scapegoat, a priestess destined for the temple and a strolling
actor who lived for pleasure. A strange trio, who should have
been wholly incapable of escaping from the forces of order.
And yet they were continuing their mad adventure, playing
with their pursuers and with every twist of fate.

This insolent good luck would not last. Kel, Nitis and
Bebon were doomed, and their illusory successes would end in
nothingness. They would never decipher the coded papyrus,
and when they discovered the truth it would be too late, much
too late.

Should the conspiracy be abandoned? No, that was out
of the question, for no alternative existed. The end was
approaching, and some of the consequences would be cruel;
it was impossible to avoid them. The conspirators' leader
regretted nothing. The implementation of the initial decision,
taken a long time ago, had demanded patience and skill. And
acquiring allies one by one had been perilous.

Now there was only a little more of the road to travel, but
the leader of the conspiracy could not control the unfolding
of the final events. However, there was no cause for anxiety.
The road was entirely traced out, and presented no pitfalls.

The deaths of innocent people? Inevitable. It was no use Kel struggling; he would come up against unscaleable walls and would lose his head as a result.

Bebon vomited vast amounts of water. Astonished to be still alive, he felt his arms, legs and head. The boat had sunk, but he was in one piece!

Standing up, he found that he was on a bank of the Nile with a thick covering of reeds. A shoebill was perched on the top of one, watching him.

'Nitis! Kel! Where are you?'

The shoebill flew away.

Still shaky on his feet, Bebon forced his way through the dense reeds. He relived the terrifying storm, felt the wind's wild breath, tried to hold on to the boat's hand-rail. The boat was travelling at incredible speed, leaping from wavetop to wavetop. At that speed, wouldn't it go beyond Thebes?

North Wind's back was to the mast. He was managing to keep his balance, and defying the heavens. He was the captain of this lost vessel, the only one capable of fending off disaster. Kel and Nitis were huddled together in the cabin, Kel desperately trying to protect his wife and prevent her from being injured.

Hours elapsed; the night seemed never-ending.

A monstrous wave lifted the boat and hurled it towards the bank. Bebon closed his eyes, convinced that he would never open them again.

But he had, and now he was walking once more, searching for his companions as he called to them in vain.

Dizziness overwhelmed him and he sat down. So he was the only survivor . . . This was horrible! Life, this life which he had loved so much, now seemed insipid and cruel. Resuming his life as an actor would be unbearable.

Overcoming his tiredness, Bebon stood up and headed for the river. Hapy, the spirit of the flood, would bring him peace.

'Where are you going, Bebon?' murmured a familiar voice. 'Haven't you had enough water already?'

'Kel! Are you hurt?'

The scribe was covered in so much mud that he was unrecognizable.

'Just scratches.'

'And Nitis?'

'She's washing. Her tunic is in tatters.'

'What about North Wind?

'Only some cuts and bruises. He's asleep.'

'You know, eventually I'm going to end up believing that the gods really are protecting us. Surviving a storm like that, then finding each other again, alive ... I must be dreaming.'

The two friends embraced.

Then they joined Nitis, who was gently stroking North Wind.

'The storm of Set spared us because of your presence,' she told him gratefully. 'Without you, we would have died.'

'Judge Gem should believe we're dead,' said Kel hopefully, 'and stop pursuing us.'

'I'm going to try and find out where we are,' said Bebon. 'Don't move from here; the reeds will hide you.'

The Nile had swallowed up the Bow of Neith, the obsidian amulet depicting the two fingers separating the sky and the earth, the bag of precious stones and the Greek knife. At Nitis's feet lay the fragments of the Answerer statuette. By transporting them safe and sound to the river's eastern bank, it had fulfilled its role.

While they waited, Kel and Nitis each traced the signs from the coded papyrus in the sand. Their memories did not fail them, but the text remained incomprehensible.

North Wind woke and pricked his ears. A boat was coming.

'Fishermen,' said Kel, 'and Bebon's with them.'

He parted the reeds, and the boat grounded beside him.

'These good people have offered us their hospitality,' said the actor.

'We can't pay them anything.'

'They have just had a good catch and are happy to invite some poor travellers to share their meal. I explained to them that our trading-boat was shipwrecked and that we lost everything.'

'Here, near Thebes, the storm wasn't very violent,' said the head fisherman. 'Let's go to our hut. We'll make a fire and grill the fish.'

North Wind got to his feet stiffly and painfully.

'Do you have any fabric that my companion could use?' asked Kel. 'Her tunic was torn.'

The head fisherman cut a piece from a cloth meant for repairing his sail. Despite this makeshift garment, Nitis's beauty dazzled the fishermen.

'What were you transporting?' asked one of them.

'Jars of wine,' replied Bebon.

'Ordered by the High Steward of the Divine Worshipper, no doubt?'

'No, we were going to Elephantine, without stopping off at Thebes.'

The fishermen's hut stood on a rise overlooking the Nile, which was now calm. The fishermen laid down their spears and baskets, made a fire and passed round some rustic beer.

'You've come a long way,' observed the head fisherman. 'When the river's angry, it doesn't usually give back its prey.'

'We were lucky,' said Bebon. 'The sight of your fish is making me ravenous!'

Three large fish were grilled: a mullet, a mormyr and a Nile perch. The perch was over two cubits long, with a silvery-white belly and flanks, and an olive-brown back.

Sitting leaning against Kel, Nitis whispered a few words in his ear. When the portions were handed out, he discreetly stopped Bebon eating any of it. The fishermen, though, enjoyed its firm and tasty flesh.

'You must tell your story to the river-guards,' said the head fisherman. 'That will prevent them searching for you in vain. We can take you to their nearest post.'

'There's no need,' Bebon assured him. 'Just show us the way, and we'll get by.'

The head fisherman seized his spear. 'The way will be a very short one, my friend. We are river-guards.'

58

The soldiers delegated by Judge Gem to intercept suspects formed a circle round their prisoners and threatened them with their spears.

Unarmed, Kel and Bebon were powerless. Exhausted and in pain, North Wind did not feel able to fight.

'Who are you?' demanded the leader of the raiding-party.

'Traders,' replied the scribe.

'The judge is searching for a murderer whose description corresponds to you, a very beautiful young woman who is a priestess in Sais, and their accomplice, a strolling actor. A witness saw them disappear on a boat belonging to the traitor Pefy – at least he's stopped conspiring.'

'What happened to him?' Kel asked.

'The commander of the Abydos garrison killed him because he refused to surrender.'

'Pefy was loyal to the king,' protested Nitis.

The soldier smiled. 'So his fate interests you, does it? According to our information, that corrupt minister knew your family well and had no difficulty recruiting you. Your escapades end here, my friends. We're going to hand you over to the judge, you'll be sentenced to death, and we'll be handsomely rewarded.'

'I don't think so,' said Nitis serenely.

The soldier tightened his grip on the handle of his spear.

This particularly dangerous trio was said to be almost in-vulnerable, but clearly that was just a stupid rumour. This time the criminals would not escape. Unable to fight, they would have to give up.

'I am a priestess of Neith,' confirmed the young woman, 'and my spiritual master taught me to decipher signs and symbols. No one can oppose the word of the gods, and they have decided that you will fail.'

'Are you hoping to defeat us by using magic spells?'

'I don't need to.'

Ready to use their spears, the mercenaries exchanged worried looks.

'Follow us and stay calm,' ordered the officer.

'You have made a fatal mistake,' said Nitis, 'and even the most skilled healer could not save you.'

'A healer? What are you talking about?'

'Eating Nile perch, the incarnation of Neith, in the presence of one of her priestesses, is an unforgivable sin. By breaking this taboo, you have poisoned yourselves. Your blood is darkening, obstructing your lungs and paralysing your limbs. Can you not feel your strength ebbing away?'

Feeling ill, one of the soldiers dropped his spear and fell to his knees.

'Pull yourself together!' commanded the officer. 'This sorceress is simply trying to frighten us.'

A second Greek collapsed.

'Stop behaving like women!'

When the third collapsed, the officer broke out in an unhealthy sweat and his vision began to blur. Brandishing his spear, he tried to stab Nitis, but Kel leapt forward, blocked the blow and easily disarmed him.

Bebon did not need to move. All the soldiers lay lifeless on the ground.

'If I'd eaten any of that fish . . .' said Bebon.

'I stopped you,' Kel reminded him.

'It looked so delicious that it almost drove me mad.'

'We must go,' said Nitis.

'Let's use these soldiers' boat,' suggested Bebon. 'The way we look, the river-guards won't trouble us! A family of poor fisherfolk is no threat to state security.'

'Access to Thebes must be strictly controlled,' Kel pointed out.

'We'll land to the north of the city, away from prying eyes.'

'And then?'

'We'll improvise. Are you giving up, so close to the goal?'

The quartet left the sinister encampment and returned to the riverbank. Hesitantly, North Wind consented to step down into the boat. Bebon took the oars and, after a long period in the hot sun, passed them over to Kel.

A river-guard boat hove into view, with two archers at its prow. As they passed, they cast a contemptuous glance at the boat's miserably clad passengers.

'Good fishing?' called one.

'Not very. We're going home,' shouted Bebon.

Kel speeded up. Other boats slid past on the Nile, and heavy trading-vessels sailed along in the middle of the river.

'Stop here,' advised Bebon.

The boat bumped gently against the bank.

North Wind was happy to be back on dry land again, and Nitis gazed for a long time at a tall acacia-tree, almost identical to the largest sacred tree at the temple in Sais, which blossomed on the twenty-third day of the first month of the flood.

'We must meditate,' said Nitis. 'We are in the presence of a shrine of Neith.'

The actor did not disagree with the priestess, who spoke the words of veneration. The sun lit up the acacia's delicate leaves, which shone with new-born brilliance. An ibis comata, the incarnation of the radiant spirit, flew off towards the heavens.

'I know a path which leads to the outskirts of Thebes,' said

Bebon, 'but it will be watched. And we haven't anything with which to buy decent clothes and food.'

'Let's climb up the bank,' suggested Nitis.

At the edge of the path they found two baskets full of fish, and a strap.

'The goddess is continuing to help us,' said the priestess. 'Bebon, use a dead branch as a staff and pretend to be a poor fellow with a painful back. I'll follow you at a distance with North Wind. He'll carry the baskets, and I'll say I'm a fish-wife. The guards will let us pass, and I'll sell the fish in the market and buy clothing and sandals. You, Kel, mix with a group of farm workers going to an open-air inn. Joke, talk, and don't show the slightest sign of nerves. We'll meet at the way out of the market, on the city side.'

Bebon was amazed. 'You know this area?'

'I am discovering it. The words of Neith's acacia-tree were clear and specific; we must follow its recommendations.'

For his part, the actor hadn't heard a thing.

Kel was not happy about being separated from Nitis.

'If we respect the goddess's instructions,' she said, 'we'll overcome this new obstacle.'

Bebon cast a sidelong look at the talking tree. The plan it had set out was very risky, but he didn't have a better one.

59

High Steward Sheshonq, who had a keen interest in ancient writings, inspected his huge house of eternity on the west bank of Thebes.* The columns of hieroglyphs were inspired by the *Pyramid Texts*, telling of the soul's incessant transformations in the celestial spaces, and the eternal journey of the radiant spirit. Throughout his long career, Sheshonq had benefited from the teaching of the Divine Worshipper. Initiated into the divine Mysteries, he directed a college of theologians who scrutinized the Tradition and provided artists, painters and sculptors with the themes they were to use when decorating tombs.

The house of death was, in reality, a house of life. Human existence was a simple and rapid transit, with no meaning except in terms of the afterlife. Sheshonq liked to meditate here. Deep within the apparent silence of the walls covered with ritual scenes, the gods were speaking. And nothing was more vital than to hear their voices.

'You are needed urgently, High Steward,' he was informed by his secretary, embarrassed at disturbing his superior's reflections.

'Is it really urgent?'

'I fear so.'

* Tomb number 27.

With regret, Sheshonq tore himself away from the tranquillity of his house of eternity.

The Scribe of the Treasury was waiting for him at the door of the tomb, visibly annoyed. 'High Steward, this situation is intolerable! I beg you to act without delay and in a decisive manner.'

'Before doing so, may I have an explanation of what has happened?'

'The Scribe of the Flocks was supposed to deliver three fat oxen and five geese to me this morning. And what came? One ox and two geese, without a word of explanation or apology. As for the Scribe of the Granaries, he has summarily reduced supplies to the bakery in Karnak. In other words, it will not produce enough bread for everyone who works there. They deserve a good beating. In your place, I would replace them immediately with competent administrators.'

'I shall deal with these problems,' promised Sheshonq.

'With severity, High Steward. Otherwise, chaos will ensue.'

Sheshonq had often heard this speech. The Scribe of the Treasury was meticulous in the extreme and constantly complained about his colleagues, accusing them of unforgivable errors even before the errors had been committed. The Scribe of the Fields drank too much, the Scribe of the Granaries was distracted by family quarrels, the Scribe of the Flocks wasted hours chatting, and the Scribe of the Boats had difficulty in distinguishing what was important from what was not.

Sheshonq spent a large part of his time correcting their mistakes and resolving conflicts. Nevertheless, his subordinates loved their work and never counted the hours they spent doing it. At the weekly meeting, the High Steward managed to smooth over resentments, to everyone's benefit. He knew the importance of listening to both sides of an argument, and never gave anyone preferential treatment. Knowing his integrity and impartiality, the scribes regarded him with respect and trust.

Just like previous days, this one promised to be long and

busy. Passing from office to office, Sheshonq would soothe tempers and re-establish harmony. The temple would continue to function despite human weaknesses, and the service of the gods would be ensured.

In addition to this usual work there was the delicate task of dealing with Henat. According to the Divine Worshipper's physician, he had taken the bait, but he was a cunning and suspicious man, who might only be pretending to believe this decisive testimony.

Sheshonq went to Henat's house, whose entrance was strictly guarded. He congratulated the officials on their alertness and had Henat informed of his visit.

The house was charming. The wall-paintings depicted beds of cornflowers with larks soaring overhead and, while gazing at these delicate masterpieces, it was easy to forget the difficulties of the outside world.

Henat soon appeared. 'Has the Divine Worshipper replied to my request, High Steward?'

'Unfortunately not – she has not answered mine, either. In the absence of firm instructions, I must calm the tensions between the scribes who head the various sections of the government. It is a real headache!'

Henat suppressed a smile. This admission corresponded to the report from the head of his network. The High Steward was helpless, and restricted himself to expediting current matters while he waited for the death of the old priestess, who no longer granted any audiences, even to Sheshonq.

'I am very sorry to speak of this sad eventuality, but . . . how will the succession be handled?'

'The Divine Worshipper chooses a spiritual daughter, whom she links with the throne in order to train her. On the death of the mother, the daughter ensures that all the proper ritual duties are carried out.'

'Has this choice been made?'

'Not officially. However, Her Majesty has never concealed

her intentions. She wishes to adopt a young priestess, Nitocris, who is a keen student of sacred lore.'

It was obvious, thought Henat, that the honest steward was keeping nothing back. In fact, Henat had already learnt all this from his head informant. Shy and reserved, young Nitocris lived as a recluse in Karnak and would never attain a degree of radiance comparable to that of the current Divine Worshipper.

When he thought of Kel, Henat felt like laughing. So much effort and so many risks, and all in vain! Even if he had succeeded in meeting the Divine Worshipper, he would merely have seen a woman on her deathbed, incapable of helping him.

'I have arranged a banquet in your honour,' Sheshonq said happily. 'The officials from the temples on the west bank will be there, and they are delighted at the prospect of meeting you.'

'I am sorry to disappoint them, but I shall not be present at these joyful celebrations.'

The High Steward looked devastated. 'Have I offended you in some way? Have I committed a serious error, have I—'

'Don't worry, High Steward. You are in no way at fault, and I thank you for your perfect welcome to Thebes. Moreover, I shall tell the king about it and I hope to see you confirmed in your office. The new Divine Worshipper will have great need of your experience. Continue to run this beautiful Theban province exceedingly well.'

'I shall try,' Sheshonq assured him, 'but your refusal . . .'

'There is a simple explanation: I am returning to Sais. This has been a delightful stay, and I have greatly appreciated your hospitality. Since I do not wish to force the door of a dying woman, I prefer to return to my office, where numerous matters await me.'

'Perhaps I could try one more time . . .'

'Pointless, cut in Henat. Please inform me of the date of

the burial ceremonies. A representative of the king will be in attendance.'

'I hardly dare ask a favour of you . . .'

'Dare, High Steward.'

'Would you give the king an assurance of my absolute loyalty?'

'I shall not fail to do so.'

Sheshonq, the true head of the Theban province, thought Henat, bowed the knee with the suppleness of a reed. What a satisfactory and reassuring outcome! There was only one drawback: the skilful courtier was hoping for a promotion which he would not obtain. At the court in Sais, he would not be of any use. Here, he controlled the situation to Ahmose's benefit.

'Will Thebes have the pleasure of seeing you again?' asked the High Steward.

'That is for the gods to decide,' replied Henat.

Sheshonq himself undertook to facilitate Henat's departure. And when he saw him leaving the Karnak port, he congratulated himself on having successfully implemented the plan devised by the Divine Worshipper.

60

As it emerged from the canal leading to the landing stage of the temple in Karnak, Henat's boat encountered another, laden with guards and soldiers. On deck, seated under a sunshade, was Judge Gem! As the two vessels slipped past each other, Henat called out to him.

A skilful manoeuvre brought the boats alongside, and the two men withdrew into Gem's cabin.

'Are you leaving Thebes, Henat?'

'Indeed so.'

'Has the Divine Worshipper assured you of her perfect cooperation?'

'I didn't see her.'

'Is this some kind of joke?'

'I am certain that she is gravely ill and will not live long. She does not even receive her High Steward and will offer no help to anyone, so I am returning to Sais. And you should do likewise.'

'It is not for you to dictate what I should do, Henat. I shall conduct my investigation as I please.'

'An investigation which is dragging on for ever!'

'You think so?'

The judge's ironic smile made Henat curious. 'Don't forget your obligations, Gem,' he said. 'You must pass on to me all the information you acquire.'

'Your obligations are the same, are they not? But I do not have the feeling that you are respecting them.'

'Your feelings do not interest me.'

'On the other hand, one of the major facts relating to my investigation should interest you greatly.'

Henat was in a position of weakness. And since the judge was hoping to savour a partial triumph, he granted him that pleasure. 'Will you reveal it to me?'

'Like for like. What did you find out in Thebes about Kel and his accomplices?'

'Absolutely nothing.'

'Do you expect me to believe that?'

'If the murderer had been spotted, my informants would have informed me.'

The judge seemed convinced. 'I have decapitated the conspiracy,' he revealed.

'You have arrested Kel?'

'His leader is dead.'

'His leader . . .?'

'The finance minister, the traitor Pefy. He was sheltering his accomplices in his house in Abydos and enabled them to get away. The commander of the Greek soldiers ran him through with his spear – he acted without orders, so he will be punished.'

This matter-of-fact statement of the facts astonished Henat.

'I have informed His Majesty,' added the judge, 'so he knows that my investigation has taken a decisive step forward. Pefy wanted to take power by using the services of a band of criminals led by Kel.'

'Is Kel still alive?'

'Probably not. A storm seems to have led to his death and those of his main accomplices, Nitis and Bebon. All the sailors I questioned said they must have drowned – though I have not found the bodies.'

'The crocodiles and other fish will have eaten them.'

'Possibly.'

'Do you still harbour doubts?'

'I would have preferred to see the bodies.'

'Perfectionism is not necessarily a virtue, Judge Gem.'

'Do you think you can teach me my job?'

'Instead of wasting your time looking for dead people, go back to Sais.'

'I have not yet concluded my investigation. I and I alone will decide when the time is right.'

'Thebes is a most agreeable city, and High Steward Sheshonq is a notable host. You are sure to enjoy some delightful moments of relaxation.'

'I intend to work, not doze. And I hope that I shall have the assistance of your agents.'

'That is for the king to decide.'

'He will reply favourably to my written request,' said the magistrate. 'Help me to gain time.'

Henat considered this. 'Go to Ramses' temple of a million years and – using my name – contact the man who produces the best-quality papyrus. He is the head of my Theban network.' The judge would be disappointed, for Henat's man would have no vital information to give him.

'Thank you for your cooperation.'

'The Kel affair is ending for the best, don't you think? We're rid of that criminal and his allies. You have avoided a trial which would have ended in the death penalty. A great success, Judge Gem. The king will be well pleased with what you have done, and you certainly deserve a few days' rest in Thebes.'

'I have absolutely no need of rest, and I must remind you that I am planning to conclude my investigation here.'

'By arresting ghosts? Enjoy the benefits of life for once.'

'That is hardly your philosophy, or so I imagine.'

'The charm of Thebes will surprise you. Don't forget to come back to Sais.'

'Have a good journey, Henat.'

The two boats parted, and the judge's headed for the quay at Karnak. The official in charge of the temple's security greeted the judge with deference.

'Your official accommodation is ready, Judge,' he said. 'The High Steward asks you to excuse him, as he cannot meet you until tomorrow because of an administrative emergency.'

The detached house formerly occupied by Henat had been cleaned, and a swarm of servants were preparing to satisfy the judge's every desire.

'This place does not suit me. Find me a building in the city centre. I need at least ten offices for my colleagues, a room for meetings and quarters for the river-guards – two other boats will be arriving shortly, and I shall station my men on both banks.'

'I must consult the High Steward, and—'

'That is an order,' barked Gem. 'His opinion will change nothing. I shall spend only one night in this house.'

A plump-cheeked cook introduced himself. 'Dinner will comprise two main courses, of—'

'Cancel it. I shall make do with a bowl of bean broth.'

'As regards wine, I suggest—'

'Bring me water.'

Indifferent to the villa's elegant interior, the judge sat down outside, in the shade of a sycamore tree, and yet again read Kel's file. Should he close it once and for all?

A guards officer came to report. 'News of the men posing as fishermen, Judge – bad news, I'm afraid.'

'Were they attacked?'

'Apparently not. They were found dead at their camp.'

'What was the cause of death?'

'According to an army doctor, food poisoning. It seems they ate poisoned fish.'

What a strange affair. Could Nitis have used a drug? And Kel, of course, had poisoned his colleagues at the Interpreters' Secretariat . . . The judge did not close the file.

61

Favourite,* the Divine Worshipper's dog, demanded to be stroked. Immediately Juggler, the little green monkey, nipped his tail, signalling that playtime had begun. These two faithful companions brought great joy to the heart of the Divine Worshipper.† Dedicated to the cult of Amun, her divine husband, she had no children. Her symbolic marriage guaranteed the continuance of creation and drove back chaos. The earthly representative of the primordial feminine principle, mother of all living beings, the Divine Worshipper had shared the secret of Amun at her coronation, and thanks to the daily practice of the rites, their communion could not be damaged.

'Love's Sweetness', 'Mistress of Charm', 'Rich in Favours', 'Regent of All Women', the queen governed the cosmos and the entire earth. Filling the temple's rooms with her fragrance, she had an enchanting voice and played celestial music.

* *Hesyf-Ma'aty*, 'Her Favourite [or: the One Whom She Praises] in Righteousness'.
† Her name was Ankh-nes-nefer-ib-Ra, 'May the King Live for Her [or: Life Belongs to Her], the Heart of the Divine Light [Ra] is in Perfection', Heqat-neferu-merit-Mut, 'Regent of Perfection, Beloved of Mut (the divine wife of Amun, whose name means both 'Mother' and 'Death'). As with the pharaohs, these names were written inside a cartouche. This outstanding woman occupied the highest sacred office in Thebes for some sixty years.

As was done every day, she was purified and dressed in a long tunic, cinched at the waist by a belt. A priest tied a red band of fabric about her brow; at the back, it held a knot from which two fabric strips emerged and floated about her shoulders.

Despite her great age, the Divine Worshipper was in excellent health and endowed with inexhaustible energy. Communing with the gods wiped away the years, and the priestess's beauty and majestic bearing remained untouched. She felt no nostalgia for her youth, and thanked Amun for granting her so much happiness.

'No curious eyes?'

'Majesty, the temple is completely sealed.'

The Divine Worshipper went to the Akh-menu, the 'Most Radiant of Monuments', the temple built by Tuthmosis III and designed for the initiation of the High Priests of Karnak. Here, the great Mysteries of death, resurrection and enlightenment had been revealed to her.

She halted before a cube-shaped statue representing the great sage Amenhotep, son of Hapu, reading a papyrus which lay unrolled across his knees. Endowed with supernatural life, it had to be purified so that no infection could sully the granite. So the Divine Worshipper anointed it with water from the sacred lake, the earthly reflection of the primordial ocean.

Then a priest handed her a torch and opened up the way to a brazier. Another ritual priest handed her a skewer. At its end was the wax figurine of a rebel, its head cut off and hands tied behind its back. The Divine Worshipper cast it into the fire. The sounds that came forth were like the moans of a man being tortured.

Once the enemy had been burnt, she drew her bow and mimed firing an arrow towards the four points of the compass. This rite shattered the forces of evil, preventing them from darkening the skies and obscuring the radiance of the gods.

The journey of those she was awaiting was at last coming

to an end. After surviving many ordeals, they had reached Theban territory. However, a number of dangers still remained, and it was by no means certain that their mission would succeed.

The flame went out.

Slowly, the Divine Worshipper walked towards the two shrines dedicated to Osiris which she had had built along the route to the Temple of Ptah. Following a little paved pathway, she entered the shrine of Osiris, Neb djefau, 'the Master of Foods'.

Associated with the festival of the royal soul's regeneration, the god offered him spiritual and material nourishment. So one saw depictions of Pharaoh Ahmose, followed by his *ka*, his creative power, and wooden structures built at the time of the ceremony. The king was offering wine to Amun-Ra, accompanied by Maat, and the god was handing the Divine Worshipper the sistra, whose vibrations dispelled malevolent forces. Snakes spitting fire hid these mysteries from outsiders, who were torn to pieces by terrifying guards who had the heads of crocodiles or wild beasts, and who were armed with knives.

At the heart of the shrine the coronation of Osiris took place, according to the Abydos rites. The Divine Worshipper came often to experience them in her mind, preparing herself to pass through the gates of the invisible world.

Her High Steward, friend and confidant Sheshonq was clearly a part of what she did, since he featured on one of the walls of this temple.

He was waiting for her there, away from prying eyes.

'Majesty, Henat has left Thebes, believing that your end is near. As he no longer regarded you as a danger, he decided to return to Sais.'

'But his spy network remains in place.'

'It does not worry me greatly, for I know all its members. Their leader is not very active, and should not cause us any serious problems. On the other hand, I am concerned about the arrival of Judge Gem and a host of river-guards. When we meet, I shall try to find out his plan of action.'

'Be extremely careful. The judge is obstinate and meticulous, and he will not relax his efforts. Now, the travellers we have been hoping for are drawing near.'

'Then they are still alive!'

'The gods have protected them. But the final stage will be difficult and perilous; one false step will sentence them to death.'

'If he believes you are dying, will Judge Gem not decide against pursuing his investigations?'

'He is obsessed with arresting Kel, and nobody can persuade him to give up.'

'I was hoping for some respite after Henat's departure,' sighed the High Steward. 'But we should perhaps prepare ourselves for worse. Contacting Kel and his friends will be particularly difficult.'

'You have solved many insoluble problems before, Sheshonq.'

'Your Majesty's trust honours me, but I have never come up against the guards or King Ahmose's legal system.'

'You have a priceless asset: experience. When faced with brutality, you can employ cunning.'

'But will Judge Gem give me a chance to do so? He is sure to set traps, and Kel is at risk of falling into them.'

'Try to thwart them and open up the path to Karnak. We can still save Egypt.'

Sheshonq bowed. 'I shall do the impossible, Majesty.'

The Divine Worshipper's faint smile was more than reward enough for the High Steward. He admired her innate nobility, her exemplary dignity and her unequalled radiance. To serve her and save her from disappointment, he would give his life.

62

After playing the invalid for so long, Bebon had ended up with a painful back. Leaning heavily on his staff, he did not look much like a dangerous malefactor on the run. Yet he was stopped at one of the checkpoints controlling access to Thebes.

'Where are you going, my fine fellow?'

'To see the healer in the northern district.'

'Are you a peasant?'

'A ploughman. I have a bad back, and I can't work.'

'The healer has good hands; he'll soon cure you.'

Taking care to limp, Bebon went to the fish market, which occupied a large part of the quay. Before long he spotted Nitis, who was selling the last of her superb fish to appreciative customers prepared to pay top prices. They paid with tunics, sandals, foodstuffs, some small vases which would be easy to trade: the bartering was a great success.

'Have you seen Kel?' Nitis asked.

'Unfortunately not. But he'll get past the blockade, I'm sure. The guards are mainly interested in couples and scribes.'

Nitis filled the baskets with her acquisitions. North Wind stood up and consented to carry them. Bebon followed them to the exit from the market, on the city side. A patrol passed them but paid them no attention.

'I'll wait here,' said Bebon. 'Try to rent a place where we can get changed.'

The northern district of the city of Amun was bustling with activity, because of the number of storehouses taking in goods. People talked loudly, traded, loaded up their donkeys and planned deliveries.

Time passed. Bebon started to worry.

A group of peasants approached, led by two oafs who were glad to be in the city. At the rear was Kel!

Bebon signalled to him, and he left the group. The friends leant against a wall in the corner of an alleyway. A short time later, Nitis came to fetch them and took them to the ground floor of a three-storey house. The building was being restored, and was being used for storage.

'It's not what you'd call a palace,' said Bebon, 'but here we are in Thebes! I can't quite believe it.'

'This city may be our tomb,' said Kel. 'How are we going to get to see the Divine Worshipper?'

'Her right-hand man, High Steward Sheshonq, seems more accessible. He's the most important man in Thebes, because he runs all the government departments and maintains the province's prosperity.'

'What if he turns out to be hostile?'

Bebon's face fell. 'Then we'll have to run for our lives.'

'We haven't reached that stage yet,' said Nitis. 'And we all need some sleep.'

Judge Gem took possession of his new quarters. He inspected each office and divided up his assistants throughout the requisitioned building. His secretary arranged the papyri and wooden tablets on shelves and set out the furniture as the judge liked it. Delivery-men brought all the materials they needed, notably ink, styli, brushes, gum, palettes, wiping-cloths and a large number of baskets.

In a few hours, the command centre would come to life. Opposite, several houses had been emptied of their tenants, who had been rehoused elsewhere, and reserved for the guards and soldiers who had just arrived in Thebes.

The judge sensed that the last phase of his investigation would be played out here. Kel and his accomplices had eliminated the 'fishermen', avoided the blockades and reached their destination. But they had still to get through the gates of Karnak. And this insane course of action would have served only to bring them into contact with a dying woman who was incapable of helping them.

Was the Divine Worshipper really dying? Ordinarily, it was impossible to deceive Henat, who, by returning to Sais, had declared his certainty that she was. And if Bebon was working for him, wouldn't he soon hand over his 'friend' Kel to justice?

The arrival of the High Steward interrupted the judge's thoughts. This imposing, plump and kindly individual exasperated the judge at first sight.

'I had given up hope of meeting you,' said Gem dryly.

'Vital government matters prevented me from welcoming you, and I beg you to forgive me. This large province is not easy to run, I can tell you.'

'Everyone has his problems.'

'Are you comfortably settled in?'

'This will suffice.'

'Would you not prefer a quiet house surrounded by a garden, so that you can rest more easily?'

'I have no intention of resting. I am here to arrest a vicious criminal and his associates.'

'I heard that they had all drowned,' said Sheshonq in surprise.

'Do not trust rumours.'

'Are the people of Thebes in danger?'

'I shall ensure their safety and I am relying on their co-operation, starting with your own.'

'You have it without reservation, Judge Gem.'

'Provide me with a detailed map of the city and the province, and put your security forces on alert.'

'Oh! There are not very many of them, and they only protect the temple of Karnak.'

'From now on, they will obey my orders.'

'I ought to refer this to the Divine Worshipper, but . . .'

'What is preventing you from doing so?'

Sheshonq had difficulty getting the words out. 'It is a sort of state secret, and—'

'I represent the pharaoh, and I demand to know everything. Moreover, I was planning to meet the Divine Worshipper first thing tomorrow and explain my intentions to her.'

'Unfortunately that will not be possible,' murmured Sheshonq sadly. 'Her state of health prevents her from receiving anyone, myself included. The people do not know of this tragedy, and I am at a loss to know what to do.'

'Continue to keep silent and perform your duties.'

'This evening you are invited to a great banquet in your honour. Our cooks—'

'This evening there will be a meeting of army and guards officers. I consider your presence vital.'

A large map of the Theban province had been laid out across several low tables pushed together. Thanks to the accurate work of the land-registry scribes, Judge Gem was able to obtain a good idea of the city and its surrounding districts.

The sheer size of the territory to be searched was discouraging. Kel could be hiding right in the middle of the city, in the country or in a temple which opposed Ahmose's policies.

The first vital move: half the troops would occupy the western bank, the other half the eastern. The entrance to the Valley of the Kings would be blocked, and access to the temples granted only to ritual priests.

Patrols would stop and question passers-by and traders at random, and many guard-posts would be set up near the official buildings; both land and river patrols would be greatly increased. Finally, a large reward would be offered to anyone who supplied the judge with useful information.

Sheshonq said nothing but he was worried. The scribe and his friends could not escape this net, and they would never meet the Divine Worshipper.

63

Dressed in a gaudy Asian tunic and luxury sandals, his hair held back by a multi-coloured band, Bebon looked every inch the Syrian merchant on the hunt for good business deals. Striding around the main markets, he was talkative and charming.

'The number of guards and soldiers here is astonishing,' he confided to a fabric trader. 'Last time I stayed in Thebes I didn't see nearly so many.'

'Exceptional circumstances require exceptional measures. Haven't you heard about the band of assassins led by a scribe?'

'Some vague rumours, yes.'

'Those wicked criminals are supposedly hiding here, in Thebes, and that's why Judge Gem has deployed so many men. Both banks of the Nile are subject to strict controls, and those vermin won't slip through the net. At least in Egypt law and order are respected.'

'Yes indeed,' nodded Bebon. 'The sooner this affair ends, the better it will be for trade.'

'Very true. And High Steward Sheshonq, a remarkable man and an outstanding administrator, cannot care much for this intervention by the central government. Thebans are proud of their relative autonomy and are always criticizing Sais's policies, albeit under their breath. Their only ruler is the Divine Worshipper.'

'Actually, I would like to offer the High Steward some high-quality perfumes, for use in the temple at Karnak.'

'You are in luck. Today he's at the mayor's office in Thebes, receiving foreign traders. Hurry up and request an audience.'

'Thank you for your advice.'

Bebon went to collect Kel, who was once more passing as an agricultural worker assisted by his donkey, which was laden with fodder. They were careful to walk slowly, carrying all the misery of the Two Lands on their shoulders.

Soldiers were guarding the entrance to the mayor's office and were searching every visitor.

The arrival of the High Steward, preceded by ten elegantly dressed scribes, did not pass unnoticed.

'When are we going to get rid of these soldiers?' one well-to-do fellow asked him. 'Thebes is a peaceful, free city!'

'It's unavoidable, I'm afraid,' replied Sheshonq. 'But things will soon be resolved.'

He exchanged a few words with the public, then entered the mayoral building, followed by the accredited traders.

As Bebon had no letters of recommendation, he had not put himself forward.

'We mustn't move from here,' he told Kel. 'At some point Sheshonq will have fewer people around him, and you'll be able to speak to him. Be brief and convincing, so as to capture his interest straight away. If he asks for a more detailed explanation, you've won. If not . . .'

A long wait began.

Late in the afternoon, Sheshonq emerged from the mayor's offices. Refusing the travelling-chair carried by bearers, he walked towards the port, still accompanied by scribes and soldiers. He boarded several boats, inspected the cargoes and checked the quality of the products on offer. Bebon was glad he had not tried to bluff his way through.

Discussions ensued with the ship-owners, traders and the

Scribe of the Treasury. Prices, quantities and delivery dates were discussed. Once contracts had been agreed, everyone congratulated everyone else and the High Steward set off again for the centre of the city.

He stayed at the Scribe of the Treasury's office for over an hour, going over the transactions that were under way. When he came out, he accepted the travelling-chair.

He's going home for dinner, thought Bebon dejectedly. Getting inside Sheshonq's vast estate posed serious difficulties. But perhaps, by studying the terrain closely, he could find a way.

The travelling-chair stopped outside an open-air tavern. The High Steward alighted and sat, alone, under a canopy. He clearly felt the need to regain his strength before a probable official banquet. The guards, scribes and bearers kept at a distance, respecting this time of rest.

This was the chance they'd been dreaming of. Bebon winked at Kel, who approached at a measured pace, following North Wind.

Weighing up the situation, the scribe decided what to do. He would take the pathway that ran past the canopy, turn off suddenly to the right, quickly cross the space separating him from the High Steward, and present his request.

Would he find the right words? A thousand and one different forms of words whirled round and round in his head, but he felt they were all dreadful. There was still the simple approach: 'I am Kel the scribe, and I am innocent of the crimes I'm accused of. If you want to save the country from disaster, introduce me to the Divine Worshipper, and I will prove that what I have said is true.'

One chance in a million. The last chance.

Kel would have liked to tell Bebon how touched he was by his courage and friendship. He would probably have to do so in another world.

His friend's gaze encouraged him: all was not yet lost.

Sometimes, a roll of the dice could win a fortune. And the gods would not abandon him at the decisive moment.

Kel advanced. Three more steps, and his fate would hang in the balance.

'Hey, peasant,' bellowed Bebon, 'you could say "Excuse me"!'

Stunned, Kel stopped dead. The guards emerged from their torpor and the High Steward awoke from his half-sleep and beckoned to his bearers.

'Incredible,' shouted Bebon. 'That filthy rogue jostled me and soiled my new tunic! Just look at it! At the very least I demand his donkey in exchange.'

Displaying the soiled hem of his tunic, he called on the guards to be his witnesses.

'Get out of here,' ordered an officer. 'You're giving us a headache.'

'I demand justice!'

'Do you want a taste of my club?'

Bebon recoiled. 'No, oh no!'

'Then go.'

The travelling-chair continued on its way.

Bebon and Kel met again some distance away, far from curious glances.

'Why did you do that?' asked Kel in great surprise.

'It was a trap. The rays of the setting sun created some strange reflections, just behind the canopy: reflections of sword-blades. And one of the soldiers lying in wait stood up too soon. You wouldn't have had time to open your mouth.'

Devastated, Kel came to the inevitable concluson. 'So the High Steward is an ally of Judge Gem! He wanted to lure me to him and deliver the prey to the hunter.'

'We can't rely on him to take us to the Divine Worshipper,' agreed Bebon.

64

'Allow me to express my profound dissatisfaction,' Sheshonq said to Judge Gem, who was busy reading the first reports from the section commanders.

'What about?'

'You used me as a lure without telling me.'

The judge fixed him with a stony gaze. 'I am conducting this investigation, and I do not have to give an account of myself to you.'

'I am the Divine Worshipper's High Steward, and—'

'You are a subject of King Ahmose, and must obey me.'

Sheshonq met the judge's eyes without flinching. 'Your conduct is unacceptable.'

'Do not cross me,' warned the judge. 'I have conducted a long and difficult battle, and now I am on the threshold of victory in this good and welcoming city of Thebes. My duty is to find the worst criminal in Egypt and arrest him. The methods matter little.'

'Even if they are illegal?'

Gem's eyes flamed. 'Confine yourself to following my instructions, High Steward, and do nothing on your own initiative. That will ensure we both have only good memories of our collaboration.'

Sheshonq withdrew. By reprimanding him and treating him with contempt, the judge had just made a mistake. The High

Steward would ensure that everyone knew about the incident, and not one single Theban would help the judge's men.

Gem requisitioned one of the many ferries that shuttled constantly between the two banks. Indifferent to the beauty of the place, he urged the boatman to make haste. At the landing-stage, he checked the security measures before climbing into a travelling-chair, which took him to Ramses II's temple of a million years.

Under the pretext of inspecting the place and satisfying himself that the local administration was functioning properly, he summoned the officials, then spoke to the leader of Henat's network, who specialized in making the highest-quality papyrus.

'I know about your role as an agent,' said the judge.

'I don't understand, I—'

'Lying is futile. Your superior authorizes you to speak.'

'I would have liked a written order.'

'If my word is not enough for you, prison will soon loosen your tongue.'

The informant decided not to argue with the judge. 'I am at your disposal.'

'How did Henat find out for certain that the Divine Worshipper is mortally ill?'

'From her personal doctor. The old lady no longer even receives High Steward Sheshonq.'

'Would Sheshonq have the courage and the opportunity to oppose the actions of the law?'

'Certainly not. He is content to manage the province's affairs, arrange sumptuous banquets and prepare his huge tomb. You have nothing to fear from him. Without directions from the Divine Worshipper, he feels lost. Reassure him by promising that he will retain his privileges, and he will obey you unquestioningly.'

'There is no secret armed force?'

'Absolutely not. And the Karnak guards are hardly great warriors.'

'Alert your men. Kel the scribe, Nitis the priestess and Bebon the actor are hiding in Thebes. Gather all information, even rumours, and inform me immediately.'

'Understood.'

The head informant decided he would not run any risks, and would produce anodyne reports for the judge. Those criminals sounded far too dangerous to take on. And if he did uncover a serious lead, he would tell no one but Henat.

Nitis, Kel and Bebon were under no illusions: the alliance between the High Steward and Judge Gem was a disaster.

'To fail when we're so close to our goal!' lamented Bebon.

'We mustn't give up,' said Nitis.

'Gem and Sheshonq are sealing up the whole province. Let's leave while there's still time.'

'And go where?' Kel asked. 'Only the Divine Worshipper can help us reveal the truth.'

'But she lives in Karnak, and we can't get in there because of the security measures.'

'Priests and craftsmen enter and leave every day,' Nitis pointed out.

'They are strictly checked,' said Bebon, 'and getting through that first blockade is no guarantee of success. The Divine Worshipper's house must be inaccessible.'

'Haven't you acted in the Mysteries at Karnak?' asked Kel.

Bebon looked embarrassed. 'The sovereign of the temple doesn't enjoy those kinds of entertainments. She prefers her permanent ritual priests to temporary guests.'

'Knowing you, you must have forged some friendships.'

'Not many. Thebes is less welcoming than it appears, and I don't know anybody important.'

'Not a single temple employee?' Nitis persisted.

'Only indirectly.'

'Then that might be a solution.'

'I doubt it. The real solution is to get out of this province and find a safe refuge a long way from Judge Gem.'

'We must all try our luck,' said Nitis. 'One of us will succeed in seeing the Divine Worshipper.'

'Impossible,' declared Bebon.

'Your indirect contact,' said the scribe, 'who is it with?'

'A decent fellow, but with no influence.'

'What's his job?'

'He's a door-keeper.'

'And who's his employer?'

'The Scribe of the Treasury.'

'You know the Scribe of the Treasury's door-keeper, and you didn't say so!'

'I forgot.'

'And whom does he know in Karnak?'

'The head gardener.'

'Wonderful! Go and see this doorkeeper, and ask for his help.'

'It's too risky. I won't do it.'

Nitis was astonished. 'You won't, Bebon? You disappoint me.'

The detached house belonging to the Scribe of the Treasury occupied a large area and was surrounded by a wall. There was only one door in the wall, and this was guarded all day by an experienced man who took pride in his work. Armed with a broom made from palm fibres, he made it a point of honour to keep the area around the door absolutely clean.

Every morning, the steward handed him a list of visitors and delivery-men. The door-keeper checked them against the list, asked them to wait and informed the steward of their presence. He was ruthless, and invariably sent away beggars and other unwanted callers.

Today, as he was about to start sweeping, he thought he

was suffering from hallucinations. 'Bebon! Is it you? Is it really you?'

'Er, yes, I'm back. And I need a small favour from you.'

The door-keeper stood stock still for a long time. Then he raised his broom furiously. 'You scoundrel! I'm going to knock your head off your shoulders!'

65

Protecting his head with both hands, Bebon tried in vain to dodge the blows from the broom.

'Stop, please!' cried Nitis.

Surprised by the young woman's intervention, the door-keeper stopped his flurry of blows. 'Are you his new mistress?'

'No, just his friend.'

'That surprises me! This debauched scoundrel gets all his lady-friends into his bed.'

'I have escaped that sad fate.'

'If you're telling the truth, thank the gods and run away.'

'Why were you hitting him?'

'Because he seduced and abandoned my little Daybreak, a pure and innocent young girl.'

'Don't exaggerate,' the actor corrected him. 'First of all, I wasn't her first lover; second, I didn't force myself on her.'

The door-keeper brandished his broom again. 'And I suppose you didn't shamefully leave her, either?'

Bebon protested. 'I did warn her that we'd have fun for a while, and then I'd have to leave. She didn't die of a broken heart, did she?'

The broom was lowered. 'No, not quite. The temple gave her a job as a bee-keeper at the edge of the desert.'

'As a doctor,' said Nitis, 'I use a lot of honey. I should like to meet your daughter and talk to her about her work.'

Favourably impressed, the door-keeper grew calmer and gave her the necessary directions to reach the hives.

Then, resuming his angry tone, he turned to Bebon. 'What is this favour you want?'

'I'd like to help a friend, a gardener who's looking for work. Will you see him?'

'Is he a debauched scoundrel like you?'

'Absolutely not!' Bebon exclaimed. 'More the serious type.'

'Bring him to me.'

The actor went and fetched Kel, whom the door-keeper looked over from head to foot.

'At least you're presentable,' he decided. 'Do you have experience, my boy?'

'I worked hard at my parents' house.'

'My friend the head gardener at Karnak is looking for temporary workers. Go to the northern gate at sunset, and say I sent you.'

Judge Gem handed the reports to his secretary. 'File them.'

'Any interesting information?'

'Administrative prattle, of no interest whatsoever.'

During the day, two witness statements had caught the judge's attention. A baker had seen Kel in a small house in the northern district, accompanied by ten armed men. And a farmer was certain he had spotted him in a palm-grove, taking weapons out of a large sack.

The soldiers sent to investigate eventually reported back.

'Well?' the judge asked their officer.

'Pure invention. These people were playing games with us.'

'An insult to justice! They will be punished.'

'With respect, sir, it would be better simply to forget the incident, otherwise nobody will dare speak again.'

'The law is the law.' Furious, Gem slammed the door of his office.

*

At the northern gate of Karnak, bathed in the rays of the setting sun, applicants were awaiting the head gardener.

'I've heard that he's a nasty fellow,' ventured a red-haired youth.

'And pretentious,' added a younger boy. 'You can't ever complain.'

'Well,' said a skinny lad, 'I won't let him order me about.'

'Nor will I!' nodded his comrade.

A square-headed, stocky man emerged from the queue and said in a loud voice, 'You four, be off with you!'

The red-haired youth was indignant. 'Why should we do as you say?'

'I am the head gardener, and I heard what you said.'

The culprits dispersed. The survivors were subjected to their future employer's inquisitorial gaze.

'You two can go as well. I don't like your faces.'

The only two left were Kel and a lanky, tired-looking fellow.

'Would you enjoy carrying yokes that hurt your neck, working all night, watering the vegetables at dawn, irrigating the orchards and gathering the medicinal herbs at dusk?'

'And when do we sleep?' asked the tired man.

'When I decide.'

'That sounds too hard for me. I'm going to try my luck somewhere else.'

'I accept your conditions,' said Kel. 'The Scribe of the Treasury's door-keeper warned me.'

'He's a good friend with a sound way of thinking. I'll take you on, my boy, but you haven't got a gardener's hands.'

'Hard work doesn't frighten me.'

'Then pick up those pots of water and follow me.'

'Into the temple?'

'Not this evening. We must attend to the gardens outside the wall, with the first night team. Try not to disappoint me.'

Overcoming his own disappointment, Kel summoned up all his courage and patience.

The Divine Worshipper gazed at the symbol of Abydos, a long pole covered with a cloth. This veiled the head of the reborn Osiris, the sight of which was permitted only to those initiated into the great Mysteries.

She recognized the High Steward's heavy footsteps. 'Good news, I hope?'

'Unfortunately not, Majesty. There is an irreparable rift between myself and Judge Gem. He dislikes me, and I cannot alter his attitude. On the other hand, his treatment of me will anger the Theban people, who will refuse to help him.'

'Has he sent out patrols all over the province?'

'Indeed so, Majesty. Worse still, he is blocking all access to Karnak and is making me appear to be his ally. In other words Kel, Nitis and Bebon regard me as a collaborator and will not dare to contact me. I do not know where they are hiding, or even if they are alive.'

'They are, Sheshonq. I can feel their presence.'

'We must face facts, Majesty: they are not going to reach us.'

'Are the gods not protecting them, High Steward?'

66

On the fringes of the desert Daybreak, the door-keeper's daughter, cared for around thirty beehives, to the great satisfaction of the master bee-keeper. The hives consisted of pots placed one on top of another and open to the bees. Inside, they made their rays of light, watched attentively by the young woman, whose task was to smoke the hives and then gather the honey.

As she was stopping up a jar destined for Karnak, she saw two people heading towards her.

'Bebon! Are you back in Thebes?'

'You're not too angry with me, are you, Daybreak?'

'You left me only good memories. And is this delightful person your wife?'

'No, she's a healer who'd like to make your acquaintance.'

'I use a lot of honey,' explained Nitis, 'because it has remarkable curative properties. I'd like to assist you while I'm in Thebes.'

'Why not? In exchange, you can teach me the rudiments of medicine.'

'Gladly.'

The two women took to each other immediately, and Bebon felt neglected.

'Are you married, Daybreak?' he asked.

'I'm in no hurry. I won't ask you the same question.'

'Because of all the problems about my work, I couldn't be a good husband.'

'What's happened?'

'I'm giving up the life of an actor: too much tiredness and too many journeys. I'd like to settle down here in Thebes and find steady work in the service of the temple.'

Daybreak thought for a moment. 'There is one possibility – but it won't be easy.'

'I don't mind a challenge.'

The head cook at the temple's outdoor kitchens gave Bebon a sceptical look. 'So you want to work for me, do you?'

'Daybreak the bee-keeper recommends me.'

'A fine young girl. Well, I'm looking for a kitchen assistant, and I don't mean a lazy one.'

'Do I look lazy?'

'You start now or you leave.'

'I'll start.'

'I have the priests' lunch to prepare. Go and clean the kitchen and sharpen the knives.'

The equipment was remarkable: cauldrons, ladles, bread-moulds, grinding-mills, ovens, copper plates used by the pastrycook, wooden spoons. Using a piece of basalt, Bebon sharpened the long, oval-bladed knives.

The head cook was impressed. 'You'll do, my lad.'

'My speciality is stew.'

'I warn you, I hate empty boasts. And the priests at Karnak like good cooking.'

'Give me a chance.'

The head cook hesitated. 'I won't tolerate failure.'

Bebon set to work immediately. Using the recipe he'd got from a delightful former mistress, he used ox-tongue, ribs, thigh, liver, the windpipe and vegetables. And he cooked it on a gentle heat, keeping a constant eye on it.

When he had inspected the other kitchens, the head cook came and tasted it.

'Excellent,' he declared in surprise. 'The priests will love it.'

'I'd be happy to deliver it to them.'

'My assistants and I will do that. You can serve us up some large portions of this good dish. We eat with the customers.'

Carrying a yoke with heavy pots of water hanging at either end was exhausting, but Kel did not complain. He was hoping that he might soon manage to get inside Karnak.

Had Nitis and Bebon found jobs that would enable them to get past the security checks? By each trying their luck on their own, they would be less easily spotted.

The scribe was finding this separation hard to bear. Without Nitis, he felt lost and had lost all joy in life. Only the need for the truth gave him the energy to pursue this insane quest.

All through the night, his neck painful and his bent back aching, he advanced step by step and emptied the water from the pots into the irrigation channels.

The head gardener interrupted him. 'Come with me. We must deliver flowers to the temple for the morning offering.'

Kel was to carry some beautiful white lotus-flowers, while a colleague carried irises – 'The Divine Worshipper likes them,' he confided to Kel.

'Have you ever seen her?'

'No, never.'

'Do you know where she lives?'

'That I do know. I've delivered flowers to her residence.'

The boy supplied the details, and Kel memorized the route he must take.

The head gardener had a long discussion with the guards. Then the wooden gate opened, and the flower-bearers followed him into the temple precinct.

Kel's decision was made: he would deliver the lotuses to the appointed place and then run at top speed to the Divine

Worshipper's house. Taking advantage of the darkness, he would try to get inside and speak to her. Caught unawares, the priests would put up only feeble resistance. Aware that what he was about to do was madness, Kel called upon Nitis to help him.

But he barely had time even to look admiringly at the buildings, for ten guards instantly surrounded the bearers of the offerings.

'You're going no further,' said an officer. 'Hand over the flowers to the ritual priests.'

'This isn't usual,' protested the head gardener. 'I—'

'Orders from Judge Gem. Go back outside.'

67

Daybreak's bees produced honey of exceptionally fine quality. It was not used as a food; all of it was reserved for use by doctors in Thebes. Nitis admired the girl's skill, and made sure to pass on some medical information to her – for example, a compress soaked in honey helped to heal burns.

'I have to deliver ten pots to the Divine Worshipper's doctor,' said Daybreak. 'Will you come with me?'

'Gladly. You can tell me about this extraordinary temple.'

Happy to be together, the two young women found the journey all too short. Daybreak described the pillared gateways, the obelisks, the great courtyards, the hypostyle chamber, the houses of the permanent priests and the residence of the Divine Worshipper, whom she had had the good fortune to meet.

'She is a beautiful woman, with a look in her eyes that is both gentle and commanding. Age has no hold on her. As the wife of Amun, she tames his power and maintains harmony by celebrating the rites. She is the true pharaoh of Egypt. The other one, the one in the North, is only interested in the Greeks and the army.'

A queue of people was waiting outside the main entrance to the temple. That morning, Judge Gem had doubled the number of soldiers on duty and strengthened the checks and controls.

The senior officer was a childhood friend of Daybreak's, and had not given up hope of marrying her.

'Delivering honey, are you?'

'Ten sealed pots, for Her Majesty's doctor.'

'Official order slip, if you please.'

'Here it is.'

The officer checked it. 'The desert air has made you even more beautiful, Daybreak. Would you consider having dinner with me?'

'I have an enormous amount of work to do at the moment. But I'll think about it.'

'You promise?'

'I promise.'

'You may pass.'

Nitis tried to slip in with the bee-keeper.

'Stop!' ordered the officer. 'Who are you?'

'A friend,' replied Daybreak. 'She's helping me carry the honey.'

'I'm sorry, but nobody who is not known to us may enter.'

'Can't you make an exception?'

'Judge Gem's instructions are law. I'd lose my job.'

'I only have two arms, and there are ten pots!'

'I'll call for a priest. You,' he said to Nitis, 'don't move from here. I must question you and check your identity.'

He helped Daybreak carry her pots inside and found her some help. When he returned to the guard-post, Nitis had vanished.

Although she was facing Judge Gem, Daybreak did not lose her composure.

'Where and how did you meet this woman?'

'I was tending my hives when she came to see me. She was recently divorced, and looking for work.'

'What is her name?'

'Achait – she's Syrian. She has three children, and she was crying poverty. I needed someone to help me, so I took her on.'

'Wasn't she accompanied by one or two men?'

'I only saw her.'

'According to the officer on duty, you called her "a friend". That's a curious word to use of an employee.'

'Her misfortunes touched me, and we got on well.'

'If you're hiding anything, however small,' warned Judge Gem, 'you will be punished.'

'I've told you everything.'

'That woman ran away,' the judge reminded her, 'so she did not have a clear conscience.'

'Perhaps I was gullible,' said Daybreak, 'but one can't be suspicious of everybody.'

'In future, be less gullible and obtain proper information before taking anybody on. Now leave.'

That judge had all the arrogance of the senior dignitaries from the North, and he obviously disliked Thebans. Glad that she'd lied to him, Daybreak hoped he wouldn't catch the healer.

'There's an emergency,' the cook told Bebon, who was busy cleaning the ladles. 'Have you any specialities besides stew?'

'Lamb grilled on skewers.'

'Excellent! Get to work. You have three hours.'

'But the ladles—'

'I'll get someone else to clean them. And I'll bring you the meat.'

Bebon cut it into small cubes which he marinaded in oil with chopped onion and a little salt. He would then put them on skewers and grill them.

North Wind had nothing to complain about in terms of his new job or his food. He carried kitchen utensils, bags of condiments and herbs, and enjoyed the leftovers of a wide variety of dishes. His calmness reassured Bebon that Nitis and Kel must still be free. But had they succeeded in contacting the Divine Worshipper?

He, on the other hand, had failed completely and had no prospect of success. Because of the new measures imposed by Judge Gem, a new kitchen assistant would be sent for checks and would be questioned in detail.

At noon, the cook went to the oven and took out some loaves shaped like papyrus stems.

'How is your lamb?'

'As tasty as anybody could wish.'

'Thats fortunate, because our customer is a food-lover and difficult to satisfy. And my reputation is at stake.'

'Who is it?'

'The closest friend of High Steward Sheshonq. He writes copies of the *Book of Coming Forth by Day** for the tombs of senior Theban dignitaries. He has an exceptionally fine hand, apparently, but his talent doesn't prevent him appreciating the finer things in life. Every week he has lunch with Sheshonq. This time, he is putting us to the test. It's a remarkable privilege, believe me.'

The scholar was an austere, self-contained individual. As soon as he arrived, he sampled a cube of grilled meat and a piece of bread. Sweat ran down the cook's brow.

'Acceptable,' pronounced the scribe. 'Tomorrow you are to deliver six skewers of lamb and two loaves to the High Steward's house.'

Bowing very low, the cook thought of the benefits he would derive from this success. A supplier to Sheshonq and his best friend!

As for Bebon, he had other ideas.

When there was a break, he went to the stables. 'Take me to Kel and Nitis,' he whispered to North Wind.

* Often incorrectly called *The Book of the Dead*.

68

'What do you think?' King Ahmose asked General Phanes. 'And be honest.'

'Your son Psamtek conducts himself as a fine soldier, Majesty. I have seldom seen an inexperienced young man make so much progress in such a short time. He has proved courageous – indeed, almost reckless – never gets fatigued, and carries out exercises perfectly. His reputation is already growing among the troops, and he will be a respected leader.'

'Continue his training, Phanes. And continue to be ruthless.'

'You can rely on me, Majesty.'

Ahmose rejoined his wife, who was arranging a banquet for the army's senior officers: a boring dinner, but the king regarded it as vital.

'Excellent news, my dear,' he said. 'Psamtek is going to become a true army commander, capable of defending the Two Lands. We can be proud of him.'

Tanith smiled sadly. 'Will you teach him how to govern the country soundly?'

'I shall do so in time,' promised the king. 'This evening, we shall congratulate some fine men and encourage them to remain vigilant.'

'Will Psamtek be there?'

'Of course. Now, I shall cut short my last meeting of the

morning, and we'll enjoy a boat trip before lunch.'

When Ahmose returned to his office, Udja and Henat were waiting for him. They looked extremely grim.

'Be brief,' the king ordered. 'The weather is beautiful, and I want to enjoy the charms of the countryside.'

'Judge Gem has deployed security forces all over Thebes,' said Udja. 'According to him, Kel is hiding there.'

'That affair no longer interests me. The traitor Pefy is dead, and the conspirators have been silenced. Their sole achievement was the destruction of my helmet. However, we shall allow the judge to act: by patrolling Thebes, he will stifle any thoughts of opposition. And the next Divine Worshipper will not cause us any problems. Is our friend Kroisos ready to set sail?'

'He has delayed his visit, Majesty,' said Henat.

'Do we know why?'

'According to a message from one of our agents, which reached the Interpreters' Secretariat, he is going first to Samos to meet the tyrant Polycrates. From my point of view, Polycrates is not a very reliable ally.'

'You are mistaken, Henat. Like all the Greeks, Polycrates admires Egypt and supports me unreservedly. He is only too happy to supply us with soldiers and receive rich cargoes in return. Send him a warm letter and tell Kroisos we hope to see him again soon.'

Eager to return to the queen and spend some delightful time with her on the water, Ahmose dismissed his advisers.

The city was sleeping peacefully. Gazing into the darkness, the leader of the conspirators saw their plan unfolding implacably. The final phase was approaching.

They could still change the course of destiny and be content with the present situation. But success was close, and nobody was going to prevent the leader savouring victory. The surprise would be total, and the reactions to it derisory. And if a few stubborn people insisted on resisting, they would pay with their lives.

There was just one last obstacle ... The conspirators' leader must be convincing and use the right arguments to rally the final dissenter to the cause. But, even if those arguments failed, the plan would be implemented anyway.

In a thoroughly bad mood, Judge Gem went to the High Steward's palace. His last conversation with Henat's head informant had produced nothing useful. That useless idiot was content to get by on a good salary, and didn't demand any effort whatsoever from his subordinates. It was pointless to rely on him to find the trail that would lead to the murderous scribe and his accomplices.

The High Steward's personal manservant greeted the magistrate.

'Go and fetch your employer.'

'He is resting and—'

'Wake him.'

The servant did not argue.

Gem paced up and down a pillared anteroom, decorated with wall-paintings showing a multitude of birds frolicking above papyrus stems.

Dressed in an indoor tunic and with his hair uncombed, Sheshonq appeared.

'I am extremely displeased,' said the judge.

'So am I,' snapped the High Steward. 'Why are so many guards watching my house?'

'They are ensuring your protection.'

'Send them away.'

'You haven't understood anything, High Steward. I give the orders in the name of the king, and you obey.'

'Do you forbid me to come and go as I please?'

'Are you hiding any murderers?'

'Search the house and its outbuildings!'

'I intend to do precisely that.'

'And afterwards, you will apologize to me.'

'A criminal investigation involves many investigations, most of which lead nowhere.'

'Well, don't let me inconvenience you!'

'Given your position, you will not have committed the folly of sheltering conspirators facing the death penalty. But I wish to know the identity of everyone who enters and leaves your house. You will thus avoid unhealthy temptations and Thebes will avoid any scandal.'

'You are losing your reason, Judge Gem!'

'I suspect that you are behind the false reports that have been reaching the security forces in large numbers. Checking them wastes a great deal of time and effort.'

'The Theban people are only trying to help you.'

'No, they're trying to put me off the scent. But I am not deceived. Stop this stupid little game, or you will regret it.'

'Your threats are unworthy of a judge, and do not impress me.'

'You are wrong, for I am not joking. This is an affair of state, and anyone who opposes the law will be crushed.

'That reassures me, since I have absolutely no intention of opposing it.'

'Have you any information concerning Kel the scribe, Nitis the priestess and Bebon the actor?'

'None at all.'

'If you learn anything, inform me immediately.'

'Was there really any need to say that?'

Furious, Judge Gem left. Thebes was rising against him and against his men. It was impossible to search every house and watch every inch of ground. He would have to wait for the fugitives to make a mistake.

69

The scholar who specialized in the *Book of Going Forth by Day* was overjoyed at the prospect of sharing a delicious meal with his friend High Steward Sheshonq, and discussing the final layout of this collection of a hundred and sixty-five chapters, heir to the *Pyramid Texts* and the *Sarcophagus Texts*. The first part was devoted to funeral ceremonies, the second to the journey of the deceased to paradise, the third to the court of the gods and the revelation of the Mysteries to those who were 'of just voice', and the fourth brought together the words of knowledge, endowed with the power of the Word. Customers selected a certain number of chapters, beautifully illustrated, and these extracts had the same value as the whole book. A fine theologian, Sheshonq took an interest in every detail and offered the learned scribe new ways of expressing very ancient ideas. For example, he emphasized the importance of the symbolic fusion of Ra, the sun of day and the creative light, and Osiris, the sun of night and the light of resurrection.

Serious thinking, however, did not prevent good eating. Did the righteous not take part in an eternal banquet, whose food was brought by the sun's boats? Dressed in a robe of immaculate linen and new sandals, discreetly perfumed, the scholar left his house, thinking about the papyrus he would soon finish. It was extremely detailed work, requiring a perfect knowledge of the texts and a steady hand.

Deep in thought, he crossed a small palm-grove near Sheshonq's huge estate. Suddenly, an arm wrapped itself round his throat, choking him.

'Don't resist and don't make a sound, or I'll cut your throat.'

The sight of the butcher's knife put all thoughts of struggling out of his mind.

The attacker dragged his hostage into a gardener's hut, where his accomplice was waiting, armed with a club. Utterly terrified, the scholar almost fainted away.

'Pull yourself together, my friend. You're not dead yet.'

'You . . . I recognize you. You're a cook!'

'I was,' admitted Bebon.

'I'm not rich, I—'

'We're not interested in your wealth,' cut in Kel, 'but in your friend Sheshonq. You're going to tell us the best way to enter his house.'

'Impossible!'

Bebon brandished the impressive butcher's knife. 'Then goodbye.'

'Listen to me, I beg you! Sheshonq's whole estate is surrounded by guards. Judge Gem has put him under constant watch, and checks everyone who enters or leaves. Sheshonq is furious about it, and has made many protests, but he cannot oppose the decisions of the judge, whom he detests.'

'He detests him?' Kel was astonished. 'The High Steward is not the judge's ally?'

'His worst enemy would be more accurate! He thinks he is capable of protecting the murderous scribe and . . .' The scholar stopped, his gaze faltering. 'Are you . . . Are you that scribe?'

'I haven't murdered anyone.'

'It is the truth,' declared Nitis.

Her sudden appearance astounded the scholar. 'The priestess, the scribe and the actor . . . You're alive!'

'And you,' cut in Bebon, 'are telling us lies. Sheshonq and Gem are allies and have set a trap for us – and you're the bait.'

'No, I swear that's not true!'

The knife menaced him.

'Sheshonq wants to meet you and help you. He has contrived to have the judge sent enormous amounts of false information and, following his recommendations, the Theban people are refusing to help the judge's men.'

'I believe you,' said Nitis. 'We must meet the Divine Worshipper with all speed, and only the High Steward can take us to her.'

'At the moment, he cannot. Judge Gem has him watched day and night.'

'Can he not elude his watchers?'

'I don't think he has much room to move.'

Bebon did not trust this frightened scholar. 'What do you and your friend Sheshonq talk about when you dine together?'

'The *Book of Going Forth by Day*. He is interested in the words of knowledge, and I show him different ways of writing them. The hieroglyphs contain the secrets of creation.'

Nitis and Kel looked at each other. They had just had the same idea.

'Give me your palette and a brush,' said Kel. He wrote down the coded text, then handed the palette to the scholar. 'Read this out loud.'

The scholar frowned. 'I . . . I can't understand a word of it.'

'That is the cause of all our misfortunes. Show this text to the High Steward, and tell him to give it to the Divine Worshipper. There is no doubt whatsoever that she will be able to decipher it.'

'Is it so important?'

'The future of Egypt depends on it.'

'Of course, you will need an answer. Where will I find you?'

Kel told him the address of the house Nitis had rented in Thebes.

'I promise I will do my best,' said the scholar. 'May I go now?'

Kel nodded, and Bebon watched his precious hostage walk away.

'He'll denounce us and send Judge Gem to us, along with a whole army,' predicted the actor. 'Well, as we've accomplished our mission, let's get out of this net before it's too late.'

'I'm staying,' decided Kel.

'So am I,' declared Nitis.

'This is madness!'

'Only the Divine Worshipper can proclaim my innocence,' Kel reminded him, 'and we must remain at her disposal.'

Bebon gave up the fight. He didn't feel he could ever persuade this stubborn pair.

70

Kel and Nitis were asleep in each other's arms, North Wind was standing guard outside the rented house, and Bebon was pacing up and down. They had returned separately to their refuge, fortunately managing to avoid the patrols.

But this, thought Bebon, was only a temporary respite. Soon they would fall into the hands of Judge Gem, and the High Steward would not tell the Divine Worshipper about them. In short, they faced total failure, prison and death. The Thebans would not lift a finger, and the relentless judge would at last have his triumph.

Someone scratched at the door. Armed with the butcher's knife, Bebon went over. More scratching. Why didn't North Wind show himself? Either he had been neutralized, or the visitor was not an enemy.

Bebon opened the door a fraction. By the light of the moon, he saw the anxious face of his erstwhile hostage.

'Are you alone?' Bebon whispered.

'Of course! I had difficulty finding you. Let me in.'

Still suspicious, Bebon searched the scholar and looked around outside. The area seemed deserted, and North Wind was dozing. He let the scholar inside, and woke Nitis and Kel.

'Did you see the High Steward?' asked Kel.

'I showed him the coded text. He cannot decipher it, but he will give it to the Divine Worshipper as soon as he can.'

'Doesn't he see her every day?' Nitis asked in surprise.

The scholar hesitated. 'To prove Sheshonq's sincerity and trustworthiness, I shall have to entrust you with a state secret. Officially, the Divine Worshipper is dying and receives no one any more. Sheshonq meets her in secret, far from prying eyes and ears.'

'In other words, Judge Gem believes she can't help us!' exclaimed Kel.

'Whatever you do, don't move from here, and wait for Her Majesty's instructions.'

An interminable day passed very, very slowly. So as not to arouse the curiosity of neighbouring traders, Bebon and North Wind pretended to make deliveries, and they brought back food and water.

At last night fell.

Bebon started to pace again. Sometimes he believed in the scholar's honesty; sometimes he yielded to dark thoughts. Nitis and Kel did not bother with useless words and experienced every moment of their love as if it were the last.

North Wind scratched at the door.

The scholar rushed in, clearly very agitated. 'The High Steward showed the coded text to the Divine Worshipper,' he said in a trembling voice. 'Two keys are necessary to unlock it. She has only one, the key of the ancestors.'

'Where is the second?' Kel asked.

'In the western burial ground, in the form of four vases dedicated to the sons of Horus.'*

'Does Her Majesty know their precise location?'

'Unfortunately not. Only one man can tell you: the head embalmer.'

'Contact him at once.'

'I'm sorry; we fell out and are not on speaking terms.'

---

* Canopic vases.

'What did you quarrel about?'

'That sinister man thinks of nothing but profit. The High Steward ought to have replaced him a long time ago, but he does his work well and nobody complains. As she is officially dying, the Divine Worshipper could not summon him to Karnak. And he will not respond to the High Steward, as he has probably stolen those priceless vases, which were made for Sheshonq's predecessor, a former member of the Interpreters' Secretariat and a great lover of coded language. He told our Queen, "I have inscribed my masterpiece on those vases."'

At last, thought Kel, things are starting to go right!

But the scholar seemed downcast. 'I fear you have come up against a dead end. The embalmer will never talk. The investigation into the disappearance of these treasures has not been concluded, and that thief will keep his secret.'

'Well, he doesn't know me,' said Kel. 'Find me some luxurious clothes and a silver ingot.'

'Are you planning . . . to buy them?'

'Can you think of another solution?'

'I warn you, that thief is cunning and suspicious. If I were you, I'd give up.'

'If you were me, you'd have died a long time ago. If I were to spoil the chance the gods have offered me, it would lead me to nothingness.'

Nitis voiced no objections.

'And I suppose I'm to play the role of your sandal-bearer?' enquired a dejected Bebon.

'How did you guess?'

'We won't even get across the Nile.'

The scholar said, 'The soldiers don't check all the ferries. The High Steward owns three, and one of them is reserved for his foreign visitors. A Lebanese nobleman accompanied by his servant and his donkey wouldn't be investigated.'

Hands on hips, Bebon could not hide his astonishment. 'So now you're having ideas! Have you quite finished?'

310

'Er, no. The ferryman will be informed about the plan and will talk to the officer on guard at the landing-stage. He'll explain that you speak very little Egyptian and that you want to visit the parts of the temples of a million years that are open. A guide, also informed in advance, will accompany you. In fact, though, he will take you to the head embalmer. Then it is up to you.'

'Thank you for your advice.'

'We probably won't see each other again. May the gods continue to protect you.'

'What about the clothes and the ingot?' Bebon asked worriedly.

'The High Steward will remove the ingot from the treasury in Karnak tomorrow. Be at the port market when the sun reaches its zenith. A tall Nubian broom-seller will give you the clothes and the ingot. I am happy to have known you and, personally, I wish you good luck.'

After the scholar had left, Bebon exploded.

'It's superb – a superb trap! Fine words, fine intentions, a fine plan and a fine trio of credulous idiots who believe in the impossible!'

'Thanks to you,' commented Kel, 'we're used to that. If he were in the judge's pay, we would already have been arrested.'

'Caught red-handed stealing a silver ingot, right in front of the people of Thebes, would be even better! Let's stop dreaming, please, and leave this city.'

'We've just learnt vital information,' said Nitis. 'Would you really give up the chance to act on it?'

'It's probably all made up.'

'I don't think so.'

Bebon sat down heavily. 'It's a trap, I tell you.'

71

The head embalmer at the Theban burial-ground was both envied and loathed. Envied because his salary included numerous tips; detested because he carried out dirty work by extracting the viscera from dead bodies, a vital task before transforming the remains into an Osirian body and the basis for resurrection.

Also, he exploited the situation extremely well; a situation which was particularly favourable because of the shortage of tombs. The government authorized him to sell off entire tombs or parts of them to individuals in search of a final dwelling. Each transaction earned him a large profit, and he also received secret payments when he carried out first-class mummifications, demanding many special products and tools. So he left the poor and the ordinary folk to his assistants. Summarily embalmed, they would be dried out by the desert sand. He knew how to wield the sharp knives, the curved blade used to extract the brain, dissolving substances, preservatives and perfumes. These costly and sometimes rare substances were subject to a flourishing trade.

Death brought wealth to the head embalmer, who was sure of never lacking clients wishing to have a perfect mummy and a comfortable house of eternity. The moment had come to raise his prices.

'Someone is asking for you,' his assistant told him.

'An official from the east bank?'

'No, a stranger in expensive clothes.'

'A future customer, eh? Let him wait a moment. This one will pay handsomely!'

To Bebon's surprise, the plan had unfolded without a hitch. The broom-seller, the clothes, the silver ingot, the official at the ferry, the guide . . . Not one jarring note. At the landing-stage, the checks had been a mere formality.

Now he and Kel were in a sinister place, a sort of village of embalming workshops. Strange smells assailed the nostrils, and the employees moved around silently, their shoulders drooping. Even North Wind seemed uneasy.

'So this is the trap,' said Bebon. 'We're going to be turned into mummies. Have you seen the expressions on those fellows' faces? They turn my blood to ice.'

'We're close to our goal,' said Kel imperturbably.

'A strange end, in the middle of all these embalmers!'

A low-browed forty-year-old came to fetch them. 'The head embalmer is waiting for you.'

The walls of his lair were blackened with smoke. On low tables lay disturbing tools with sharp blades.

'Send your servant away,' he said.

Bebon was only too happy to return to the fresh air.

'Where are you from?' the embalmer asked his visitor.

'I am rich, very rich, and I will pay a good price for what I want.'

'A laudable intention. And what do you want? A first-class mummification and an ancient tomb charged with magic, I assume?'

'You're mistaken. I want a treasure.'

The embalmer was curious. 'I think you're talking to the wrong person.'

'No, I'm not. My information is quite specific. I want four

313

vases dedicated to the sons of Horus; they belonged to High Steward Sheshonq's predecessor.'

'Oh, that old story! They got lost.'

'But you know where they are.'

'I'm not a thief!'

'I didn't say you were. This is a simple commercial transaction: you sell, I buy.'

'I haven't got this treasure.'

'Would you refuse to exchange it for two silver ingots?'

A long silence followed this question. The embalmer had difficulty controlling his emotions as he tried to envisage the extent of his new fortune.

'It's an old story. But my memory might come back to me ...'

'Take your time,' said Kel.

'Two silver ingots ... You're mocking me! Show them to me.'

'I'll give you the first one.'

The embalmer's eyes bulged. He caressed the ingot.

'The second,' Kel went on, 'you will receive after giving me the four vases.'

'What if I decide to make do with this one?'

'You won't have long to enjoy it. My friends dislike dishonesty.'

'I was only joking! Come and fetch what's owed to you.'

The embalmer led the scribe into the burial-ground, to a place near the temple of Deir el-Bahari. There, immense tombs had been excavated, made up of raw brick superstructures and vast open-air courtyards, leading to numerous underground chambers. The walls were covered with scenes inspired by the *mastaba* tombs of the age of the pyramids,* thus continuing the golden age.

* *Mastaba* is Arabic for 'bench', and describes the superstructure of these monuments.

'This is the house of eternity of Sheshonq's predecessor,' said the embalmer. 'His sarcophagus rests at the bottom of a very deep well. After burial it was filled with sand, so that the dead man's riches could not be stolen. But there is another well linked to the cave by a vaulted passageway. I think I recall that the four vases were hidden there.'

'You lead the way.'

The embalmer removed a few bricks and, from a hiding-place behind them, removed a knotted rope. He fixed it firmly to a post and began the descent.

Kel followed hesitantly. He must remain vigilant at all times, for his guide clearly had only one thought in his head: to get rid of this rich fool. The embalmer didn't believe there was a second ingot and would be content with the fortune he had so easily acquired.

They reached the bottom of the second well. A narrow corridor led off from it.

'You've arrived just in time,' said the embalmer. 'I was planning to fill it with sand next week.'

'And lose the vases?'

'What do you take me for? I had another hiding-place in mind.'

'Get them out.'

The embalmer made one of the stones in the passageway pivot round. 'Come and see.'

The four vases rested inside a niche. They were true works of art, made of alabaster and wonderfully elegant.

As Kel was removing the first one, the embalmer ran off. He climbed the rope remarkably quickly and, once at the top of the well, shouted down, 'You shall have a fine tomb! Nobody will ever find you under the mass of sand that will enshroud you.'

The embalmer did not enjoy his success for long. Something hard hit the back of his neck; his vision blurred and he lost consciousness.

The blow from Bebon's club had been hard and precise. Kicking away the inert body, he fixed the rope back in place.

'Are you still down there, Kel?'

'I've got the vases!'

'Bring them up carefully – don't break them!'

The task was easily accomplished.

'North Wind and I had to put that filthy rogue's two assistants out of action,' explained Bebon. 'They were rather slow on their feet. They and their employer will have terrible headaches.'

He took back the silver ingot.

'We'll give it back to the temple,' decided Kel.

Bebon had been afraid of something like this, and unfortunately it would be no use arguing.'

With great care, Kel laid the vases in North Wind's panniers, and the trio headed for the landing-stage.

72

Thanks to the efficiency of the High Steward's men, the return journey to Thebes went smoothly. At the far end of the quay, away from prying eyes, Kel traded his expensive tunic for a peasant's kilt. Taking different routes, he, Bebon and North Wind returned to their refuge, where Nitis awaited them.

She knew the moment she saw Kel's face.

'You've got them!'

The two lovers fell into each other's arms. Bebon quickly removed the vases from the baaskets and asked North Wind to stand guard outside.

'When you two have finished pouring out your hearts to each other,' said the actor, 'we'd better get to work.'

The first vase bore a man's head and contained the deceased man's liver. Bearing the name of Imset, it opened up the way of the southern sky to the soul. The second, which had a baboon's head, bore the name of Hapy and housed the spleen and the stomach; it guaranteed a happy journey to the west. The third, Duamutef, with the head of a jackal, contained the lungs and windpipe. It corresponded to the light from the north. Finally, falcon-headed Kebehsenuf contained the intestines, vessels and channels removed from the body by the embalmer. Its power brought the east to life.

Together, the four sons of Horus took part in the process

of transmutation of the individual's mortal remains into an immortal Osirian body. Linked together, they recreated the interior of Osiris's being and brought him back to life during the celebration of the rites.

Now the friends had to find the code the vases bore.

Kel read the texts, which were perfectly clear. These benevolent spirits drove away visible and invisible attackers, watched permanently over the man who was 'of just voice', led him to a new awakening and preserved his life beyond the ordeal of death.

There was no sign of coded writing.

Initial disappointment gave way to a determination to solve the mystery.

'The recipient of these items was a master of hieroglyphs,' Kel reminded the others. 'Let's try to read them backwards.'

A waste of time.

In turn, Kel and Nitis tried to apply different coding systems; but in vain.

'Perhaps we're using the wrong method,' she said. 'What if the secret lies within the signs themselves?'

Bebon and Kel brought the torches closer to the vases. The light threw the hieroglyphs into relief.

'Look! The *I* of Imset and the *H* of Hapy are much more deeply engraved than the other letters.'

'*IH* . . . an allusion to the sistrum of the gods?' wondered Kel.

The names of the last two sons of Horus don't contain this anomaly,' observed Nitis, 'but their meaning is highly instructive. Duamutef is "He Who Venerates His Mother" – in other words, Isis-Hathor, embodied by the Divine Worshipper, one of whose most important ritual acts is to wield the sistra in order to drive away evil.'

'What about Kebehsenuf?' Bebon asked, much impressed.

'That's "He Who Refreshes His Brother": Osiris was brought back to life by the celestial water.'

'That doesn't help us much,' complained the actor.

'Yes, it does. When the Divine Worshipper has this information, she is sure to be able to provide us with the final key, whether it's her own sistrum or the water of regeneration from the sacred lake.'

'That's one step we can't take,' said Bebon. 'Judge Gem has turned Karnak into an impregnable fortress. Clearly he wishes to isolate the Divine Worshipper, even if she is dying, and make it impossible for her to help us.'

'I have an idea,' said Kel.

The actor bit his lip. Yet again, he feared the worst.

And he was not disappointed. Kel's plan proved to be sheer insanity.

'There's only one problem,' he said when he'd finished. 'How do we pass the details on to Sheshonq?'

'We can't.'

'I have a suggestion,' said Nitis.

'I'll never get through the security barricade!' Bebon protested.

'No, you won't. But your friend Daybreak should be able to manage it.'

The actor was not unhappy at the prospect of seeing the pretty woman again. They could relive pleasant memories and enjoy the present. As for the rest, it was up to the bee-keeper to decide.'

Judge Gem was depressed. Another ten rumours and denunciations to check. In Thebes, hundreds of people had spotted Kel and his accomplices, whose number varied considerably according to the witness reports. And all these investigations had produced absolutely no results.

People were making mock of him. Urged on by the Sheshonq, the entire city was in league against the state's representative and preventing him from carrying out his mission. Should he attack Sheshonq directly? No, it would be of no use. The Thebans venerated the Divine Worshipper and admired her High Steward.

At one time the judge had wondered if Bebon was a spy in Henat's pay, trying to infiltrate Kel's network. That hope, too, had gone. Bebon would already have betrayed Kel and obtained a large reward.

In hostile terrain, powerless despite all his guards and soldiers, the judge sometimes felt a kind of dizziness. Although he did not doubt Kel's guilt, he wondered if someone had perhaps been using him.

The coded documents in the judge's possession remained mute, and he still lacked certain explanations. Could the ruling power have manipulated him, too? Most unlikely. Heat, exhaustion and repeated failure were the cause of these nonsensical thoughts, which were unworthy of the head of Egypt's judicial system.

Gem set to work again and consulted the list of visitors to the High Steward. Alas, every one of them had been identified. However, the conspirators would have to make contact with him, so the judge would have to rely on his greatest virtue, patience.

Bebon might be a rogue and a liar, but he was also a wonderful lover. Daybreak had no regrets about yielding to him again. She had spent an exciting and entertaining night, and would have liked to delay the unpredictable actor even longer.

At the end of these pleasurable hours, how could she refuse him the favour he asked, particularly since she liked the young woman who had helped her to carry the pots of honey?

At sunset, the bee-keeper went to the men guarding Sheshonq's house. 'I have brought an order of honey for the High Steward,' she said.'

'Wait here. We'll tell his steward.'

The steward was preparing for a banquet, and was annoyed at being interrupted. 'What's this all about, young woman?'

'I want to see the High Steward.'

'Why?'

'I'll tell him myself. If you value your job, don't send me away.'

Troubled by this, the steward decided not to take any risks and ventured to disturb Sheshonq, who recognized the bee-keeper.

'I didn't order any honey,' said Sheshonq in surprise.

'Yes, you did,' said Daybreak with heavy emphasis. 'Don't you remember? You said you needed a pot of my finest honey, because it contains vital substances.'

'Ah, yes, I remember now, and I shall very much appreciate those properties.'

It hadn't taken Sheshonq long to understand. Making sure that nobody was around, he opened the pot. In it was a wooden tablet covered with hieroglyphs in Kel's writing.

The scribe's proposal was unbelievable. The High Steward would submit it to the Divine Worshipper anyway, but she was bound to find it quite unacceptable.

73

Modestly attired, Nitis came to the great gate of Karnak with North Wind. Kel and Bebon joined her, arriving separately by different routes.

Bebon kept asking himself why he was taking part in this insane adventure. They hadn't the smallest chance of success, would lose all the benefits of their previous efforts and would be taken back to Memphis aboard a prison-boat. But no argument could dissuade Kel or Nitis from carrying out this madness.

'Halt!' ordered the guard.

'I am delivering precious items to the Divine Worshipper,' said Nitis calmly.

Her beauty stunned the soldier, but he must respect the rules. 'Go to the suppliers' entrance. The guards there will check your identity.'

'When you see this treasure, you will let me pass.'

Kel and Bebon removed the four vases from North Wind's panniers. Each raised two to the heavens.

'See!' shouted Kel. 'See the sons of Horus! They recreate the life of their father Osiris, and we have come to offer them to the Divine Worshipper!'

Silence fell over the temple forecourt. Struck dumb, the guards stepped back. In moments, a crowd had gathered and was pushing forward to see what was going on.

An officer was the first to regain his composure. 'Are you ritual priests? You don't look as if you are.'

'Let us pass,' insisted Nitis.

'Certainly not. Orders are orders.'

'Beware the anger of the gods.'

'You talk like a priestess! A priestess . . . and two men . . . the scribe and the actor!'

The officer was trembling with excitement. He had just identified Kel the assassin and his two main accomplices! The reward would match the magnificence of the achievement.

'Arrest them,' he ordered his men, 'and inform Judge Gem.'

The soldiers approached hesitantly. The four vases might give out a dangerous energy.

'You're in no danger,' the officer assured them. 'They aren't even armed.'

Bebon savoured his last few moments of freedom, wishing that he had been able to persuade his friends to listen to reason.

Brandishing spears and swords, the soldiers surrounded them.

Suddenly there was a strange, low sound. The great gilded wooden gate of Karnak opened slowly.

All eyes turned towards the frail figure that appeared on the threshold.

Dressed in a long, clinging white gown, a broad gold collar about her neck, the Divine Worshipper was wearing the ceremonial crown: a headdress imitating the pelt of a vulture, symbol of the goddess Mut, surmounted by two small horns evoking Hathor, and two tall feathers at whose base a sun was being born.

Thebans rushed up from every direction. Most of them had never seen their queen before. Happy and admiring, they bowed as a sign of respect.

Nitis, Kel, Bebon and even North Wind knelt down.

As for the soldiers, they stood aside. Dry-throated, unable to master this situation, the officer rejoined the ranks.

'Majesty,' said Nitis, 'we make offering to you of these four vases which belonged to one of your servants, and which were stolen from him. May the justice of Maat continue to govern the sacred city of Thebes.'

'Stand up,' said the Divine Worshipper. 'You shall be my guests.'

Bebon couldn't believe his eyes: the plan was working!

'Arrest those criminals immediately!' shouted Judge Gem breathlessly, elbowing his way through the throng.

Grumbles of complaint rose from the crowd.

High Steward Sheshonq physically restrained the judge. 'Control yourself. Her Majesty has just granted hospitality to these bearers of offerings, who now belong to the brotherhood of ritual priests.'

The judge pushed Sheshonq away, and the crowd grew angrier.

'Arrest those criminals!' the judge demanded a second time.

The soldiers stood where they were, their weapons lowered.

'Calm yourself,' the High Steward advised him. 'The words of the Divine Worshipper have the force of law, and these three ritual priests are now under her protection. To harm them would arouse the people's fury, which you would not be able to quench.'

The judge raged at his helplessness. They were there, close enough to touch and yet out of reach!

He addressed the Divine Worshipper: 'Majesty, hand these criminals over to me.'

The look in her eyes reduced him to silence.

She turned round, and North Wind followed her across the threshold of the temple. Nitis, Kel and Bebon were at his heels, forming a small procession.

And the great gate of Karnak closed once more.

74

'You are confined to your house,' Judge Gem informed the High Steward, 'and I am going to order the troops to invade the temple and arrest the criminals.'

'A twofold mistake,' said Sheshonq. 'If you prevent me from carrying out my duties correctly, the government of the province will become disrupted, and the king will be angry with you. As for invading Karnak, the domain of the Divine Worshipper, do not even think of it! You would provoke a popular uprising and commit a crime against the throne for which the pharaoh would never forgive you.'

Unfortunately, the High Steward was right.

'Since you now know where Kel is,' suggested Sheshonq, 'you can lift the security controls which are inconveniencing so many Thebans.'

'The temple will be under permanent watch,' warned Gem, 'and none of those three criminals will be able to get out.'

'I don't doubt it,' said the High Steward. 'Will you come and dine with me this evening?'

'I think not.'

'You are making a mistake. My cook's creations are unequalled. If you change your mind, even at the very last moment, you will be welcome.'

Judge Gem felt torn. On one hand, he was furious at not being able to arrest this trio he had at last managed to track down; on the other, it was a consolation to see them as prisoners in Karnak.

In the end he decided to let patience dictate his actions. Although it was more than clear that she was not dying, the Divine Worshipper might not live much longer. The woman who succeeded her would doubtless wish to rid herself of these inconvenient guests, and would hand them over to justice.

Bebon was dazzled. He would love to have played the role of a god in the immense pillared hall or beside the sacred lake, which was the largest in all Egypt. The obelisks that pointed at the skies dispelled harmful energies and captured creative ones, the expressions of divine power.

The sacred domain of Karnak was a true city in itself, constantly bustling. But he must defer his exploration of it, for the Divine Worshipper, Kel and Nitis were in a hurry to know the secrets of the coded text at last.

The old lady's sovereign elegance took his breath away. She had been a queen since her birth, and the god Amun could not have found a better wife.

In the shade of a wooden canopy beside the lake, servants had set out chairs, a low table, a sheet of papyrus and writing-materials. Here the Divine Worshipper had conversed with Pythagoras before initiating him into certain Mysteries. Favourite was gnawing a bone, while Juggler was eating figs.

'Now,' she said to them, 'tell me your story in detail.'

Kel, the principal accused, spoke first; then Nitis added further details. When Bebon's turn came, he had nothing to add.

'Write the coded text.'

Checked by Nitis, Kel did so. They had studied it so often that memory could not fail them.

The Divine Worshipper asked a ritual priest to bring her the Power-sistrum and another to fetch a heart-shaped vase filled with water from the sacred lake.

'The ancestors possessing the code were the sons of Horus, and their disappearance prevented us from discovering the truth. By finding them, you have given me the chance to use my own keys. Clearly, this assembly of hieroglyphs is the product of an enchantment. We must first dispel it.'

The Divine Worshipper moved the sistrum above the text.

High-pitched, metallic sounds assailed Bebon's ears. The old lady's slow movements unleashed an appalling din, which was only just bearable.

Eventually, calm returned. The text was unchanged. Had the magic of the sistrum, which could unleash the enlivening power of Amun and appease destructive forces, been ineffective?

'One organ escapes the protection of the sons of Horus,' said the Divine Worshipper, 'and that is the heart. It is never placed in one of these vases. The seat of the conscience and of thought, it must be extracted from the body, washed and rendered immune from decay. Then the embalmer replaces it in the chest or replaces it with a heart made of stone, in the form of the scarab of metamorphoses. We must therefore purify this text by ridding it of its darkness.'

The queen of Karnak poured the water on to the signs. Nitis and Kel were disappointed to see that, again, no changes took place. Three times, the Divine Worshipper unhurriedly repeated the action. Noting the failure, Bebon felt a kind of despair. The adventure was ending disastrously.

Then, almost imperceptibly, some of the signs began to fade. Others followed, and the process speeded up. In the end, only about fifty hieroglyphs remained.

A first reading produced partial results. Kel conquered the last obstacle: several words had to be deciphered backwards.

Then the truth appeared, the truth that had caused so many crimes. The last part of the document read:

We, Queen Ladikeh, will change the destiny of Egypt by destroying the ancient customs and the throne of the pharaoh. The north-eastern border of the country will be opened, with the aid of the Greek officers, and the country freed from Ahmose's oppression. The Emperor of Persia must act cautiously and await my signal. Together, we shall triumph.

'Ladikeh is Queen Tanith's former name,' recalled the Divine Worshipper. 'So treason has rotted the very heart of the state!'

'We must warn the pharaoh at once,' said Kel.

'I fear it may be too late.'

'Majesty,' ventured Nitis, 'summon Judge Gem and persuade him to leave immediately for Sais. He will show this document to the king and prevent the worst.'

75

The skies over Sais were grey and heavy. King Ahmose had a bad headache and did not want to get out of bed, and the gloomy weather did not incline him to devote himself to affairs of state.

Scarcely had he eaten his breakfast when Henat requested an audience.

'Majesty, the situation is grave!'

'What now?'

'A report from one of our agents in Palestine. Unfortunately the Interpreters' Secretariat took a long time to translate it and pass it on to me.'

'A revolt by the sand-travellers?'

'The Persian army is marching straight towards Egypt.'

'Are you daring to mock me?'

'Indeed not, Majesty. Supplied with food by the desert nomads, the enemy is moving fast.'

'Are you certain this report is not pure invention?'

'A second agent speaks of an attack by sea. The Phoenicians and the tyrant Polycrates of Samos are apparently collaborating with the Persians.'

'That is far from likely! My Greek allies would never betray me.'

Ahmose called for a cup of red wine and dressed quickly. He told his steward to summon his most senior officers to a council of war. Egyptian military power would crush the invader.

'Don't bother,' said the icy voice of Queen Tanith. 'It is all over.'

The king could not believe his ears. 'What do you mean?'

'Your army will not fight.'

'You are mad!'

'For many years I have been waiting for this moment,' revealed Tanith, her eyes blazing. 'You saw and understood nothing. I, the scorned and deceived Greek woman, I was able to persuade your allies to detach themselves little by little from a second-rate pharaoh and to rally to the Emperor of the Persians. Kroisos and his wife, Nitetis, delighted to avenge her father whom you murdered, gave me invaluable help. As an ambassador, Kroisos persuaded the Greek princes to abandon you. And it was also he who planned the invasion, by buying the chiefs of the sand-runner tribes and the Palestinians. The Persians have encountered no resistance; their army and their fleet are making swift progress and will soon reach the Delta.'

Ahmose was having difficulty in breathing. 'My war-fleet is ten times better than theirs, and will destroy it! My foot-soldiers and my cavalry will annihilate their troops. Phanes of Halikarnassos will lead my Greek soldiers to a brilliant victory!'

Tanith smiled cruelly. 'You poor, foolish creature! You sold the defence of your country to the Greeks without even noticing. Phanes and the senior officers obey me implicitly. Your commander-in-chief handed Kroisos the keys to the Egyptian defence arrangements, and not a single Greek will fight against his new master, the Emperor of Persia.'

'Udja will command my admirals!'

'Udja knows where his interests lie. As he values his life and his privileges, he has chosen to hand over the entire Egyptian fleet to the Persian navy. No boats will be sunk, and Cambyses will be magnanimous towards those dignitaries who submit to him. This palace no longer belongs to you.'

A fierce pain tore through Ahmose's chest. 'Udja ... Udja has betrayed me, too?'*

'He has adapted,' said the queen sarcastically, 'and will become a faithful servant of the emperor. As for the head of your spy service, Henat, I rendered him deaf and blind. Without the Interpreters' Secretariat, he thought of nothing but internal disputes and his trivial battle against Judge Gem. If he proves reasonable, we shall offer him an honorary position. As for the judge, he will be eliminated. The ancient justice of Maat, on which you have so often trampled, will be replaced by that of the Persians. At last, Egypt will vanish.'

'Our son, Psamtek ... He will make the people rise up and resist!'

'Does that witless creature really want to get himself killed?'

'Tanith! He is our son!'

'It is up to him to choose his camp. If he chooses wrongly, he will die.'

The pain intensified. Unable to breathe, Ahmose had to sit down.

'What a pleasure to see you suffering and dying! Fascinated by the Greeks – who regard you with contempt – you have led Egypt to decadence and ruin. Soon it will be nothing but a province of the Persian empire. The day I destroyed your helmet I destroyed your magic, and the affair of the murderous scribe served me wonderfully well. That rebellious innocent and his accomplices have earned themselves a fine execution in a public square.'

'Tanith ... This is just a nightmare! You don't hate me so much!'

The queen burst out laughing. 'Lazy, drunken, a libertine

* The treason of General Phanes, the collaboration of Udja-Hor-resnet and the active complicity of Kroisos are historical facts.

and a failed warrior, a gullible ruler incapable of judging those around him . . . You deserve your fate.'

'Sais is my capital. It will resist to the end.'

'Phanes will offer it to Cambyses, and everyone will bow before the Persian emperor. You may rely on me: he will enjoy a triumphal welcome.'

Ahmose's eyes rolled back in his head, the muscles in his face tensed, and he had not even the strength to put his hands to his chest as he collapsed.

The queen smiled. She would have him buried in the tomb intended for him, so as not to shock the common people, who were still attached to the ancient customs. The Persians would swiftly impose theirs.

As she left her dead husband's bedchamber, Tanith met Henat.

'Majesty, I must see the king again as a matter of urgency!'

'Ahmose is dead.'

'Dead! And this terrifying news . . .'

'What do you mean?'

'It is incomprehensible. The Persians have encountered no opposition and are heading for Sais!'

'We must recognize defeat, good Henat. That way we shall save many lives.'

'Majesty, that would mean . . . a Persian occupation!'

'Would you consider resisting them?'

His reflections were brief. 'I do not see how I could.'

'Then accept reality, and you will remain as palace director.'

Henat yielded.

'Prepare for Cambyses' arrival,' ordered Tanith. 'He is to have a sumptuous reception.'

76

In the depths of the night, the Divine Worshipper took Nitis to the goddess Mut's *icheru*, or sacred lake, which was shaped like the crescent moon.

The old woman gazed at the silvery waters, rippled by a cool breeze.

'This is the matrix of the world,' said the Divine Worshipper. 'Mut is at once mother and death: the mother who gives us earthly life, and death which brings us back to the life of the cosmos. On this anxious night, she has decided to manifest herself in her most fearsome form.'

A lioness sprang from the darkness and came to drink the waters of the lake. The silence was absolute. Nitis could hear her tongue lapping.

Sated, the animal turned her head towards the two women. Her eyes became blood-red, her back arched, and she seemed poised to attack. The confrontation seemed endless. Then the lioness grunted, scratched the ground with her claws, turned and disappeared.

'Many times during my reign,' said the Queen of Karnak, 'I have made her submit. She has lain at my feet, I have stroked her, and I have turned her power back against the demons. Today all I can do is prevent her from devouring us. Her fury remains entire, and she heralds suffering and destruction. Our rulers have betrayed Maat, and the hour of the gods' vengeance is approaching. The Eye of Ra will burn our world and the lioness will be nourished by the blood of human beings.'

'Can we not prevent this disaster, Majesty?'

'We deciphered the coded papyrus too late.'

'Perhaps Judge Gem will arrive in time and persuade the king to destroy the conspiracy.'

The Divine Worshipper said nothing.

Bebon was relaxed and becoming accustomed to his new life in Thebes. Since the judge's departure, the temple of Karnak was no longer ringed by guards. Coming and going as he wished, the actor paid frequent visits to Daybreak and happily transported her pots of honey.

It had not taken him long to discover the city's best taverns and to make friends with merry fellows who enjoyed women and good wine. However, he missed travelling the country, playing the roles of the gods. But it was only a matter of waiting a little while, because once King Ahmose had been enlightened he would get rid of the queen, have the conspirators executed and inflict a stinging defeat on the Persians.

In the final analysis, that madman Kel had been right to struggle against fate. United for ever with Nitis, who had become a priestess of Hathor and a follower of the Divine Worshipper, he occupied the post of Scribe of the Archives, and gorged himself on the old documents kept in the House of Life at Karnak. Enjoying perfect love, the pair rarely left the temple enclosure. It was pointless to talk to them about a return to Sais. And North Wind, who had been classified as an elite donkey, was settling into his comfortable new life, too.

Invited to a banquet by the High Steward, Bebon abandoned himself to the barber, the manicurist and the perfumer before donning a fashionable wig and an elegant pale-beige tunic. Knowing how talented Sheshonq's cook was, he had eaten a very light meal at midday. Among the guests there were sure to be a few delightful Theban women, interested in knowing all about his adventurous life.

He was cruelly disappointed. The only people there were the Divine Worshipper, Sheshonq, Nitis and Kel. And the atmosphere was hardly one of rejoicing.

'I call all the gods to this evening meal,' the Divine Worshipper prayed. 'May they gather around us and be nourished by the subtle essence of the food.'

Taking a little from each dish, she put together a meal destined for the invisible world.

Suddenly, Bebon sensed strange presences. Although a sceptic, he had to admit that the old lady's prayer had been answered.

'Let us savour this moment of peace, in which the world beyond and the world below are in communion,' she urged. 'Now we may eat and drink.'

She passed around a cup of wine and shared out the bread. Osiris was the blood of the vine, and the cereal crop that came back to life after the death of the grain; and in this way he sustained life.

Sheshonq did not even taste the delicious marinated fish. 'I have terrible news,' he announced, close to tears. 'Cambyses, the Persian emperor, has crushed the feeble army raised by Psamtek, the son of King Ahmose. And both father and son are dead.'

'Has Sais been conquered?' Nitis asked.

'Sais and all the other towns in the Delta. Memphis itself has just fallen. General Phanes has made a pact with the enemy and Udja has agreed to collaborate. In order to destroy any spirit of resistance, Cambyses has killed the Apis bull. Henceforth, the law of the strongest will be imposed upon Egypt.'

Tears flowed down Nitis's and Kel's cheeks. Bebon was a skilful enough actor to appear impassive.

'The Persians are continuing their conquest,' added Sheshonq. 'Their next objective is Thebes.'

'We shall resist!' Kel promised.

'We do not have the means,' said the Divine Worshipper. 'And Cambyses will not dare to attack Karnak. But you must leave. To you, Nitis, I give a chest containing the sacred fabrics designed to appease the dangerous lioness. It also contains the shroud of Osiris used during the celebration of the Mysteries. With its aid and your knowledge as a priestess of Neith, you shall preserve our wisdom and pass on our values. You, Kel the scribe, are to be initiated tonight, and you shall know the secrets of the heavens, the earth and the stars' matrix. You will breathe with a new life, and you will become a spiritual son capable of fighting for our freedom. At dawn, you shall leave Karnak together. Only a couple like you can triumph over misfortune.'

'Where are we to go, Majesty?' Nitis asked.

'To Nubia. A letter of safeguard written by me will enable you to cross the border at Elephantine. Then you will follow the track along the banks of the Nile. A sign from the heavens will enable you to reach a village whose headman worships Amun. There, you will be safe and will prepare for Maat's return to Egypt.'

77

After the night of his initiation, Kel felt no fatigue. His mind had been opened to the spiritual realities taught at Karnak for centuries. The time was approaching to leave the temple and the Divine Worshipper. He thought of his superior at the Interpreters' Secretariat, murdered because he ought not to have kept the coded papyrus and tried to decipher it. But the queen and her accomplices had decided to kill everyone in the secretariat, so as to render Egypt deaf and blind and enable the Persians to prepare for their invasion unbeknown to King Ahmose, who had too much trust in his Greek allies. And he, Kel, had served as the perfect scaapegoat, on the recommendation of his Greek 'friend' Demos, who had subsequently been eliminated.

The gods were avenging themselves on a government which had ignored the way of Maat. At Nitis's side, Kel would continue to fight, gathering together those who opposed the Persians. Even if their chances of success appeared very slim, they would not give up.

'I'll come with you,' said Bebon. 'North Wind and I need to stretch our legs.'

'The journey is likely to be dangerous.'

'Can you see me staying here on my own? In Nubia we

shall make fine masks and I shall put together a troupe of divinities capable of acting out the great myths.'

The two friends embraced.

North Wind took the lead, heading a group of sturdy donkeys laden with food, flasks, clothing, products for cleansing the body, writing materials and weapons.

'You must leave at once,' the Divine Worshipper told Nitis.

'I would so dearly love to stay with you!'

'Your destiny lies elsewhere. You and Kel form a couple worthy of ruling the country. Yet you must fight in the shadows, deriving no benefit from your efforts and without ever losing heart. Except for Bebon, have no friends and rely only on yourselves. The time of misfortune and opposition is coming, and you are the sole embodiment of hope.'

Nitis, Kel, Bebon and North Wind bowed before the Divine Worshipper, and the procession set off for the South.

'Tomorrow, Majesty,' said the High Steward, 'the Persians will reach Thebes.'

'It is time for you to take refuge,' said the Divine Worshipper.

'You know me: I am a sedentary man. Leaving you would be an unbearable punishment.'

'Cambyses will not spare us, Sheshonq. He will kill us and try to destroy Karnak. Thanks to the gods, part of the temple will survive, but those faithful to Amun will be slaughtered.'

'I have endeavoured to serve you faithfully and to contribute to the happiness of the province. To run away would be contemptible.'

Accustomed to controlling her emotions, the old lady confined herself to a look of gratitude, which moved the High Steward almost to tears.

'We must go to my funerary shrine at Medinet Habu,'* she decreed. 'There, I shall carry out the final act of my reign by adopting Nitocris, the last Divine Worshipper.'

As she crossed the Nile, the sovereign thanked the gods for granting her so many favours. Throughout her long life, the wife of Amun had striven to capture his benevolent power and spread it around her.

The walls of the shrine were covered with columns of hieroglyphs, summing up the main themes of the *Pyramid Texts*. The old lady described to young Nitocris the principal rites that raised her to the highest spiritual office in the land, and talked to her for a long time about the duties of her position. Thus the transfer took place outside human time and space, as if the Persian invasion did not exist.

'Nut, the sky-goddess, surrounds the living with the circle of her two arms,' said the Divine Worshipper. 'She will be our magical safeguard, and our essential being will be protected from all evil. Our *ka* will not be detached from us.'

The mother and her spiritual daughter returned to Karnak. Favourite and Juggler were delighted to see their mistress.

From the sun-drenched temple roof, they saw the Persians charge forward, laying waste everything in their path and yelling as they attacked the great gilded wooden door, after trampling on the corpse of High Steward Sheshonq.

'I am afraid,' admitted Nitocris.

'Stay close to me and close your eyes,' ordered the mother.

Soon the assassins' footsteps echoed on the stone staircase.

---

* Cambyses not only ordered the destruction of Ankh-nes-nefer-ib-Ra's shrine but had her mummy burnt. However, we can still admire the houses of eternity belonging to other Divine Worshippers. And the sarcophagus of Ankh-nes-nefer-ib-Ra, a masterpiece of Egyptian art, was found by the French expedition of 1832. As the public authorities considered it uninteresting, it ended up in the British Museum. Its inscriptions, which are widely misunderstood, speak of the Divine Worshipper's spiritual destiny.

Her eyes raised to the heavens, the Divine Worshipper spoke the words of transformation into Light.

After crossing the border at Elephantine and the First Cataract, the caravan led by North Wind entered Nubia.

Bebon had all he needed, and had even found the journey pleasant, but he was becoming impatient. This famous sign was a long time coming.

A large bird with a very long beak was perched at the top of a tree, watching them. As they approached, it spread its long wings and wheeled above them.

'It is the *ba*, the immortal soul of the Divine Worshipper,' declared Nitis. 'It is feeding on the sun's rays and will guide us to our destination.'

Indeed, the bird did not leave them for a moment. It led them to a village where the soldiers from the Elephantine garrison and a number of civilians had taken refuge. These people all realized that they could not oppose the Persians, but they neverthess wanted to form a resistance movement and, little by little, win back the territory that had been lost. They had chosen a leader, to whom they brought the new arrivals.

Bebon was filled with consternation.

'No, not you!'

'It is indeed I,' declared Judge Gem, 'and you no longer have anything to fear, since the truth has been established. When I arrived in Memphis, I learnt of the death of King Ahmose. As a Persian victory was inevitable, returning to Sais would have been stupid – I would have been killed on the spot. So I decided to gather together those who had the courage to continue the fight. At my age, the burden of command promised to be a weighty one. But you folk are young, and able to take it from me.'

Bebon was preparing to voice serious objections when a beautiful Nubian woman, dressed in a purely decorative kilt of palm-fibres, offered him something red to drink.

'It is a herb tea called *karkade*,'* she explained. 'Its freshness drives away dark thoughts and gives energy. You are a very fine warrior, I can sense that.'

Bebon did not disillusion her. 'Where do you find this plant?'

'A little way from the village.'

'I'd love to see your garden.'

'Come, I'll show it to you.'

Judge Gem sat down on a mat. 'Our actor is going to enjoy his new life. I, on the other hand, made a terrible mistake, and when justice loses its way a country is destined for disaster. I shall make good my error by fighting under your command, Kel, and we shall drive the barbarians out of the Two Lands.'

At the end of a frugal dinner, which Bebon did not attend as he was too busy gathering herbs with his new teacher, Kel and Nitis climbed a sand dune, gilded by the rays of the setting sun. North Wind lay down at their feet.

Their eyes turned towards Egypt, they promised themselves that they would liberate their tortured homeland.†

---

* Translator's note: aka hibiscus tea.

† In 405 BC Amyrtaios of Sais, with the aid of resistance networks, succeeded in driving out the invaders and became king. Pharaonic Egypt then experienced its last period of freedom and sovereignty until 342, the date of the second Persian occupation. This was followed by further invasions: Greek (333), Roman (30), Christian (in AD 383 an edict ordered the closure of the temples), Byzantine (395) and Arab (639). The dynasties are no more, but their message remains.